GONE

Also by Glenna Thomson

Blueberry
Stella and Margie

GONE

GLENNA THOMSON

BANTAM
SYDNEY AUCKLAND TORONTO NEW YORK LONDON

BANTAM

UK | USA | Canada | Ireland | Australia
India | New Zealand | South Africa | China

Bantam is part of the Penguin Random House group of companies
whose addresses can be found at global.penguinrandomhouse.com

Penguin
Random House
Australia

First published by Bantam in 2024

Cover photography by Getty Images/Southern Lightscapes-Australia (landscape)
and Shutterstock/Leadidge (shed)
Cover design by Christabella Designs © Penguin Random House Australia Pty Ltd
Typeset in 11/17 pt Sabon LT by Midland Typesetters, Australia
Printed and bound in Australia by Griffin Press, an accredited
ISO AS/NZS 14001 Environmental Management Systems printer

A catalogue record for this
book is available from the
National Library of Australia

ISBN 978 1 76134 550 0

penguin.com.au

MIX
Paper | Supporting
responsible forestry
FSC® C018684

We at Penguin Random House Australia acknowledge that Aboriginal and Torres Strait
Islander peoples are the Traditional Custodians and the first storytellers of the lands
on which we live and work. We honour Aboriginal and Torres Strait Islander peoples'
continuous connection to Country, waters, skies and communities. We celebrate
Aboriginal and Torres Strait Islander stories, traditions and living cultures;
and we pay our respects to Elders past and present.

To Alistair

It was bad luck that my sister, Rebecca Bundy, disappeared in the week before Christmas in 1984. Most people were distracted with last-minute shopping and catering plans for family visits. Others were probably preoccupied with getting as far away from the good cheer as possible.

Then, two days after Rebecca went missing, Jacob Healy, a local sheep farmer, shot and killed his pregnant wife and their three lovely blonde-haired kids. When he'd satisfied himself they were all dead, he drove his ute to the dam, walked into the centre of it and turned the gun on himself. A murder-suicide investigation followed. Perhaps because of the time of year it became one of those stories that made world headlines. Family photos covered the front pages of all the newspapers, and it was the lead story on radio and TV news. It seemed to go on for weeks, even after the funerals. White coffins buried in the Maryhill cemetery.

The Healy investigation took its toll on the local police resources, and perhaps their empathy was stretched thin too. It meant that Rebecca's disappearance quickly became a cold case. Those two events – Christmas and the Healys' murder-suicide – worked against my family and had devastating long-term consequences.

The other point I'll make about the lack of police interest in Rebecca's disappearance was that she'd run away once before, and came home when she'd cooled down. It's true she'd been talking about going to Queensland over the school holidays. That possibility was always a live option. But as the days and weeks went on other leads emerged that added to the confusion and uncertainty. Anyway, Rebecca slamming the back door behind her always followed an argument with our mother.

I was fourteen years old when Rebecca vanished. I was young, and a lot of what was going on around me didn't make sense until I was older, particularly relating to my mother's mercurial and increasingly alarming behaviour.

But I was there on the day Rebecca disappeared. I watched her hurry away. If I close my eyes I can still see her, the way her hair seemed to float behind her as she fled behind the toilet block at the showgrounds.

That was thirty-eight years ago.

I'm now ready to share my story from the beginning about what I knew and what I've found out since.

ONE

1984

On the last day of the school year the bell rang ninety minutes early. It was a hot day, and the Gyle–Maryhill bus wasn't due for ninety minutes, which meant that twenty-three of us had a long time to wait. It was Rebecca who suggested we all go to the showgrounds to hang out in the shade of the Moreton Bay figs. She picked up her schoolbag and headed off without looking back to see if anyone followed.

The showgrounds were a short walk from school, along a concrete path beside the Deveron River and across the railway line. We filed through the granite pillars and quickly settled under the row of giant trees. The boys organised themselves to play cricket. Andy Knightly propped up his schoolbag to be the wicket and someone produced a bat and ball. I perched on a concrete bench with Rachel Cooper and Andrea Goodman to watch them play.

Rebecca sat away from us, her head bowed to a book she held against her chest. None of her friends caught our bus and it had been a long time since she'd been bothered with any of us, including me. That wasn't always the case. Rebecca and I had been close for most of our lives. She changed when she started thinking of herself as grown-up and me still as a kid. By the time she turned seventeen the three-year age gap between us somehow seemed much greater.

As if Rebecca felt me looking at her, she raised her head and for a moment we held each other's gaze. Nothing in particular was communicated between us, perhaps a silent acknowledgement that we were there together in the shade, and that night we'd sleep under the same roof – with our long history as sisters ahead of us. When Rebecca turned back to her book, sunlight filtering through the branches caught her auburn hair and I noticed again how similar she looked to our mother. That's what was always said in our family, that she took after Mum, and I took after Dad.

I turned away from Rebecca when the boys started arguing whether Shaun Taylor had been caught out, or the ball was dropped. The smell of cigarettes wafted from behind the toilets. In the mid-distance, a bearded man and his black dog wandered across the exhibition ring towards the pavilion, where every year one of Mum's decorated wedding cakes was displayed at the show. I was hungry and thought of the fish and chips I'd eat later at Maryhill's local shop where I worked three times a week. Warm air touched my skin and, in that moment, I remember being happy.

Then through the showground's granite pillars dust rose behind a yellow Volvo. There was no mistake, it was our mother's car because we were the only family in the district to own one in that egg-yolk colour. She was driving fast towards us, and I didn't under-stand how she knew we were there. I felt uneasy. Out of the car, she slammed the door and strode towards Rebecca. Our mother's nostrils flared, and her mouth was open as if trying to take more air in to her heaving lungs. The cricket game stopped. All the kids became still, staring.

Everyone knew our mother, Diane Bundy. Not only because she baked and decorated all the wedding cakes for the local brides, but because she was beautiful and glamorous. That's what we all saw when she zeroed in on Rebecca. Even in rage it was possible to see how striking she was, in a sleeveless white-and-yellow polka-dot dress and white patent leather sandals, her thick auburn hair tied up high on her head and kept in place with a green scarf.

I felt afraid and wished Dad was there because he knew how to handle Mum and Rebecca. At home they fought constantly. A few days earlier they'd argued when Rebecca said she'd like to go to Queensland with her best friend, Jasmine Vasilakis, for the Christmas holidays. I didn't think she was serious, just talking out loud about an idea. But Mum shouted at her, told her she was forbidden. Rebecca yelled back saying she was seventeen and could do what she liked. The arguing only stopped when Dad came inside.

Rebecca closed the book, then stood and put her shoulders back as if bracing for whatever was coming from Mum.

'You stole money from my purse,' Mum said, stabbing the air in front of Rebecca's face. 'One hundred and seventy-five dollars is missing. The cash payment from Lauren Reinhart's wedding cake is gone. It was in my purse last night.'

'I don't know what you're talking about,' Rebecca said.

'Don't you lie to me. Where's the money?'

'What is wrong with you?' Rebecca replied, eyes darting to see who was watching.

'Get in the car, right now,' Mum said, then turning to find me, she yelled, 'Eliza. And you too.'

I picked up my schoolbag.

But Rebecca wasn't going anywhere.

'Rebecca, get in the car right now,' Mum snapped.

'I'm catching the bus.'

'What's got into you?'

'Nothing. What's got into you?'

Mum's voice was low and slow, a dangerous sign. 'What have you done with my money?'

'I haven't got your money.' Rebecca replied so normally she sounded convincing.

I headed towards the car hoping they would follow and the public scene would end.

'Come on,' I called.

They ignored me.

'Let me see inside your bag,' Mum demanded.

Rebecca snatched up her schoolbag and dropped it behind her. 'Don't you dare touch it.'

'Give it to me,' Mum said, stepping forward.

'Just leave me alone, for fuck's sake.'

Mum was crazy if she thought she could physically wrestle Rebecca's schoolbag off her, or force her into the car. But she tried. With a lunging step, she grabbed Rebecca's arms, pulling her forward. I couldn't think what to do. I was startled, stopped breathing. Rebecca was hard-eyed when she yanked away, forcing Mum to fall onto her knees. I've never forgotten how demeaning it looked, as if Mum was begging at Rebecca's feet. Then to my horror Mum's body went completely limp as she dropped onto the talc-like dirt and started crying with bursts of screaming, something I had never seen or heard before.

All the kids openly gaped down at her. The white dress Mum was wearing with the yellow polka dots was filthy in the dirt. The green scarf that tied up her long hair was loose; strands fell across her wet face. One of her sandals had come off.

I still didn't move. Should I have helped my mother to her feet? Told her to shut up? Instead, I took in all the staring faces, wondering what they were thinking. Then, as a ripple of wind moved through those mighty trees, Andy hurried forward, put his hands under Mum's arms and lifted her up. She was looking around for her missing sandal when Rebecca backed away.

So Mum didn't see Rebecca disappear into the deep shadows of those Moreton Bay figs and vanish behind the toilet block. But I did. I saw the way her hair sat lightly on her shoulders as she went. A thin girl wearing a too-short blue-and-white check school uniform. In her right hand she gripped her schoolbag, and in her left she held the book she'd been reading. She didn't look back, but walked fast and with purpose.

*

I followed Mum to the car and sat in the front passenger seat. Behind the wheel she snapped down the visor and stared into the mirror. She clicked her tongue, sniffed and blinked as she studied her face. Then she reached into the backseat and plucked a tissue from her black shoulder bag.

'Do you want me to go and get her?' I asked.

'She can get the bus,' Mum said, dabbing watery mascara stains from under her eyes.

All the kids had moved deeper into the shade and gathered around each other. Shaun was waving his arms acting out the pulling and pushing between Mum and Rebecca. Andrea's head was back, laughing. Rachel was flat-faced, staring at me in the car. What they had witnessed was a rare thing, gossip fodder, and I hated my mother for what she had just done to me and our family.

'How could you do that in front of everybody?' I asked.

'Rebecca's a thief and needs to be held to account.'

'What makes you think she took it?'

'Simple. Because I had the money last night and now it's gone.'

I thought of Mum's red purse that she kept in her shoulder bag. 'That doesn't mean Rebecca took it.'

'You know she's been carrying on about going to Queensland with that Greek girl, Jasmine whatever-her-name-is. So she would've taken it for that. It's obvious.'

When Mum turned to face me she exaggerated her grin by raising her eyebrows, clown-like, as if something was funny. A whiff of her Chanel No. 5. There was lipstick on her teeth and her makeup had mostly worn off. I always thought she looked better, or less complicated, without it. She turned back to the mirror and gathered her hair in her hands, retied the green scarf and tugged it tight. She was acting strangely and I understood then, perhaps for the first time, something wasn't quite right with her. I wanted Dad.

With the air-conditioning on high we drove out of the showgrounds. As we passed the pavilion the bearded man and his black dog, who I'd seen about fifteen minutes earlier, were there. The man, wearing a blue shirt and jeans, was standing beside a tap while his dog lapped from a stream of water. For certain he'd seen the fight between Mum and Rebecca. I turned, as he did, and we looked at each other. Dark eyes, narrow face, trimmed beard, shorter than my father. I'd never seen him before, which was unusual in a small country town. As Mum drove through the showground gate I turned for one final look at him, and was surprised to see he was still watching us.

*

The way Mum clenched the steering wheel she could've powered us up the mountain with the sheer force of energy in her body. We sped under the double-bridge overpass that carried all the traffic between Melbourne and Sydney. We passed the familiar horse studs, farmhouses, rusted cattle yards, and the views across dry hills dotted with granite rocks and eucalypts that had survived for months without much rain.

Up ahead was a straight stretch of road, just past Hedge End Lane, where the locals knew they had a good kilometre to safely overtake a slow vehicle. It happened all the time: a revved car suddenly appeared from behind to pass an unhurried driver or a heavy truck. Even though Mum was probably on the legal speed limit, a black ute with a roo-bar and P-plates came up behind, tailgating, edging close to pass. Back then, those bitumen roads were too narrow to carry two vehicles so it was common practice for the driver in front to move partly onto the verge allowing the passing vehicle to overtake safely.

'He's an idiot driver,' Mum gasped, as the Volvo tyres gripped the gravel.

We both knew it was Bull Tennant driving that ute. No one else on the mountain drove like him, as if galloping a stallion into battle. In the seconds it took him to power ahead, I glimpsed his forward-looking stare, a man trying to put distance between us as fast as he could. His arm moved down as he went up a gear.

'He should have his licence taken off him before he kills someone,' Mum said.

Bull wasn't his real name. Until Cheryl, his grandmother, gave him a second-hand .22 rifle for his thirteenth birthday, we called him Ashton which, at the time, was a posh name for a country kid. Armed with a gun to shoot foxes for the bounty money – ten dollars a scalp – his nickname quickly became Bull when it was obvious he was a bull's eye shot. He lived with Cheryl in an old weatherboard house down near Earls Creek, on a bend where willows bowed low into the shallows. I'd heard the rumours how Bull's mother left him with Cheryl when he was a baby saying she'd be back in a couple of weeks, but she didn't return.

From early on, Rebecca and I knew we weren't to have anything to do with Bull or Cheryl, *those people*. I don't remember Mum ever explaining why, we just understood to steer clear of them, and for a while we did. There were obvious differences between them and us, things to judge and be wary of. Bull's school uniforms were always second-hand and either too big or too small. His school lunches were basic, white bread, no fruit, never anything homemade. There was also Cheryl's noisy, dented green Cortina. And their only toilet was outside. It was never said out loud that they were poor, lesser. Even so, a shameful prejudice was instilled in us.

But we caught the bus with Bull every day, and until he quit school at sixteen, we got to know him and worked out for ourselves that he was all right. Better than all right. He was smart and funny. During those bus journeys up and down the mountain the three of us bonded. No, that's not quite right. It was more that Bull and Rebecca hit it off and I was the little sister hanging around, taking everything in. Either way, the three of us accepted each other and having a secret from our mother elevated our friendship, made it all the more important or special.

There's something else I should mention about Bull. At school he was often in fights with other older and bigger boys. He had a temper, but from the way I saw things, it was because he was provoked. Perhaps Bull was a target because he was a natural threat. What I mean is, he was strong and defended himself like a street fighter, played dirty, kneed balls, broke noses, twisted arms, cracked ribs, bent fingers. He'd been suspended a few times, once for bringing tinnies of beer to school. Another time he was thrown off the school bus after bashing Ryan Taylor for saying something about Cheryl's Cortina. No one ever dobbed, otherwise he would've been expelled from school, for sure. By the time he left, when he was sixteen and just completed Year 11, he had a reputation for being the undisputed toughest kid in the school, which rendered him immense respect among all the students. And that hard-earned deference carried right through to when he was older, until he eventually left the mountain and never returned.

Bull was a couple of years older than Rebecca – and when his shoulders broadened and he grew to six foot four, bought his ute and started smoking Marlboros, all that maleness packaged together was something to take notice of. For sure, every girl in the district noticed him, including me, but it was Rebecca who Bull always adored. Sometime earlier in the year, perhaps it was in February, she started seeing him on the sly. It was also around that time Bull was questioned by the local police, something to do with his gun licence. I know that afterwards he tried to avoid the cops, but whenever they came across Bull on the road, he was pulled over so they could check out his car, hassling him about how roadworthy his ute was.

In those days, Rebecca used to confide in me so I could cover for her, tell lies to our parents about where she was when she was with Bull. I knew that sometimes they went to the deserted workman's cottage on our apple orchard, or even to Bull's place. If they went to other places I wasn't told.

Up ahead, Bull's ute grew smaller, red tail-lights flashing as he disappeared around the next bend. His sudden appearance on the road behind us, then overtaking, all happened so fast it wasn't until he was out of sight that I wondered if Rebecca was in the passenger seat beside him. Was she slouching down, hiding from us? It would have made perfect sense if she'd gone to a public phone and asked Bull to pick her up in Gyle and drop her off at the bottom of our driveway. The more I thought about it, the less certain I was about what I actually saw.

'Does he come into the shop?' Mum asked.

'Who?'

'Bull.'

The answer was occasionally. He bought Marlboros, Coke, sometimes a hot meat pie with sauce. I only worked in the shop Tuesdays and Fridays after school, and all day on Saturday which meant I didn't see him very often.

'He must come into the shop sometimes,' Mum insisted.

'Not that much.'

'Have you ever seen him with Rebecca?'

I acted like I didn't hear the question and stared out the window. Paddocks flew by, cows were sitting under the shade of peppermint gums.

'Have you?' Mum repeated, kneading the steering wheel with her hands while glancing at me.

'What do you mean?'

'It's a plain question. Have you ever seen Bull Tennant and Rebecca together?'

'Of course not,' I said, but in my mind were flashes of the times I'd seen Rebecca get into Bull's ute after school. He always parked in the same spot, across the road and down about a hundred metres towards the BP service station. And I knew their weekend meeting place was a twenty-minute walk for Rebecca up to the corner of Fosters Lane and Marion Road. It wasn't far from Bull's home, perhaps a half a kilometre or so.

The shop was up ahead, on the right. The grapevine threading along the verandah railings was heavy and overdue for pruning. Long free-hanging green tendrils were searching for something to cling on to. A decorated pine Christmas tree was in the window, fairy lights flickering.

When Mum pulled up out the front, she asked if I wanted my dinner put aside.

'I'll eat here.'

'Greasy fish and chips again?'
'They're not greasy,' I said.
'It's your waistline, not mine.'
I closed the car door and Mum accelerated away.

TWO

Every Friday night the shop stayed open until eight pm. It was fish and chip night on the mountain, the only local takeaway within thirty kilometres, and everybody, except my family, went mad for them. Robyn Hart, who owned the shop and lived out the back with Gary – her mostly absent husband – made the best chips of any I'd ever had, then or since. Whenever I'm served chips or fries as part of a meal, I'm transported back to that shop and Robyn's secret deep-frying method. Something to do with canola oil and the cooking temperature. She took phone orders and spaced the pickup times ten minutes apart.

From the moment I walked into the shop, I was Robyn's assistant and did as she asked, sometimes taking the fish and chip phone orders, or selling everyday things like newspapers, milk, bread, cigarettes, sliced ham, packet biscuits, and whatever else. And because it was only a few days from Christmas there were displays of Christmas cards and decorations for customers to buy. Also Judy Stoner's Christmas cakes, puddings and mince tarts. 'O Come All Ye Faithful' was playing on the cassette recorder that sat on top of the storage cupboard beside the sink. A ceiling fan whirred on high speed.

The thing I loved the most about working in the shop was using the cash register. Aside from Robyn's constant praise and cash payment, it was the reason I worked there. I couldn't help showing off, striking the keys, the sound of the drawer pinging open, the speed I could count out the change without making a mistake. Robyn often told me and others that I was the best help she'd ever had. Once when I was behind the counter and my mother came into the shop, Robyn put her arm around me and proudly said, 'This girl of yours is amazing. I only have to tell her something once and she gets it. She's a little champ, this one.' I'm sure Robyn thought she was paying Mum a compliment for having such a capable child. Still, after all these years, I can hear my mother's response, 'Tell me your secret, she's hopeless at home.'

With a blue apron over my school uniform, I took my position behind the counter. Soon the door buzzer rang. Cheryl, Bull's grandmother, was first off the rank for her fish and chips. She was a tiny woman with a wrinkly but pretty face, sharp eyes, an easy smile with a wide gap in her front teeth. A faded blue and black bird-looking tattoo was on the side of her neck, partially hidden by her thin grey hair. A green sleeveless cotton dress clung to her body. Thongs on her feet. I hadn't seen her in a while, perhaps a couple of months.

'How are you, Lizzie?' she asked, the only person who ever abbreviated my name. My mother forbade it. Same for Rebecca; only Cheryl called her Bec.

'I'm good,' I said.

'What're you doing for Christmas?'

'Dad's picking peaches and watering. So we'll all be at home. What about you?

'Having a quiet one. Maybe we'll sit down at the creek. You and Bec can come along if you want.'

16

Cheryl wasn't stupid. She knew my mother looked down on her, yet she would've also been fully aware she had the prize. Her glorious grandson was in a secret relationship with Rebecca. And so, Cheryl inviting us to join her and Bull on the bank of Earls Creek on Christmas Day would've required us to sneak away. Perhaps she enjoyed the idea of that.

When I put her parcel of fish and chips on the counter – two flake, three dollars of salted chips, four dim sims and two potato cakes – she reached inside her shoulder bag and I saw that her fingers were swollen and crooked. I'd noticed her arthritic hands before, but they were worse this time, and I thought it'd be difficult for her to craft her pottery. Cheryl sold her ceramics at the local farmers' markets; as far as I knew it was her only income.

When we were younger I went to Cheryl and Bull's place a few times with Rebecca, always on the quiet. We'd been rabbiting with Bull and his ferret, named Snoopy. A couple of evenings, when our parents left us at home by ourselves, we went shooting foxes with him too. Other times we just hung out at their place. We could eat chocolate biscuits, whatever was going, without being berated about putting on weight or spoiling our dinner. I'd seen inside Cheryl's workroom, a gable-roofed cabin surrounded by tall rhododendron and camellia bushes. Inside was a square stainless-steel kiln that looked like an oven. Hanging from the rafters were slow-turning ceramic chimes that caught light coming through the casement windows. Her potter's wheel, and stool, were positioned in the centre of the room. Against the walls were benches filled with work at various stages of production. Everything was large, oversized. There were bowls, vases, plates, some with slashes of bright glazing.

With Cheryl's order on the counter between us, I waited as she fumbled with her purse, carefully opened it and tried to pinch her fingers onto a ten-dollar note.

'Here, Lizzie, can you grab that tenner out for me. My hands are playing up.'

With the note in my hand, I did my expert best at the cash register. Ping went the drawer, then I counted out the change.

'Enjoy your dinner,' I said.

'Bull will eat most of this,' she said, smiling, showing that gap between her front teeth that was more intriguing than unattractive.

The carols droned on. Away in a Manger. Silent Night. Hark! The Herald Angels Sing. I hated them all.

Robyn's system worked. Every ten minutes the door buzzer rang as someone entered the shop for their hot, sweaty parcel of fish and chips with salt and a wedge of lemon. Only a few customers had the extras, dim sims or potato cakes.

I knew the names of everyone who came into the shop, and they knew me. I was the youngest Bundy girl, Eliza, the dark-haired one who looked like her father. Which wasn't a bad thing, I just didn't look like my mother or Rebecca.

Next Jacob Healy was standing in front of me to collect his order. While waiting he amused himself by staring at my small breasts, a tiny sneer on his half-handsome face. Of all the customers, I detested him the most. When I gave him his order and took a twenty-dollar note from him, he didn't let go, forcing a little tug of war between us. And, as I counted out his change, he curled his fingers upward, making it impossible for us not to touch. I glanced across at Robyn, who was standing at the deep fryer. But I could never tell her how Jacob behaved when I served him because his pregnant wife, Sinead, was Robyn's best friend. Sinead often came into the shop to see her, the two of them with their heads together talking. Sinead was always showing Robyn the latest outfit or toy she'd bought for the kids. Other times it was the professional photographs she had taken at every child's birthday. Once when Sinead was out of earshot I'd heard Robyn say, more to herself than to me, that Sinead was *a spender*. And I knew that sometimes Sinead bought groceries at the shop on credit, the only customer I was aware of who had that privilege. Either way, Robyn and Sinead often went out the back to Robyn's house, leaving me with Sinead's three blonde kids. I kept them quiet by giving them chocolate Paddle Pops. Even in winter those kids loved ice-cream.

Rebecca knew the children a lot better than me. She'd been regularly babysitting at the Healy place for about eighteen months, since Sinead started part-time nursing at the aged care facility in Gyle. She got off the school bus at the bottom of their driveway, usually on Mondays and Thursdays after school, and sometimes full days on school holidays. Her job was to supervise them, feed them dinner, bathe them, and have them ready for bed, so Jacob was free to get on with his farming work. When Sinead came home from her shift at about seven o'clock – the times varied – she or Jacob dropped Rebecca off back at our house. I'd once asked Rebecca what she thought of Jacob, but she didn't feel the same as me. 'He's nice,' she'd said.

Her attitude towards Jacob perplexed me. I was left wondering if I was just too uptight, that perhaps I needed to loosen up a bit and play along with him. But that always felt awkward and so I never did.

Time passed, and in between customers coming and going, I ate my own serve of fish and chips. Robyn gave me a can of Fanta.

'Here, love, to wash them down.'

*

At eight, when Robyn closed the shop, I headed home. It was still light, no glare. A warm breeze lifted the smell of ants and eucalyptus.

The rustle of dry bush and the quiet buzz of insects. Walking along the dirt track beside Josephs Road, scanning for snakes, my mind turned to the fight Mum and Rebecca had had earlier at the showgrounds. My body tensed with fresh shock that it had actually happened.

Across the bridge and a left turn up our gravel driveway, a long and tall cypress hedge on the left. Opposite were rows of Red Delicious and Jonathan trees with growing apples, still green, hard and small, not much bigger than walnuts. Along the length of each row black polypipe was suspended on wire about thirty centimetres off the ground. Dad had the pump going, water was dripping.

Our driveway was long, started with a flat stretch, then over a crest it curved in a wide arc. Up ahead, on the right, was our red clinker brick house, surrounded by a lush garden, shaded by old maples, liquidambars, oaks. In the distance was Dunny Hill; its granite peak looked like an enormous scar. It had been named Duncryne Hill by the Scots who settled on Taungurung land, but the name had never stuck. Aside from official maps, it was known locally as Dunny Hill.

Around the back, I pushed the metal gate open and entered the concrete courtyard. To the left was a half-full woodshed covered in ivy, opposite was our rarely used outside toilet. Beyond was a sloping concrete path that led to the packing sheds and cool stores. A row of potted red geraniums lined the laundry wall. Through the open door, the washing machine was vibrating on spin. Dad's work boots were beside the back step, which meant he was home after delivering a load of peaches to the distributor in Coldstream.

Inside the porch, Ripper slowly lifted himself from his basket to greet me. He was our mongrel, mostly kelpie with a bit of border collie, and going by the size of his head and paws, the vet said, he had some labrador in him too. He was a much-loved tired old thing.

Dad took him as a pup from a neighbour on Rebecca's second birthday, which made him almost ninety in human years. I scrunched his ears and asked him how he was. He lifted his face with an open mouth, his way of smiling. His eyes were cloudy, so I guessed it was my voice he understood because he barked whenever strangers came to the back door. Ripper returned to his basket, turned a circle as if trying to work out which way hurt less when he dropped.

The kitchen and living area was one large light-filled room. Beside the buffet was our decorated pine tree that Dad had cut down in the state forest. Layers of Christmas cards were displayed on rows of string that stretched around the walls. Mum did that every year, her way of demonstrating how popular she thought we were. There were probably a hundred or more cards hanging up there.

No one was around. I opened the glass door to Mum's workroom where she decorated her cakes. A long bench, a high stool, cupboards with closed doors. She wasn't there.

Up the carpeted hallway.

'I'm home!' I called.

Rebecca's bedroom door was open so I knew she wasn't home yet. I peeked in. Everything was as expected. Her bed was made, the green bedspread was smooth, no wrinkles. The top drawer of her dresser was open, it was where she kept her underwear and socks. The usual books on her desk; the bottom drawer was where she hid her contraceptive pills in a cloth purse. The wardrobe door was ajar. A Madonna poster on the wall. Perhaps something was different. I gazed around the room trying to work it out. Nothing. So, I turned away.

The house was quiet.

Dad and Mum's bedroom door was closed.

I knocked and went straight in. The room was dim. A ceiling fan slowly turned. Mum was lying stretched out on a white sheet.

21

Dad was sitting beside her holding her hand. An empty tea mug and a box of tissues was on the bedside table. Crumpled tissues were on the floor.

'Has Rebecca phoned?' I asked.

'I've just been telling your father about her stealing my money so she could run off to Queensland with that Jasmine girl,' Mum said in a pathetic voice I'd heard before.

'No, she's not called,' Dad said in his quiet way.

I looked down at Mum. 'Did you tell Dad how you fell in the dirt and cried and made a fool of yourself in front of everyone at the showgrounds? If Rebecca hasn't come home it's your fault.'

I was surprised when Mum started shivering all over as if she was very cold, her jaw juddered. Dad patted her shoulder as he gently rolled her onto her side. The long line of her body, the deep curve of her waist and rise to her hip. She'd changed her clothes since the showgrounds and was wearing a blue denim dress with a long zip up the middle. Bare feet, red toenails. Dad pulled the top sheet and a cream cotton blanket up from the bottom of the bed, covered her and lightly tucked her in.

'What do you know about Rebecca going to Queensland with Jasmine?' Dad asked me.

'Nothing. It's just talk. Something that would be fun to do, but not serious.'

'I've already told you,' Mum said, trying to sit up. 'That's why she took the money. It was in my purse last night. I know it was. And it was gone this morning. How dare she. I worked so hard on Lauren Reinhart's cake for that money.'

It was true that Mum worked most days, and often into the small hours, on her wedding cakes. She didn't do it for the money because Dad's orchard was productive and we seemed to have everything we needed, more than other people we knew. I'd say now that all the baking and decorating helped focus her mind and gave a task for her restless hands. It calmed her and offered her something to be proud of.

I remembered that night Lauren Reinhart came to the house to go through Mum's albums to choose her cake. She handed Mum a sample of the pink crepe the bridesmaids' dresses were being made out of so she could match the colour with the icing flowers.

'It'll all work out,' Dad said, patting Mum's shoulder. 'She'll be home soon. Get some rest.'

I followed Dad down the hallway to the kitchen.

'It was pretty bad,' I said. 'She screamed at Rebecca and attacked her in front of everyone.'

We looked at each other and I waited for him to say something, to react somehow. All he did was go to the buffet drawer, take out the phone book and thumb through the pages.

'Who're you calling?'

'Jasmine, to see if Rebecca is there,' he said.

I watched him dial, and swallow before he spoke. I glanced around thinking that for sure Rebecca was with Bull, not Jasmine.

Dad nodded to himself when he heard the news that the Vasilakis family hadn't seen or heard from Rebecca. He hung up.

'What about Bull?' Dad asked me. 'Reckon she's with him?'

Heat rose on my neck as I turned to fill the kettle.

'Eliza?'

I turned around. 'She knows not to have anything to do with him.'

'That's not answering my question.'

Dad stared at me, challenging me with his silence. But I was remembering the last time Mum and Rebecca had a bad fight.

It was late November. A Saturday. The house was quiet, organised, dishes drying in the rack beside the sink. We'd just finished lunch and Dad had left the house to attend to some orchard task.

Mum was at her workbench rolling out royal icing for a cake. I was bored, and uninterested in any suggestion Mum had for me that ranged from cleaning my room or folding washing to dusting the buffet shelves. As for Rebecca, she had quietly left the table and disappeared into the bathroom, then her bedroom. When she reappeared, I shrank with worry. Her hair was teased, smoothed, sprayed. Black eyeliner and lashes. Pink lips. A low-cut black t-shirt and denim shorts that showed the shape of her filly-like legs. A small brown bag slung over her shoulder.

Mum looked up. 'Where do you think you're going dressed like that?' she asked.

'Out,' Rebecca said, pacing fast, eyes directed at the porch door.

'No, you're not.'

Rebecca kept going.

'Stop right there,' Mum said, getting up from her workbench, apron speckled with white icing dust.

The walls vibrated when Rebecca slammed the door behind her.

'I forbid you to go out,' Mum roared, yanking the door open. 'Do you hear me?'

'What's your problem? I've done nothing wrong.'

'You need to ask permission before going out.'

'Why? So you can say no?'

'No daughter of mine is going anywhere dressed like that!'

'Fuck off,' Rebecca said.

A slap.

I didn't see Mum hit Rebecca, but I heard the power of it, and Rebecca's scream.

The wire back door opened and a stillness entered the house.

Dad came in from outside to see what the fighting was about. It was always like that when he came into a room, we all became quiet and still. Perhaps it was a kind of respect because we instantly settled down, even Mum. It was a remarkable thing to witness, a man with a naturally soft voice, no volume to it, who commanded authority but in a caring and placid way, like some schoolteachers can do.

'What's going on?' I heard him ask as I stepped forward.

Dad stared through his round wire-framed glasses, first to Mum then to Rebecca, waiting for an answer. He was a tall man, wiry with narrow shoulders, and a full head of dark brown hair. And even though his face was weathered from a lifetime of summers and winters outdoors there was nothing hard or rough-looking about him.

If anything was going to embolden Rebecca it was being hit by Mum.

'She just slapped me across the face,' she cried.

'She's going out, Maurie,' Mum said, 'and she won't say where, but probably with that Jasmine Greek girl, and that Plockton crowd.'

Plockton was a small farming town about twenty kilometres from Gyle, marginal flatland only suitable for cropping. Dad took his time, pinching his bottom lip while he looked at Rebecca.

'We've talked about this,' he said to her. 'We don't want you seeing Jasmine outside of school. And we're not having you going anywhere with those Plockton kids.'

'But I'm not doing anything wrong,' Rebecca protested.

'I'm not saying you are,' he said.

'Then what's your problem?'

'Because you're still young and we don't think they're a good influence.'

'I'm nearly eighteen.'

'That's right. You're seventeen years old and in my opinion you're far too young to roam wherever you want.'

'Well, I'm not staying here,' Rebecca said, turning and walking away.

'Rebecca,' he called out in his soft voice.

She glanced around at Dad, took a firmer grip on her shoulder bag strap and said, 'I hate it that you don't trust me.'

'We've discussed this before and had an agreement.'

'Telling me I have to do something is different to me agreeing.'

'Don't you dare defy your father,' Mum said, her voice shrill, off key.

If only she'd shut up and stayed quiet, because Mum speaking like that to Rebecca was equal to slapping her a second time. 'I can't stay here with her,' Rebecca said.

The wire door smacked behind her, leaving Dad and Mum standing side by side watching her go.

Dad turned to me. 'Do you know where she's going?'

'No,' I said bravely, in absolute loyalty to my sister. Yet, the night before she'd told me she was meeting Bull. That a group of them were catching up at the waterhole where a swing rope hung from a river red gum, magnificent in its girth and stretch into the centre of the water.

Dad lifted his glasses and rubbed the bridge of his nose, then placed them back in position. 'When will she be home?' he asked Mum.

'How on earth would I know?'

'Do you know where she's going?' he asked her.

'You think she tells me?' Mum glared back at him.

'Perhaps we need to take a different approach,' Dad said.

'Like what? Let her do whatever she wants and ruin her life?' Mum was yelling now.

I left them and went to my bedroom. Facedown on my bed, I felt the pull of wanting to be somewhere else, not having to answer

26

to anyone. That was the first time I understood why Rebecca wanted her freedom and would fight for it.

She didn't phone until that evening, saying she wouldn't be home until the next day. And she hung up before Mum, who took the call, could ask any questions. But at least she had phoned. Later the next day when Rebecca did walk in through the back door, Mum ignored her, didn't speak to her for a few days, walked out of the room when she came in, silly behaviour. It only changed when Dad asked Rebecca to apologise to Mum, which she did in a short sharp voice.

Fast forward four weeks to the madness at the showgrounds. Rebecca wasn't home and she'd not phoned yet to say where she was, or when she'd be back.

The kettle boiled.

'Want tea?' I asked Dad.

'You've not answered my question about Bull Tennant. Do you know if Rebecca is with him?'

'I don't know where she is,' I said.

'Your mother told me Bull passed her this afternoon coming up the mountain.'

'Yeah. He did, but so what? He was probably just driving home from work.'

'So what's going on?' Dad asked.

'Why am I in trouble? I've done nothing wrong.'

'You're not in trouble. I just want to know if Rebecca is seeing Bull after your mother and I have been very clear she's not to have anything to do with him.'

There was nothing for it, except to own my lie and make it real.

'I don't know,' I said.

Dad took a step forward. 'Eliza, are you telling me the truth?'

'Yes, I am,' I said, pushing my shoulders back, standing straighter. 'And what's Bull got to do with Mum throwing a fit today in front of everyone? It's her who should be in trouble, not Rebecca, or me, or Bull, or Jasmine, or anyone else. If it wasn't for Mum doing that, Rebecca would be home right now.'

Dad was always a composed person so I didn't expect – and have never forgotten – the way he lowered himself into a chair, took his glasses off as he bowed his head and covered his face with his hands. Still, I can hear the deep-down, almost silent groan, like I'd punched and winded him. I was frightened because I'd never seen him weak like that before. I was forming the words to take it all back and tell him the whole truth, and my part in it, when he spoke.

'Go off to bed, Eliza,' he said, without looking at me. 'You've had a big day and have work tomorrow.'

'But Dad.'

'I told you to go off to bed,' he said quietly.

I did as I was told.

*

I slept heavily and woke to magpies carolling. Breeze through my window lifted the lace curtains, and with a sudden smack of memory, I was out of bed and rushing down the hall to Rebecca's bedroom. Her door was open, so she wasn't home and my body tensed before I'd even stepped inside. Everything was the same as before. I opened her wardrobe, clothes hanging as expected. Shoes and boots scattered on the wardrobe floor. Her brown shoulder bag. Cardboard boxes, folders, more novels, an extra blanket on the top shelf.

I turned to a sound.

At the window, I yanked the curtains back, and gasped to see Bryce Jones standing outside Rebecca's bedroom window. He was Dad's full-time orchard hand, who also worked in the garden a couple of half days a week. We were both startled, but he quickly recovered, gave me a quick wave before turning his back to continue deadheading a pink rose bush. Bryce was in his late thirties, olive-skinned with long dark hair that he sometimes wore in a ponytail. His eyes were a bright icy blue, unusually piercing. Rebecca and I always avoided him. He'd worked for Dad for about three years, and sometimes Mum asked him to deliver her wedding cakes, especially those in Benalla where he lived with his mother.

I closed the curtains and went to the kitchen.

Dad was pouring hot water from the kettle into Mum's favourite mug, white bone china with tiny violets.

'Rebecca's not home,' I said.

He shook his head.

'Has she called?' I asked.

'No.' He removed a teabag, added milk.

'So what now?'

'I'm going to phone the police.'

'Why?'

When he turned towards me, I saw his face was grey, unshaven, and through his glasses his eyes looked smaller. 'Because this is the first time in her life she's never phoned us to say where she is.'

I knew then that Rebecca must be with Bull. It was the only thing that made any sense.

'You go off to the shop,' Dad said, walking towards the hallway with the mug of tea, taking it to Mum who was still in bed.

'Why doesn't Mum get up?'

'She's just tired. See you later,' he said, glancing at me before disappearing down the hallway.

THREE

Christmas carols looped through the tracks, one after the other, high-pitched and jolly. Robyn was out the back in her house. Gary had arrived home from a hay carting job, so my instructions were to call her if I got busy and couldn't manage. Even though I didn't particularly like any of the customers, I waited for them to arrive so the monotony of the day would be broken. I flicked through the women's magazines that I'd already gazed at. And there I went, far away from the mountain, across oceans into another world where famous actresses with beautiful hair and clothes lived. My Meryl Streep and Debra Winger phase.

It got hotter as the morning went on. Out the front a listless breeze fluttered through the vine. Everyone who came into the shop was old, red faced, sweaty. Cora Engelman, from three doors up, stood at the counter like she was ecstatic to have an outing even though she'd only walked a hundred metres. She was a retired horse farrier who wore her dead husband's clothes. Every Saturday, at roughly the same time, she bought *The Age* newspaper and a packet of Werther's toffees. As I was counting out her change, I saw Dad drive past in the direction of Gyle. His gaze was forward-looking, blank, not taking any notice of the shop, which was unusual.

Normally, he'd peer across to try and see me behind the counter, then wave. By then he would've phoned the police about Rebecca. Fear tightened my chest; how strange it was to realise Rebecca was suddenly missing, like she'd magically vanished. But then, maybe she was already home.

Customers came and went. Sinead Healy went down the back to speak with Robyn, leaving me with her three young kids who I kept happy by giving them each a Paddle Pop. Sinead was about six months pregnant and my skin shrank at the thought she had sex with Jacob Healy. Next, five men wearing black leather arrived on motorbikes. They bought hot meat pies with sauce, and soft drinks, then sat out the front talking to each other. They weren't real bikies, but clean-shaven men from Melbourne who took long rides on the weekends. Later, skinny cyclists pulled up after peddling all the way up the mountain from Gyle. They were the same as the bikers, city people who used the shop as a resting place. They didn't buy anything but refilled their bottles from the tap near the phone box, then sat in the shade of the grapevine to drink and talk.

As the sun burned brighter and tilted west, a black ute with P-plates arrived and parked under the plane tree, the roo bar almost touching the thick motley trunk.

Bull.

I watched him unclip his seatbelt and open the car door. A cigarette wedged in the corner of his mouth. Before he came inside he slowly crushed his smoke under the heel of his boot. The buzzer went, four strides and he was at the counter.

'How you going?' he asked, not wanting an answer. 'What's going on with Rebecca?'

I opened my mouth and stared back at him.

'What's she doing?' he said.

'She didn't come home last night. I thought she was with you.'

Bull leaned forward, stared at me. 'What do you mean?'

'We don't know where she is. She had a fight with Mum and took off. So I thought she'd be with you, but I've not said anything about that.'

'She was supposed to come with me to the Winton racing trial this morning. But she didn't show.'

'Really?'

'Yeah. She didn't turn up.'

'I didn't know that,' I replied.

Bull's brown eyes became small, intense. 'So where is she?' he asked.

I told him about the fight at the showgrounds the day before. How Mum turned up and screamed at Rebecca, accusing her of stealing money, and that she tried to drag her into the car. Bull stood with his legs slightly apart, hands in his jeans pockets, listening carefully to everything I said. So I kept on going, trying not to exaggerate, and I didn't, yet even to my own ears it sounded like a made-up story.

'Then everything went to hell because Mum ended up on the ground and started howling. Everyone was watching. It was pretty fucking bad,' I said.

I had never spoken the word *fuck* out loud before so the word hung in the air and I felt both surprise and pride at having said it in front of Bull.

'Then what?'

'Rebecca took off the back way into town. Mum figured she was going to get the school bus, but she didn't come home. And she's not with Jasmine, so I figured she was with you.'

Bull looked around as if he might see Rebecca walking past the shop.

'Dad's phoned the police this morning.'

'Why?'

'Because we're all worried. Mum's in bed upset.'

'That doesn't make any sense,' he said, as if talking to himself.

'I think she's just got the shits with Mum and will come home when she's ready.'

Another swear word had just popped out and I felt more equal to Bull.

'So where do you think she is then?' he asked.

'For all I know she might be home already.'

'Give me some Marlboros and a Coke.'

No please or thank you, but his voice was kind so it didn't bother me. When he plucked a ten-dollar note from his wallet, I caught a glimpse of a photo of Rebecca in the front slot. Tilted head, big smile.

I handed over the smokes and Coke, counted out his change.

'You reckon you can let me know if she's home then?' he said. That was his dilemma. Bull couldn't phone our place, or just appear on the back doorstep.

'Maybe she's gone to Queensland like she's been talking about,' I said.

'No. She was going to the Winton car trials with me this morning.'

'What about Queensland then?'

'She wasn't serious about that. Yeah, maybe a cool thing to do, but she wasn't going.'

Bull seemed certain and I immediately believed him.

'I'll let you know what's going on,' I said.

He nodded approval and I was happy to have pleased him. And when he left the shop, I kept my eyes on him until he reached his ute. In one smooth movement he opened the door and folded himself behind the wheel. He took a moment to light a smoke, and as he sped away he glanced in my direction and gave me a little wave.

When Bull was gone, the dust taking a minute to settle, I stood behind the counter feeling lonely, left out of things, impatient, waiting for something important to happen in my life. I glanced at the clock. Ninety minutes to go.

*

Finally, I was free. Outside it was hot and dry, everything was slowly baking. The idea of it ever raining again seemed unlikely. The main street was deserted, parked cars and not a person in sight. Magpies warbled. Other birds joined in.

When I walked into the porch, Ripper lifted his head and followed me with his half-blind eyes as I stepped into the kitchen. A burned toast smell. The table was clear, the sink empty, a tea towel hung over the oven handle. A pedestal fan oscillating across the room flicked the butcher's calendar and the hanging Christmas cards.

'Hi,' I called, 'I'm home!'

A sound deep inside the house. A door opened or closed. Perhaps the scrape of a chair. Faraway muffled talking. Then soft footsteps.

I opened the cupboard beside the sink, took out a glass, filled it with water, and drank.

When I turned Dad was standing in the kitchen at the hallway door. He wasn't wearing his usual work gear, but his good clothes, brown trousers with a sharp crease down the front, and a beige short-sleeved open-necked shirt. His dark brown hair was parted and neatly combed. Something was wrong. Even though Dad was dressed tidily, as if he was going out somewhere, his face was lined in a new way and he looked very tired.

As I stepped towards him a flash of lightness crossed his face.

'Have you heard anything from Rebecca?' he asked.

'No. I thought she'd be home by now.'

'We've got no idea where she is,' he said.

'What did the police say?'

'To wait a bit. That she'd come home.'

It was then I should've told Dad about Bull coming into the shop, that he was looking for Rebecca too, that she hadn't shown up that morning at their meeting place to go to the Winton car trials. I hesitated because I'd already bald-faced lied to him about what I knew. At the time, I believed my silence was what Bull and Rebecca expected of me.

'I can't make sense of it,' Dad said. 'I phoned Cheryl Tennant to see if Rebecca was there with Bull. But she's not. What do you think of this idea she's gone to Queensland? Your mother thinks that maybe she has.'

'I don't know.'

Dad slowly rubbed his eyes with his fingertips as if massaging them, his glasses moving up and down on the bridge of his nose. He kept doing that in a distracted way, like trying to work something out. Suddenly he looked up, as if remembering I was there.

'I need to check on your mother,' he said, turning away and closing the hallway door behind him, separating me from him and Mum.

So there I was, standing in the kitchen, my feet planted on the green patterned vinyl. Cool air from the whirring fan brushed my skin. Staring deeply into the dining table, an idea came.

The flywire screen gently closed behind me as I walked out the back door.

FOUR

Our back garden was neat with leafy trees, trimmed shrubs, and beds of flowers. Pots were filled with daisies and pansies. The roses were out, all colours, mostly red. Wisteria draped across the two water tanks. In the distance Dunny Hill stood out against the wide blue sky; its granite peak looked pink and warm as if glowing from inside. It was too late to be going up there on my own without telling anyone, but I turned towards it anyway, following a feeling.

The dirt track was powder-soft from the tractor and trailer tyres that constantly pounded the dry hard ground. A long row of pines on the left. On the right, Granny Smith and Golden Delicious were in full leaf with small hard fruit growing. Up ahead was a dam, the surface half-covered with pink water lilies, like a troupe of resting ballerinas. The track elbowed left at the dam bank where a plot of clingstone peaches was being drip watered. The light was getting weaker. Small flocks of cockatoos flew into the state forest. The only sound was the soft padding of my footfall on the dusty track, which eventually narrowed into a driveway.

The workman's cottage was on the left, hidden behind a dense windbreak of wattles, banksias, eucalypts. When my grandfather William Bundy was an orchardist, a full-time workman and his family had lived there. Over the years different families had come and gone. But Bryce Jones lived on a small property just outside of Benalla with his mother, who bred Gotland sheep for their wool, so the cottage hadn't had a tenant for about three years.

Into the driveway. Dead grass. Scarecrow-looking plants from lack of water and neglect. Through the open wire gate and along the footpath, and – as was second nature for a country kid – my eyes searched for coiled or moving snakes. Beside the front stairs was a giant liquidambar with small thirsty green leaves curled over like tiny hoods. Up the stairs and onto the verandah. Dead blowies covered the sills. The front doorknob turned, but was stiff, so I put my shoulder to it and pushed. Inside, hot stale air and the stink of dust and mice.

'Rebecca?' I called into the living room. 'It's me.'

I spoke loudly, believing she could hear me.

'Dad and Mum are freaking out and Dad's been to the police. Bull is looking for you too.'

My voice was loud and echoey, like I was shouting inside one of our big cool stores where the apples were kept before being trucked to market. There was another sound – a whisper, or nearby breathing, but it could've been white noise, or my imagination. I didn't know why, but I was scared, my heart was pounding.

'Rebecca!' I called, looking around, half-expecting her to silently step out from behind a door. I stood still and listened. Nothing, only the cottage's old bones creaking in the heat.

Into the kitchen. The floorboards beside the sink were rotted and cracked. VB cans on a round timber table. Ash and butts in a glass jar on the floor beside a chair. A hole in the skirting board and plaster, big enough for my hand to reach into.

'Rebecca?' I yelled. 'Where are you?'

If she was there, she would've answered. I was certain of that.

At the lounge room window, a faded curtain was only half attached to the rod. A mantel and fireplace filled the inner wall. I turned right and went into a bedroom. On the floor was a mattress covered in a crumpled, pale yellow sheet that I recognised from home. Beside it was an open plastic bag filled with used tissues. A folded brown blanket lay on the floor beside the window. A glass jar with wilted red roses, not quite dead; my guess was they were about a week old. Rebecca must have brought them.

Standing there, a fourteen-year-old virgin, I was a voyeur imagining Rebecca with Bull's man's body on top of her. They were beautiful, strong, grown up, and I believed then I was hopeless in some way – too shy, or not brave enough, because I could never do that. A few weeks earlier, at the football club awards ceremony at the community hall, Andy Knightly had tried to kiss me. It seemed everyone was pairing up and there we were, the two of us outside in the dark standing too close, the smell of Clearasil on his skin, beer on his breath. The Bee Gees' 'How Deep Is Your Love?' coming through a distant speaker. When his hand went under my skirt, I slid to the side and ran back into the hall, gathered up my things and walked home. Two days later when we saw each other on the school bus, he seemed embarrassed too. Without a word spoken, we entered a pact where nothing was ever said, as if it never happened.

I opened the wardrobe door. Wire coat hangers, nothing else.

Then hurried out.

A quick look around in the other bedroom, empty except for a dressing table with a cracked mirror.

Back in the living room there was a tremor in my voice when I said, as if speaking to myself, 'Rebecca, please speak to me if you can hear me. I'm by myself. What do you want me to do? I'll help. But Dad and Mum are sick with worry. You need to come home.'

Rebecca wasn't there. Still, I waited, counted to ten.

Outside I walked around the back, past blackberry bushes taller than the cottage, and carefully edged my way through the dead grass to the corrugated iron shed and peered inside. The door hung open on one hinge. Golden light glinted in through rusted holes. Ancient rabbit traps hung from the rafters. A faded and stiff garden hose was looped on a hook. A kid's bike was covered in dust and grime, pink tassels at the end of the handlebars. Paint cans, shovels and spades, a pickaxe. All of it long forgotten. In the soft dirt, where I stood, there were footprints that didn't belong to me. I placed my sandalled foot inside one of them, longer and wider than mine, then turned away and looked across the back fence towards Dunny Hill.

It had been our playground when we were kids. Rebecca and I knew every wallaby track, wombat hole, hollow log. We'd been up there under the cover of cloud, during snow, or when it was dead summer dry. Sometimes Bull was with us. One school holiday the three of us built a log cabin among a copse of tall pines. We sawed and hacked those trees and squared them into shape, then filled the gaps with clay we dragged up from the dam in plastic buckets. The roof was too low for us to stand upright and we never did properly finish it. Even so, we slept overnight in it once in our sleeping bags, eating food we'd brought from home.

From the cottage shed, I could see the tops of those pines where the squat timber cabin was. A mass of dark green against a weakening blue sky. Fright surged through me, that feeling of being watched. I turned. Nothing.

I peered up into Dunny Hill.

'Rebecca!' I yelled, my voice fading into the distance.

A fleeting idea that I should go up to the cabin came and went. It felt too quiet, I was scared, but not having the right footwear was my excuse to turn away. And besides, Rebecca wouldn't be up there. That log cabin was too small and crude for anyone to go to. It was

40

just a holiday project that we forgot about as soon as we went back to school.

As I turned towards the track, a lone kookaburra flew overhead. Its wingbeats were slow, rhythmic, laboured, appearing to use a lot of energy to get to where it was going. It was headed towards our house, but then abruptly curved around and flew in the direction of Dunny Hill.

*

When I got home, Dad was in the kitchen heating up chicken soup from a can. The toast was ready. It was a rare thing to see Dad preparing a meal, the kitchen had always been Mum's domain.

'Where have you been?' he asked.

'I went for a walk. Where's Mum?'

'Still in bed. I'm taking her a tray.'

'What are we going to do?' I asked.

'I don't know,' he said.

I decided to be helpful, a good daughter making up for what I hadn't told. I opened the fridge for the margarine, spread some on the toast and cut it in half. Next, I set up the green tray with the short legs – the tray Mum served us meals on when we were sick in bed or lying on the couch – and laid an ironed tea towel on it to serve as a tablecloth, and a soup spoon on the right side. I hurried to the backyard garden and picked a budding yellow rose, cut the stem to fit neatly into a small crystal vase and put it on the tray. These were the little touches I had seen Mum do. Then I stood back and waited while Dad ladled the steaming soup into the bowl. All his actions were slow, his mind elsewhere, distracted with Rebecca and Mum, who as far as I could tell hadn't been out of bed all day.

41

When Dad disappeared up the hallway, I dialled Bull's number. Two rings, he picked up.

'It's Eliza,' I said.

'She home?'

'No.'

'You're kidding me. Right?'

I lowered my voice. 'We don't know where she is. My parents are really worried.'

Bull deeply inhaled, probably smoking.

'When did you last see her?' I asked.

'A few days ago. Tuesday.'

'Dad's spoken to the police.'

'What'd they say?'

'Not to worry, that she'll come home.'

'Okay, thanks,' he said, then hung up.

I was anxious, a little nauseous. Rebecca wasn't with Jasmine or Bull, or home, which obviously pointed to something else. It was then that the notion she'd gone to Queensland started to set in. I wasn't sure, had no feeling for it, but nothing else made sense. I closed my eyes and imagined Rebecca staring out the window of a Greyhound bus heading north. As if standing on the side of a highway, I saw her fly past, her head resting on the window, staring into the distance, not thinking about me and how I might feel about her leaving home. That's another thing that troubled me. I was alone. The house was too quiet.

I went up the hallway and stood outside my parents' half-open bedroom door, listened to their whispers, the low voices they used when they didn't want Rebecca or me to know what they were talking about. I heard Mum say something about Bull, words to the effect that he would know where she was.

I moved in closer, held my breath.

'I don't think so,' Dad said. 'I phoned Cheryl.'

'Come on, Maurie, get with it. Sinead Healy told me she saw Rebecca in Bull's car last week. The police need to haul him into the station.'

Mum's whispering voice was urgent as if some terrifying drama was unfolding. My stomach cramped because, once again, I needed to speak up, to confess everything I knew. Still, I didn't move because Rebecca wouldn't want me to do that, to dob her in, and besides, she was on a bus heading towards a long beach with palm trees. But I was confused because that made no sense. She wasn't on a bus by herself, leaving Bull and her friends behind. There was buzzing in my ears. I was uneasy, my breathing was shallow.

'Love,' Dad said to Mum, 'the police have said they'll have a word with him.'

'You're so naive,' Mum replied in a hissing whisper.

Mum's sob was more like a loud hiccup, then softer with Dad shushing her.

I left all the dishes in the sink as a protest that I was only fourteen years old and someone needed to be in charge, helping me. After all, I had worked all day in the shop, so I was tired, plus my sister hadn't come home and no one knew where she was. It was the strangest time in my life.

I went to my bedroom and firmly and deliberately closed the door to signal that no one should enter. I just sat there, enclosed inside four walls, curtains and window open. A pink-streaked sky. A moth hit the flywire screen. Sitting on my bed, I spoke to Rebecca.

Where are you? I asked.

When the answer came it was hard to distinguish between a feeling or an internal voice, perhaps intuition, but at the time I believed it was Rebecca who told me, *Don't worry. I'm all right.* I wanted to cry with relief, and feeling a bit better I climbed into bed and slept. Sometime during the night Ripper started barking. He was locked in the back porch, and because he was almost blind, it would've been a sound or smell that disturbed him. A wombat or some other creature wandering around outside. I expected to hear Dad's quiet voice telling him to settle down, to get back in his basket, but he didn't come. I thought to go to Ripper, but I was half asleep and couldn't quite rouse myself. And besides, each time after Ripper barked he went silent for long minutes, so I dozed again only to snap awake when he started up again. It was during one of those barking episodes my mind turned to that blue-shirted and bearded man I'd seen at the showgrounds – who I later learned was called Jeremy McCourty. He had a black dog at his side. I remembered how we'd looked at each other square in the eye as Mum drove away. There was definitely something unusual about that encounter.

*

I woke early and went straight to Rebecca's room, holding my breath, willing her to be in bed. I held a clear image of her. Red hair a curled mess on the pillow, eyes closed, pale warm skin, a white sheet covering her body. I stepped inside. She wasn't there.

Dad and Mum's bedroom door was ajar. I went straight in. Two long bodies lay motionless in sleep. Dad was spooning into Mum, his arm resting across her pink nightie.

When I sat beside Mum, I put my whole weight on the bed. They both woke and looked at me, blinking.

'I thought of something last night,' I said, and before they had lifted their heads, I told them what I remembered about the man at the showgrounds. The black dog. As far as I was aware, no one at that stage had said out loud that Rebecca might've been abducted. I knew things like that happened because at the shop I read the newspaper headlines and sometimes the stories. It happened more often than an ordinary person might think.

'I'm not saying he knows where Rebecca is,' I said, 'but I've never seen him before and it was weird that he was just standing around watching what was going on.'

'What do you think of that, Maurie?' Mum said, her hair in long thick ropes, unattended for a couple of days, which in itself was alarming. My mother was a vain person, and there she was, ashen complexion and deeper set eyes with purple hollows underneath. She looked unwell. Our powerful mother had become weak and pathetic.

Dad sat up, his left elbow pressed into a pillow. He was wearing a white singlet that showed his thin but muscled arms. The outline of his work shirts, which protected him from the sun, was imprinted on his body. His forearms and neck were deeply tanned and leathery, but from the elbows upwards, his arms, chest and back were milky white. His glasses were folded on the bedside table leaving him to appear incomplete; the same man, but with a narrower face and smaller eyes.

'It's worth mentioning to the police,' he said, then looking across to me, 'Your mother and I have an appointment with them in Gyle at ten. Will you be all right here by yourself?'

'You need to stay here, Eliza, in case she calls,' Mum said.

Dad put his glasses on and spoke directly to me. 'Last night, after you'd gone to bed, we had a good look in the house and we can't find the maroon travel bag. It looks like it's missing, unless you know where it is. And Mum says Rebecca's bathers aren't anywhere in her room and there's other clothes we can't find.'

'So she's gone to Queensland after all?' I said.

'Do you know where her thongs are?' Mum asked me.

'I've not looked for them,' I said. 'But when she left the show-grounds she only had her schoolbag. That means she must've come home if she's taken stuff with her.'

Mum sat up, frowned. 'Who knows what she had planned and hidden away.'

'But until you turned up at the showgrounds she was minding her own business reading a book, just waiting for the bus to take us home.'

Mum covered her face with her hands and shook her head, saying, 'That Bull Tennant knows where she is.'

Dad looked at me with warning eyes that I shouldn't upset her.

'Off you go and get some breakfast,' he said.

When Mum lay back in Dad's arms and started whimpering like an unsettled child, something shifted in me. I thought she was pathetic. Why didn't she get out of bed and do more to find out where Rebecca was?

'This is all your fault,' I said to her.

'Go on,' Dad said. 'That's enough.'

I made breakfast. Another meal on my own and with each mouthful of the milky cereal I thought of Rebecca, how she always sat opposite, sometimes softly kicking my foot under the table to get my attention, or just to hurt me, sometimes to share a private joke against our parents. Right then, sitting alone, I didn't know what was happening, but the room felt too large, me tiny on the chair, everything closing in. I started to cry, tears hot on my face. I breathed Rebecca's name and spoke to her again, asking her to come home, to hurry up because I couldn't handle her being away. I'd just grabbed a handful of tissues when Dad came into the room and, unlike the comforting support he gave Mum, he seemed irritated with me.

'Eliza,' he said, 'come on, stop that. Put the kettle on and make Mum a cuppa.'

'Dad, I need to tell you something.'

He walked over to me. 'What?'

'Bull came into the shop yesterday to ask me where Rebecca was. They were going to the Winton car trials that morning and she didn't turn up at their meeting place. He's got no idea where she is. So you have to tell Mum to leave him alone.'

Dad stiffened, stared at me, 'Why didn't you tell me this before?'

'Because Mum always goes nuts.'

Dad glanced away. 'She's got good reason to be concerned about Rebecca seeing Bull.'

'There's nothing wrong with him and I believe him when he says he doesn't know where she is. Mum's just a snob.'

'Bull drives too fast and he's got no ambition,' he said, hesitating, finding his words. 'He's got a reputation for getting into trouble and he's had dealings with the police. We don't want Rebecca getting herself into a situation that changes the direction of her life.'

'Like what? Being happy?'

'You don't know what you're talking about, so stop it.'

'That makes you a snob too,' I snapped.

Dad gave me one of his stares that had a thousand words attached to it. I felt ashamed.

'You should have told me about Bull coming to see you in the shop. Mum thinks Rebecca might've been in Bull's car Friday afternoon when he passed her coming up from town.'

'But I one hundred per cent believe him. Bull told me he hasn't seen her since last Tuesday.'

'Last Tuesday?' Dad repeated, nodding as if working something out.

I sat there confused; so many conversations and angles, I could hardly keep up. The thing was, I'd wondered if Rebecca had been in Bull's car on Friday afternoon too. I'd replayed, over and over, that moment when Bull changed gears, his forward-looking stare, the empty passenger seat. It had occurred to me that someone might've been hunched down, trying not to be seen. I wasn't convinced one way or the other.

'I've got to start the watering and pack some peaches for an order. Please make your mother a cup of tea, and some toast, and take it to her in bed.'

He left the room without waiting to hear me agree. I considered defiance, ignoring the request, but the thought of Dad's silent disapproval got me out of the chair.

When I delivered the tray with tea and toast, Mum was lying on her back, corpse-like, arms across her chest and eyes closed. I believed she was awake, so I pressed the tray down hard onto her lap so she knew I was angry with her, fed up with her laziness. Tea slopped onto the floral tea towel that I'd placed on the tray as a mini-tablecloth.

'I know you're only pretending to be asleep,' I said.

FIVE

It wasn't long after Dad and Mum left for the police station that the first helicopter came low and thundering across the orchard. I hurried outside, looked up and saw its black belly pass over the cypress hedge then disappear. Everyone on the mountain knew that sound, because Maryhill was on the flight path for the choppers that took all the north-east car crash patients to hospitals in Melbourne. When the second helicopter followed, as if chasing the first – something I'd never seen before – I immediately thought there had been a serious road crash somewhere north on the Hume Freeway. A driver had fallen asleep at the wheel. Or a drunk P-plater had skidded out of control. Maybe a roll-over on a back road where fearless young men had their secret drag races. I knew about those possibilities because in the shop I sold newspapers that reported on those types of tragedies.

I was bored, nothing to do, so out of curiosity about the two helicopters, I switched on the ABC radio's eleven o'clock news. That familiar anthem I'd heard every morning of my life when Dad turned the radio on, one minute to the hour, usually at seven.

Breaking news was delivered so fast I wasn't sure I heard properly. A family on a farm were all dead. Maryhill. It happened

49

in Maryhill. Two adults and three children. No names. I stared into the wall, felt my warm breath. Police were on the scene. There had been a shooting. More details to follow. The next story, something about Christmas shopping records being broken. I tried to piece it all together. Somewhere on the mountain there was a person with a gun who had killed people. Which family? Which children? In my mind I scanned through faces as if I might work it out. I glanced at the back door. Was I safe? Almost every farmer on the mountain had a gun so they could end the suffering of sick and dying animals. Or, like Bull, to kill foxes and rabbits, vermin he called them.

I wanted Dad, but he said they wouldn't be home until after lunch, which made no sense to me. Where were they having lunch? Why hadn't I been included, or told any details? And why didn't they come home to me so we could have Sunday lunch together like we always did? Right then, I wanted Rebecca more than anything. I would've felt safe if she had been home with me. More than that, the drama of a shooting would have equally ignited and horrified her. She'd be bright-eyed with energy trying to work out the details. She'd make phone calls.

I couldn't think who to call, so I phoned Bull, but Cheryl answered.

I asked her if she knew anything about a shooting, that it was on the news.

'Did you hear the helicopters?' I said. 'There were two of them, one straight after the other.'

'What are you talking about, a shooting? Who is this calling me?'

'Eliza Bundy,' I said.

'Why are you talking about a shooting?'

It was then I realised she was crying.

'What's wrong?' I waited, heard her hiccup as she tried to catch her breath. 'Is Bull there?' I asked.

'He's at the police station. They came and got him early this morning. I've had a gutful of you bloody Bundys. You think you can say whatever you like, and the next thing Bull is in trouble for nothing. He's done nothing wrong.'

Then she hung up.

When I put the phone back on the cradle, I went to the kitchen drawer and took out the black-handled knife Mum used to slice tomatoes, and rested it on the soft skin of my forearm. I thought of Mum's red purse with Lauren Reinhart's money in it. Rebecca walking away behind the toilet block, and my mother grinning at me in the car like she was insane. Dad glaring at me with his disapproving eyes, a controlling passive-aggressive bastard because I had to be good, always good, or he'd turn his back and walk away. And Mum acting helpless in bed. I hated my parents. There, I'd finally admitted it. *Rebecca, where are you? Help me.* I pulled the knife sideways and when the blood flowed out like escaping poison I felt I could breathe again, finally released from pain. More like I'd given myself a different pain, a lovely distraction, and I pressed a tea towel onto it to soak up all the hurt and loneliness that I had released.

I went back to bed and slept and dreamed I was with Rebecca. We were laughing. And when I woke the memory of the dream was too foggy to properly recall, but I felt better for it, lighter, a bit happier. My arm was throbbing and I peeled back the tea towel and saw the angled cut I'd made, seeping clear liquid, small bubbles of it. In the bathroom I pinched it closed, wrapped gauze around it and secured it with a knot, all the while trying to hold on to the nice feeling I had from the dream.

Back in bed I slept again. It was like I couldn't get enough sleep and when I woke I was hungry. The light in my room was dimmer, perhaps it was overcast or late afternoon. Then the memory returned, that Rebecca was missing. And there had been helicopters earlier on. I wondered if there was a link between those two things. And why was Bull at the police station?

Down the hallway, I opened the door into the living room. Dad and Mum were sitting on the couch, staring into the TV. A female reporter was standing at the top of Earls Creek Road. I was certain of that location because the bus went there twice every school day, morning and afternoon. That row of nine mailboxes: one was square, most were round, one was painted dark purple, another one was pale yellow.

'What's happened?' I asked.

They quickly shushed me, and in unison leaned forward, as they watched the aerial footage of a long driveway lined with leafy poplars. Then tall trees that surrounded a large square house with three chimneys and a wrap-around verandah. My heart went strange. It was the Healys' place on Glen Lochan Road, where Rebecca got off the bus on her babysitting nights. It was only the day before that I'd seen those kids. Elliot had helped the others with their Paddle Pop wrappers. Audrey's new gappy smile; a front tooth had recently come out. I've always liked the names Sinead chose for her children and have never forgotten them. The older two that went to Maryhill Primary were Elliot and Audrey. The little boy, who wasn't old enough for school, was Mason.

Next there was a set of swings, a trampoline out the back of the house, a blue wading pool. I imaged Rebecca pushing the children on the swings. Maybe she jumped on the trampoline with them. Or sat on the dry grass beside the pool as they splashed in the shallow water. The aerial shots were showing the whole country, the whole world, the Healys' house and backyard, as if that horrific event didn't demand any privacy. Back to the reporter standing at a distance from a police car that was blocking the entry into

Glen Lochan Road. A couple of uniformed police were leaning against an unmarked car parked further along.

I sat beside Dad. If I reached out I could touch him, so that made me feel better. I clenched my teeth, took a deep breath and held it. The cut on my forearm was pulsing. Neither parent seemed to notice the bandage or asked me what had happened, because there were more important things going on than me. I was never a problem for them, so they thought. Everything was always about Rebecca. And now there'd been people shot dead on the mountain. I exhaled and took in another deep breath.

The graphic at the bottom of the TV said the reporter was Virginia Hurley, and just as her face filled the screen the wind blew her hair across her right eye. Three children had been shot. I knew they were Elliot, Audrey and Mason. A woman had been shot too. That would be Sinead. The reporter didn't say anything about the unborn baby. I was there when Sinead showed Robyn the grey and white ultrasound, its huge head like it was floating in outer space. I knew if the baby was a girl, her name would be Gwyneth. If a boy, Fletcher.

I reached out and touched Dad's arm. I needed some kindness, some understanding about how lonely and confused I felt, but he didn't respond. I glanced at him, saw his sad face and his jaw slowly chewing something, or maybe he was grinding his teeth. I took my hand back and rested it on my heart, felt it beating against the throb in my arm. An adult male had been found with a fatal gunshot wound. That would be Jacob. There was aerial footage of his ute parked close to a large dam in a bare paddock with lots of sheep in the distance huddled along a fence. Then the reporter was saying that the police weren't looking for anyone else, and something about the drought and the mental pressure it put on families. That didn't make any sense to me. Why was having no rain and skinny sheep an excuse for anyone to die?

Virginia Hurley moved the hair away from her eye. They wouldn't release the names of the victims until the families had been notified and I didn't understand why that was necessary. Some things needed to be left private. Except for family, friends and the residents on the mountain, none of the viewers had ever heard of Sinead and her lovely innocent kids before they were murdered. So why did anyone need to know their names or anything about them when they were dead? It didn't seem right.

Then Tony Russo was on the television. He lived on Glen Lochan Road, near Marion Road, a couple of kilometres from the Healys. His wife, Jenny, was standing close beside him. She looked terrified, like Jacob was still on the loose with his gun. Tony swatted a fly and told the reporter how shocked they were.

'Lovely family,' he said. 'You'd never imagine something like this in our neck of the woods. We're a close-knit community. We never knew anything was wrong.'

Then a phone number was on the screen for people to call if they needed help. I guessed they meant for people thinking of doing the same thing as Jacob Healy. I couldn't believe that was necessary either.

And so, the Healys were all dead and the newsreader in the studio started talking about the fire risk in the Yarra Valley.

As Dad turned off the TV, Mum lifted herself from the couch and stretched her arms up high like she was just waking up. That was the moment she should've turned to me and said something, asked how I was. I rested my bandaged arm out in front on my knee so it was impossible to miss. But she didn't notice, or if she did register that her child had been hurt in some way she didn't care. She was only worried about herself. Rebecca had gone off somewhere – the third night was approaching – and yet our family crisis seemed to be more about Mum. She put her hands in her hair and retied her ponytail with a thick red hair tie, then without a word went up the hallway, where I assumed she was going back to bed.

Dad looked at me. 'Shocking business.'

'I served Sinead in the shop yesterday. She came in with the kids. I gave them ice creams,' I said, quietly.

He put his arm around me and pulled me close, the familiar smell of his sweat, the stiff strength in his arm. 'Did you? That's tough,' Dad said.

'Do you think Jacob killing his family has anything to do with Rebecca not coming home?'

Dad pulled away, looked at me. 'Why do you say that?'

'I don't know. It's just that she works there sometimes. And now she's missing and they're all dead.'

Dad stared into the wall, mouth open. 'It's just a coincidence,' he said, weakly.

'Why was Jacob's ute at the dam?' I asked.

'I'm guessing he wanted to make sure he died. That if the bullet he gave himself didn't work, then he'd drown.'

'So he killed the kids and Sinead?'

'That's what the talk is.'

'Why would he do that? You know, kill them?'

'I've heard they had financial worries. That the Healys were in a lot of debt and he couldn't see a way out of it. Not having any money and a poor rain season can get to people.'

'Why didn't he just kill himself then?'

'It makes no sense to me.'

I shifted gears. 'What did the police say about Rebecca?'

'When we got there, they were responding to this Healy situation so we didn't get to speak to anyone. But I understand they've talked to Bull.'

'He's got nothing to do with Rebecca not coming home,' I said.

'That's for the police to decide.'

I sat up and glared at him. 'I told you, Dad. He's a good person and he doesn't know where she is.'

'Well, the money from Mum's purse is gone. I'm trying to piece everything together. The travel bag is missing. And some of her clothes, mostly summer things. And she was talking about going to Queensland, so she might've gone. I just don't know. And now this crazy business,' he said, flicking his hand towards the TV.

He inhaled and closed his eyes.

'Dad.'

He didn't move.

'I know she was really upset with Mum,' I said. 'They've been fighting a lot, but I still don't think she'd leave us without saying goodbye.'

'Rebecca is a strong-minded young woman. She's always pushed the boundaries. So maybe she decided impulsively to go off like she'd been saying.'

That might have been true. Perhaps Rebecca hitchhiked somewhere, caught a bus north. There she was, moving forward, staring out a window at a flatter unknown earth, road signs with unfamiliar names, lower skies in darker hues. I got it. Rebecca had been humiliated, scandalised in public among people who would never forget what they saw. If it had happened to me, I couldn't live with Mum either.

'Maybe we could drive to Queensland and find her,' I suggested.

Dad turned to me, a lost man with a droopy face and sad small eyes behind his glasses.

'You don't know how big a place it is. I wouldn't know where to start.'

I sat there confused and sick in my stomach. Everything had changed, the world was different to what I'd always taken for granted.

'Have you had any dinner?' Dad finally asked.

'No.'

My poor exhausted father stood up and cracked eggs into a frying pan, added a little milk and whisked to make scrambled eggs. When the toast popped I spread the margarine. After he took Mum's portion on the tray into their bedroom, Dad and I ate together at the kitchen table. We didn't talk, not one word, but that was all right. I was happy for the silence because I just liked the comfort of being with him.

When we'd eaten we left the dishes in the sink and parted from each other. Dad took Mum a glass of white wine into their bedroom, something I'd never seen him do before. It was a strange time. The Healys were dead, those little kids murdered. Sinead's unborn baby would be dead too. And that creepy Jacob had killed himself. And no one knew where Rebecca was. I had the sensation of looking at myself from a distance and wondered who I was and what would become of me. My parents were doing their own thing, whatever that was, leaving me to myself.

I brushed my teeth, checked the bandage on my forearm, put on my nightie and curled up in bed. It had been another hot day, still warm, so only a sheet covered me. Through the open window magpies sang, strangely reassuring.

Once when Rebecca and I were little, she found a baby magpie on the front lawn. She called it Maggie and kept it alive with insects and worms until one day it died or flew away, we never found out what happened. I thought that maybe Rebecca had decided it was time to leave as well. I didn't actually know what to believe, or think. The only way I could feel better was to imagine Rebecca dancing, arms outstretched as she turned circles on a long white beach, looking upwards to an open blue sky. Her red hair was loose and bright in the sun. She was happy.

*

The next morning Robyn phoned to ask me to work in the shop. I didn't want to. I couldn't.

'Please,' she said. 'I've got to go to the police station. It's about the Healys. Because I was Sinead's best friend they want information from me.'

I looked around the kitchen. Mum was still in bed. Dad was out watering. Everything was deadly quiet like there was no life in our house. Last night's dinner plates and our morning's breakfast dishes were in the sink. We'd almost run out of milk and bread. There was wet washing in the machine that had been there for two days.

'We still don't know where Rebecca is,' I said. 'I probably should stay here.'

'Oh Eliza, honey, I'm so sorry to hear that. But all teenagers get cranky from time to time. She'll come home when she's cooled off.'

I thought about that, how good it would be if it were true.

'Can you be here in half an hour?' Robyn asked. 'Gary has gone away on a job, and besides he's a useless bugger in the shop. You're the only one I can leave here without worrying.'

Even though I didn't want to go, I told Robyn I would. I hung up and went to tell Mum.

She was sitting up in bed taking nail polish off her fingers; the room smelled of acetone. A green towel lay across her lap and used tissues with pink stains were on the floor where she'd dropped them.

'Why don't you get up?' I asked.

She glanced at me. 'I'm not well.'

'You're well enough to do your nails.'

'Don't you start on me. I'd like a cuppa.' When she snatched a fresh tissue from the bedside table her fingers trembled.

'Why are you shaking?'

'Why do you think, Eliza?'

I thought of hurtful things to say, that she was lazy and conceited, that she wasn't a good mother, certainly not to Rebecca, and that it was all her fault that her daughter had not come home.

'I'm going to help Robyn at the shop. The police want to speak to her about the Healys.'

'Why can't that husband of hers step up? I need you here.'

'He's gone to a hay job and, even if he was home, he's no good in the shop. And I already said I'd go.'

As I turned to leave she was shaking the red nail polish to mix it up. The tiny bead inside the bottle ticked on the glass with each movement.

'At least make me a cup of tea before you go, will you?' Mum asked, then as an afterthought in a loud shrill voice, 'Please, Eliza.'

I went to the kitchen and put the kettle on. And when I was pouring boiling water over a teabag into her favourite mug, I thought about turning the kettle nozzle so it would scald my hand. I imagined myself doing it. Knew I might. *Go on, do it*, an inside voice said. Then the moment was gone, the mug was filled. I added the last drop of milk from the carton and took the mug to Mum in her bedroom.

'Put it on the bedside table,' she said, not looking up.

'I'm going now,' I said.

'Bring back some bread and milk. And some cheese and ham.'

As I turned to leave she told me to bring one further thing home.

'Please bring me my purse. I want some Cadbury's chocolate too.'

Her shoulder bag was on the floor beside her dressing table. I took it to her but because her nails were freshly painted she couldn't touch anything.

'Take twenty,' she said. 'And bring back the change.'

As I opened the note section of Mum's red leather purse I thought of the accusation that Rebecca had stolen money from it. So much trouble had come from that one stupid thing. And there was her accuser sitting in bed sipping from the mug of tea I'd just made her. Her nails were shiny dark red.

*

Robyn's eyes were bloodshot and dazed-looking. 'I'll be back as soon as I can,' she said, opening the door that led to her house, closing it behind her. Within minutes there was dust rising from behind her car as she sped down the service road, then left onto the bitumen. She was driving too fast.

'Good King Wenceslas' was playing. Two days before Christmas and there was nothing happy or fun anywhere. I was standing in such a familiar spot, my runners planted on the timber flooring. The idea that this was me, Eliza Bundy, grown up enough to be in charge of a shop. I liked the feeling. 'Once in Royal David's City' was next on the tape. A silver Falcon station wagon drove past that looked a bit like Sinead's. I gaped in shock, realising it wasn't her and never would be again.

I spoke silently to Rebecca and told her it wasn't fair what she'd done, that she'd ruined everything and I wanted her to come home. Wherever she was, she would've heard by then that the Healys were dead and be devastated by the news. On a few occasions, she'd made it pretty clear that she didn't particularly like minding those gorgeous kids – *spoilt brats, fussy eaters, bloody little monsters* – but she always went because she wanted the pocket money. Even so, the news would've been distressing enough for her to call home to share her shock and grief with us.

I ate a Wagon Wheel and drank a small bottle of Fanta.

My first customer was Dad.

I watched his slow stride as he entered, that quiet manner he always had.

'Your mother told me you were here.'

'Robyn needed me.'

'Well, we need you at home. Mum's in bed. And I've been called down to the police station.'

'Why?'

'A few questions about Rebecca babysitting at the Healys.'

'What about that?'

'They're just doing their job, covering all bases.'

'Well, Mum's fine on her own. She was painting her nails when I left.'

A tiny flicker behind his glasses like he was working something out. 'I'll take the things she wants with me now,' he said. 'She told me you know what they are.'

I hadn't served my father in the shop before. Even then, on one of the worst days of our lives, I couldn't help showing off. I quickly gathered up the bread, milk, cheese, ham and chocolate. Then pulled the twenty dollars from my pocket and rang up the cash register like I was about to win a competition. I couldn't help smiling when I counted out the change, but I don't think he noticed how expert I was.

'What time will you be home?' he asked.

'Robyn said she'd be back as soon as she could. So I don't actually know.'

'Next time I'd like you to check with me before you agree to work outside your regular hours.'

'Why? Robyn couldn't find anyone else. It's about the Healys.'

Dad looked into my eyes and spoke with that authority I'd seen him use with Rebecca and sometimes with Mum. 'Because your sister is missing and your mother isn't coping. I need your help at home.'

After he left I felt small, and hot. I thought then if I knew where Rebecca was I'd join her and never come home. Mum was just being selfish and lazy. They wanted me to be her slave. I ate another Wagon Wheel, then a Poly Waffle, and drank half a can of Coke. Then down the hall to the bathroom, I opened the toilet lid and tickled the back of my throat and vomited. It wasn't the first time I'd done that, to stay in control, a certain lightness and secret disgust that made me feel better somehow. When the shop's buzzer rang, I ran up the hallway to sell Cora Engelman *The Age* newspaper that had a family photo of the Healys on the front page. They were all smiling, huddled up together.

'Shocking business,' Cora said.

'Yes.'

'This isn't your usual day, is it?'

'Robyn had to speak to the police.'

'Did she now?' she said, eyebrows raised. 'What do they want to know?'

'I don't know, just that she was Sinead's best friend and probably knew things.'

'Like what things?'

I blinked, had no words.

'That poor woman was pregnant.'

I bowed my head, so she wouldn't see that I was biting my lip so I wouldn't cry.

'Rebecca minds those kids, doesn't she?'

'Sometimes, yes.'

'It must be hard on her.'

'Yes,' I said, not admitting that Rebecca was missing.

'Oh well, it's a good thing you can help out Robyn. Good girl.'

'Joy to the World.'

We sold out of newspapers that day.

*

When Robyn returned mid-afternoon she was quiet and pale. She sat on a kitchen chair and covered her face with her hands and cried, her shoulders and back moving up and down with each gasp for air. I put my hand on her shoulder and she clasped it with hers.

'Can you stay until close?' she asked.

'Yes,' I said without a thought. She was different to my mother. I'd never seen Robyn upset before. Quite the opposite, she was always smiling and making jokes with the customers.

The buzzer rang so I hurried back to the shop.

Bull.

Good. A jolt of happiness.

I had his Marlboros on the counter before he asked.

'Two packets,' he said, standing with his legs apart, shoulders back, handsome as ever and somehow powerful, which was his natural self-confidence. I looked into his brown eyes but couldn't hold his gaze.

'What's going on at your place?' he asked.

'Nothing much. Dad's been called down to the police station to talk about Rebecca working at the Healys'. And I'm in trouble for not staying home,' I said, shrugging.

'What's the deal with Rebecca and the Healys?'

'Dad said the cops are just covering all bases.'

'Your parents told the police that I know where Rebecca is,' he said. 'Why would they do that?'

'It's because they've found out you've been seeing Rebecca.'

'I want you to tell them what I've already told you, and the coppers. That I haven't seen her since last Tuesday afternoon and she didn't turn up Saturday morning for the gig in Winton.'

My heart was racing.

'Where do you reckon she is?' he asked.

'I don't know. I thought she'd phone home when she heard about the Healys, but she hasn't.'

'This is all so fucked up.'

I lifted my face, looked back at him.

'You'll let me know if you hear anything, right?' he said.

'Yes.'

He nodded, dropped a ten-dollar note on the counter, and turned away before I opened the till to give him his change. The buzzer went, and when he drove off he didn't wave.

Perhaps it was fifteen minutes later that I saw Dad drive past, coming up from Gyle. He was driving slowly, didn't look at the shop. He would've been to the police to talk about Rebecca babysitting for the Healys. I didn't know what to make of that.

*

When I arrived home Mum was at the kitchen sink washing the dishes, bare feet, wearing the denim dress with the long zip. Her hair was tied up in the red band. She glanced at me over her shoulder then turned fully to face me.

'About time you showed up, missy. Your father told me you've been fraternising with Bull Tennant at the shop. And you knew things that you kept from us.'

I looked back at her, trapped.

'You knew that Bull and Rebecca were sneaking around behind our backs. Didn't you? And what's this rubbish about some supposed meeting they had lined up Saturday morning and she didn't show? Explain yourself. Why did you lie? Why didn't you tell us when we've been so sick with worry?'

'You know why,' I said.

'Go on, tell me why I wouldn't want to know where my child is and who she's with.'

'Because you hate Bull, that's why.'

'Just so you're aware, the police will be investigating all these lies and deceptions.'

'Bull isn't lying,' I said. 'He's a good person who thinks our family is fucked up.'

Mum stood straighter, eyes wide.

I felt something and turned. Dad was standing quietly behind me in the porch. He was wearing his good clothes, brown trousers, open neck shirt.

'Eliza,' he said, 'don't ever let me hear you use language like that again.'

That familiar feeling of being hot and small.

'There's washing in the machine. I've put it through the rinse cycle again. Please go and hang it out,' Dad said.

I stepped past him and out the back door to the laundry. Among the washing was one of Rebecca's t-shirts, some undies, her new skin-coloured bra. I held them to my face, damp and cold. I had the vague thought that she would've taken those things with her to Queensland. And there it was again, the settling into the idea that that's where she was.

Dad came and helped, pegged his shirts, Mum's blue slacks, my school uniform. Not Rebecca's, wherever she went she must've either been wearing it or taken it with her. But taking her school uniform with her didn't make any sense.

'What happened at the police station?'

'Just a few questions,' he said.

'Do they think Rebecca not coming home and what happened with the Healys is connected?'

'They're working through things.'

'Do you think it's a coincidence?' I asked.

Dad shook his head, had nothing to say.

'If Rebecca came home, and took the travel bag, why did she take her uniform with her? She would've changed into something else, right?'

It was like he didn't hear me or register what I'd just said.

'Eliza, listen to me. This is important. Do you, or anyone else, including Bull and Jasmine, know where Rebecca is? We're talking about a police matter, so we can't be fooling around here. It's serious, do you understand?'

'I don't know where she is,' I said. 'I've even been to the workman's cottage to see if she was there.'

'Why would she be there?'

'Because that's where she used to meet Bull.'

Dad shook his head, looked away. 'I didn't know that.'

'Everything is a secret because Mum hates Bull, but Rebecca loves him.'

'How long has this been going on for?'

'Few months.'

'So why would she go away and leave him then? And you?'

'I don't know, but Mum and her fight all the time, so maybe that's why.'

'Do you think Bull is in contact with her?'

I shrugged. 'He's been in the shop a couple of times asking where she is and what's going on.'

Dad pinched the sides of his mouth with his fingers, thinking.

'Maybe we don't mention the workman's cottage to your mother. For the time being anyway.'

He stared at me until I said, 'Okay.'

'What about the man I saw at the showgrounds? Remember I told you?'

Dad looked tired, a little stooped. 'The police wrote it down, but I think they're now concentrating on the Healys and what happened there.'

'Do you think Rebecca is all right?'

'I've got no idea where she is, or why she'd do this to us.'

When he said that, I felt something shift inside me because my father was strong and dependable and always knew how to manage everything in our family. Like that time earlier in the year when Mum and I were driving along Hedge End Lane, taking the short cut to Benalla to do some shopping. We had just passed Colin Buckley's long driveway, lined with golden poplars, when Mum realised she'd left her purse at home. She hit the brakes, abruptly put the car into reverse to return home and didn't see the Buckleys' milkcan letterbox until she'd flattened it. The crunching sound of smashing metal. The way she glared at me, the message was *shut up* and *do not say a word*. But later when Dad quizzed her about the damage to the car she told him what had happened, strangely, as if it was the letterbox's fault. And Dad, such an honourable man, went straight to the Buckleys' house to apologise, telling them he was responsible and whatever the repair costs were he would pay. I remember after that Dad was quieter than usual, and being a man of nature, he stayed outside with his apple trees for as long as the sun gave him light.

'What are you going to do?' I asked.

'Don't you worry,' Dad said, 'but please don't keep anything from me. Do you understand? It's important.'

'I won't.' I was going to him for a hug, but he stretched out his arms to keep me at a distance. Of all the things that happened in those confusing days and weeks, I remember his rejection as a marker. That moment when I understood I was alone, that my family had changed in a way I couldn't make sense of.

SIX

On Christmas Day Mum showered, washed and dried her hair, and put on a green dress with a white check pattern. She'd lost weight, her shoulder blades stuck out, her skin seemed whiter, and her eyes deeper set. She was beautiful in another way, different to her dynamic energy of the past where she sang while multi-tasking, moving between the kitchen and her workroom. Since Rebecca had run away Mum had acquired a solemn beauty of the type catwalk models have, her expression unsmiling as if always unhappy. I believed Mum had got out of bed for me so that Christmas Day could be as normal as possible. Our family ritual was opening presents and watching Mum busy in the kitchen cooking a ham and turkey with all the accompanying vegetables. Always finished off with her Christmas pudding that Dad set alight with brandy. But there was none of that. The three of us sat silently around the kitchen table like it was any other meal and ate heated-up lasagne that Cora Engelman had dropped off a couple of days earlier.

Actually, it was the first time since Rebecca had left that Mum, Dad and I were at the table together, so at least there was that. But in front of me was Rebecca's empty chair and it was impossible not to imagine her sitting in it. In my mind I conjured her image and watched her smile, cut into her food and chew. I'd bought her Madonna's latest cassette, *Like A Virgin*, for Christmas. If she had anything to give me I didn't know where it was. Earlier that morning I'd hunted in her bedroom, under the bed, in all her drawers, the top of her wardrobe, but I didn't find anything. Before lunch Mum handed me a shopping bag with unwrapped new bathers and a beach towel, and a few other things that gave the appearance of lots of presents, but I didn't want or need any of it.

The lasagne was only partially warm and hard to swallow. As we ate, our knives scratched across the plates, forks prodded into the doughy pasta. The fan flicked the calendar and frilled the rows of Christmas cards. I wanted to cry for no other reason than there was a deep trapped feeling in my body.

When the phone pierced the silence we all looked up. Dad was first on his feet, his arm stretched out, his chair upending and crashing loudly to the floor as he turned to grab the receiver on the wall. That phone was like a bomb, the thing we were all conscious of, waiting, waiting for it to explode with news from Rebecca. Mum's jaw was hard, and eyes wide as she slapped her hand over her mouth. And my whole body tingled with excitement that of course Rebecca would never let Christmas pass without calling to tell us where she was.

'Hello,' Dad said, pressing the phone hard against his ear.

He cleared his throat as if to block a sob.

'Helen,' he said.

Dad's sister, Helen Wallace. My Auntie Helen.

'No news,' he said, his voice quieter than ever like he'd been winded and couldn't fill his lungs. He leaned against the hallway doorframe listening. His eyes were closed.

'Yes, it'd be wonderful if you could come and stay for a few days,' he said.

Then Mum was out of her seat, standing in front of him, shaking her head, waving her hands in front of his face, mouthing, 'No, she's not to visit.'

Dad looked at Mum confused, still holding the receiver to his ear, trying to understand what she was on about.

'Hang on, Helen,' he said, pressing the receiver against his chest.

So Mum repeated, in a fierce quiet whisper, that she didn't want Auntie Helen to come to the orchard.

Dad seemed to cower, before nodding that he understood.

'I'll get back to you about visiting,' he said to his sister.

Auntie Helen was all right. Her husband, Uncle Leon, died from bowel cancer when I was young and I have no memory of him. My cousins are Tom and Sam, and when they were younger they would come to our place for Christmas, or we'd be at theirs in Camberwell, a suburb in the east of Melbourne. Auntie Helen was an English teacher and always gave Rebecca and me books for our birthdays and at Christmas. Sometimes in the school holidays I spent a week with them at a flat-roofed aqua house she rented in Apollo Bay.

Auntie Helen used to tell me she'd always wanted a daughter, and once when I was staying with her, in a joking way, she pretended I was hers which made me feel special, something I didn't experience anywhere else, except maybe with Robyn at the shop. Perhaps Auntie Helen felt sorry for me because she'd seen the pecking order in my family – that it was in order of beauty with my mother the most powerful, followed by Rebecca who was equally beautiful, but the younger version. In hindsight, perhaps Mum, in some strange narcissistic way, was in competition with Rebecca.

When Mum sat back down at the table her chest was heaving, red blotches on her neck and face. She glanced at me with narrowed eyes, a warning not to ask why she didn't want Auntie Helen to visit. So we sat there watching Dad shake his head as he answered

Auntie Helen's questions – that he didn't know, he'd not heard anything, yes the police were busy with the Healy tragedy, that we were doing all right, that he'd be in touch if we needed anything, that he was thankful for her call.

'We could do with her help,' Dad said when he was back at the table.

'Are you kidding?' Mum snapped. 'Help? She just creates more work. She's the last thing we need.'

Dad glanced at Mum then continued on with his lasagne.

'I'm stressed enough as it is without her being in my home,' she said.

Dad licked his lips and tried again. 'I don't think we're coping very well. Helen is practical. She's on holidays from teaching. It'd be good to have the help.'

Mum stood up, took her plate to the sink. 'She just likes being the centre of things, Maurie. Under no circumstances is she to come here.' She turned around to glare at Dad. 'Did you hear what I just said?'

She waited for Dad to answer, and when he just sat there staring into the lasagne, she opened a cupboard and plucked out a wine glass. From the fridge she took a bottle of white wine and disappeared down the hallway.

Without saying anything to me, or even looking at me, Dad pushed his plate away, stood up and went out to the porch. The wire door opened and closed, and he was gone.

*

Ripper yawned and stretched. The old boy wasn't up for a walk, so I went by myself. Christmas Day with a vast blue sky and Dunny Hill imposing in the distance. I seriously thought about running away too. It was strange thinking that there was nothing stopping me and I had good reasons. My family had fallen apart. I hated my mother. The Healys were dead. It was Christmas Day and nothing would ever be the same again.

I packed a windcheater, some water, and a block of fruitcake into my blue backpack. None of that was thought out properly, but then it felt like an emergency and I needed to hurry. The way my chest opened up as I walked up the lane towards Dunny Hill was proof that I was doing the right thing. My thongs padded in the soft dirt. Warm breeze on my skin. When I thought of Rebecca the urge to cry made my mouth loose and the only way I could stop the feeling was to hold my breath and walk faster until I was almost running.

Around the dogleg turn at the dam, the ballerina waterlilies, and up past the rows of peaches. The drippers were watering those trees, slow droplets falling to the ground. Then up to the workman's cottage. I hadn't really intended to go there, but there I was standing on the verandah. I liked the quiet, the opposite to the tense quiet at home. I sat on the step, leaned against the post, closed my eyes and tried to settle down and straighten my thoughts.

I was lonely, that was the first thing I understood. Around my body was space, nobody was close to me. I missed Rebecca, but being at the cottage I felt strangely near to her. I had another conversation with her, a silent one inside my head, and I waited until I heard her voice answering me back. I wanted to touch her, and the physical desire to reach out and hug her made my chest hurt. I let myself cry hot tears. To be noisy in the silence felt too much like my mother, so I just heaved my sadness as quietly as I could.

'Hey.' A man's voice called out.

I looked around, pushed my hair away from my wet face and wiped my eyes. Bull was standing at the side of the house. When he came to me I hid my face in my hands. I was still upset that Cheryl had been angry with me on the phone, and that the last time I'd seen Bull he seemed annoyed with me too. Plus, I was guilty of telling my father about him and Rebecca, which resulted in the police speaking to him.

He sat next to me. 'What's going on?' he asked. 'You all right?'

'Not really.'

'What's happening?'

'Today, at lunchtime, when the phone rang we all thought it would be Rebecca because if she was going to phone it would be today. But it was Auntie Helen wanting to come and stay to help us, then Mum threw a fit and said she wasn't to come. Now Dad is angry with her and I'm just upset about everything.'

Bull lit a cigarette and handed it to me. I put it to my lips, breathing in, and instantly felt the nicotine rinse through me, making me dizzy. I felt sick, but he was lighting up a second one for himself. So I took another drag and tapped the ash the way I'd seen him do it. The smoke curled and drifted in the breeze. After a few inhales I'd worked out how to swallow the rising bile and keep going.

'Where the fuck is she?' Bull asked, as if talking to himself.

'The only thing I can think of is she's really gone to Queensland. Some of her clothes are missing and the maroon travel bag isn't anywhere. I've looked for it and it's not in the cupboard.'

'I don't buy it,' he said. 'She wouldn't have gone.'

I told Bull about the dark-haired stranger with the black dog at the showgrounds, about how curious he seemed watching Mum and Rebecca fight. 'Dad's told the police about him but they're only interested in the Healys, which is fair enough because that's about the worst thing that's ever happened. But I just can't seem to forget him.'

'What'd he look like?' Bull asked.

I took my time and recalled the colour of his shirt, his beard, the length of his hair, that at one point he had his hands in his pockets, that he wasn't in a hurry to be anywhere except to watch us.

'Rebecca ever talk to you about her maths teacher?' Bull said. 'Mr Soydan, or something like that. A couple of months back she told me he pulled over in his car. Lunchtime at school when she was walking up the street. He asked if he could drive her to where she was going.'

'Really?' I shrugged. 'He's a bit of a wanker, but most kids like him.'

'How old would he be?'

'In his twenties, or a bit older. He's from Melbourne, thinks he's cool the way he dresses.'

'He gave her a book to read,' Bull said. 'You know that?'

'No. What book?'

'Sci-fi shit.'

'Rebecca doesn't like sci-fi.'

'She read it.'

'What was the book?'

'Dunno, had a purple and white circle on the cover.' Bull was grinding the cigarette butt under the heel of his boot. 'Has she ever talked to you about him?'

'No.'

We sat in the quiet, ants at our feet. Magpies carolling somewhere off in the distance. Sticky flies on our skin. The temperature and light had dropped and out in front grey clouds were building and moving forward.

'What did the coppers say to your dad about Rebecca working at the Healys?' Bull asked.

'They just asked him questions.'

'It's all crazy shit.'

'Jacob Healy gave me the creeps.'

'Why'd you say that?'

'Just the way he used to look at me when he came into the shop.'

'How was that?'

'Staring at me, thinking it was funny.'

Bull shook his head, as if he didn't quite believe me.

'Anyway,' I said, 'what're you doing here?'

'Probably the same as you, just somewhere to come when there's nowhere else.'

'I'm sorry that the cops spoke to you,' I said.

He tilted his head and glanced at me. 'Was bound to happen.'

'Mum thinks that you drove her home last Friday, after their fight. You passed us coming up the mountain.'

'Yeah, well, she's wrong there.'

'I don't understand how one minute she was standing at the showgrounds waiting for the school bus, and the next thing she takes off and some of her stuff is missing and she's not come home,' I said.

'Yeah, so how'd that happen?'

'I don't know. But she didn't have the travel bag with her at the showgrounds. So she must've come home, then gone out again. How did she do that?'

Bull lit two more Marlboros. Somehow doing the thing my parents hated the most felt like the absolute best thing in the world to do. I was getting the hang of it, holding the smoke in my lungs, slowly exhaling.

'What's your dad say about that?' Bull asked.

'He's just sick with worry and doesn't know what to do. That's why he wanted Auntie Helen to come because she's sensible, whereas Mum just stays in bed and tells us what to do.'

We smoked in the silence and I thought if Rebecca could see us now she'd be happy that Bull and I were together keeping each other company.

Parched liquidambar leaves whistled in the breeze; some fell at our feet. A few drops of rain. The flies were gone.

'Better go,' Bull said. 'Going to piss down any minute.'

'I'm staying here for a while.'

Bull stood up, watching me, thinking.

'Okay. See you around,' he said.

He walked away. His ute would be parked across the back fence on the track that was part of the state forest, no-man's-land, hidden behind a copse of acacias and peppermint gums. I watched the line of his long back, white t-shirt, those Levi's, his thick brown hair, too long. He turned and nodded at me, a tiny smile.

'Take care,' he said.

He turned away at the corner of the cottage.

Bull was a good bloke.

*

Lightning speared the ground, silver with high voltage and only a few metres from where I sat. I ran inside as the thunder came. Rain pelted the tin roof. In no time, water poured from the rusted gutters. Through the kitchen window I watched the impossibility of the dry ground absorbing so much water. Rivulets formed, carrying the flow to a blocked drain and within minutes a puddle became a large pool. Lightning and thunder, a fight between a spear and shield. It felt dangerous and I wished I wasn't alone. Rebecca wouldn't be afraid, so I put her beside me and we sat on the floor, held hands and breathed together. But since I knew that wasn't really happening – I was only pretending because I was weaker than she was – I didn't think, just stabbed my right heel against a rusted floorboard nail that was poking up as if waiting for me to attack it. The pain was good, all through my body, and I closed my eyes and breathed in to withstand it. How good it was to be distracted from one mighty pain with another. And when I turned to Rebecca she wasn't there, she'd left me.

After the rain stopped I lifted myself up and carefully put pressure on my foot. There wasn't much blood, only a weeping gouge. With each limping step I felt the hurt, let it rise up my leg.

Outside the air was cool and full of bush smells. It was like everything had enjoyed a nice long bath and was now clean. I was restless, but not keen to go home. So I sat on the verandah and emptied my backpack, pulled out the cake, broke a piece off and ate. I heard the car before I saw it. Dad's white ute rounded the corner and came slowly toward me, stopping beside the liquidambar.

He wound down his window. 'What are you doing up here?' he asked.

'Nothing.'

'I need you to come home.'

I was never going to argue with Dad so I gathered my things and limped to the car.

'What's wrong with your foot?'

'Stood on a nail.'

He reversed out and headed back to the house, down the long row of pines.

'I'm sorry that you're not having a good Christmas,' he said.

I didn't say anything, but stared forward thinking about all the things I hated about my life.

'Eliza,' Dad said. 'Have you been smoking? I can smell it on you.'

I glanced at him and didn't speak.

'Where'd you get them? From the shop?'

I nodded, yes.

The look on my father's face, the sadness that now seemed constant. He shook his head in disapproval and seeing him do that hurt me more than any punishment he could've given me.

'I'm sorry,' I said.

'We've got enough going on in the family without you playing up.'

'I won't do it again.'

'Where are they? The packet?'

'I don't have it.'

'Why don't you have it?'

'Because I only had two. And please don't tell Mum.'

Dad pulled up at the house and seemed too weary to get out of the car.

'Your mother isn't coping,' he said. 'I want you to try and make things easier for her.'

'How am I supposed to do that? She's not the only one who's upset about Rebecca. What about me? And Auntie Helen wants to come and help us and she won't let her. Now I've got to run after her. Why doesn't Mum just get out of bed and help herself?'

I can still recall that moment clearly, sitting beside Dad in the ute, the build-up of frustration, not feeling understood or loved.

'I've been thinking,' Dad said. 'Maybe it'd be a good idea for you to go and stay with Helen for a few days. Just until things settle down a bit. I need to discuss this with your mother, but how's that sound?'

'But then you have to do all the watering and also look after Mum.'

'I'll ask Bryce to help out with the watering. Keep up with things for me. That way I can be at the house more.'

I should've been happy about the suggestion of going to stay at Auntie Helen's, but it felt more like I wasn't wanted, that it was perfectly all right with my parents to have none of their children in the house with them. I was a foolish impulsive girl. Out of the car, I slammed the door, went straight to my room and slammed that door too. Within a few minutes I realised I'd trapped myself in my room because I was too proud to come out. I flicked through a book, tried to read, but I was bored, hungry and wanted to go to the toilet.

Perhaps fifteen minutes passed before my door swung open and Mum barged in.

'What's this about you smoking? I'm going to speak to Robyn about it,' she said.

'Don't you dare,' I shouted back.

'You little brat, running off this afternoon giving me and your father more things to worry about. And now you come home stinking of cigarettes that you stole from the shop. You girls are going to be the death of me.'

'I hate you,' I spat.

I saw it coming. As she raised her hand I flinched. Then Dad was there, his face a tight grimace, wild eyes. He stepped between us and pushed me into the hallway. When I turned I saw him gripping the door handle, and as he pulled it shut, he put his other hand on Mum's shoulder, pinning her against my bedroom wall. My heart was racing, blood smashing through me. Never before had I seen my father so unrestrained and angry.

I listened to their argument through my closed bedroom door, Dad speaking in a loud husky whisper and Mum in a petulant whine. A desperate husband trying to coax his desperate wife to act differently, to be calm and in control.

'You promised me you wouldn't speak to Eliza about the cigarettes,' Dad said.

'You're too soft on her, Maurie.'

'Stop being like this, please.'

'Why am I in trouble with you when Eliza was the one smoking?'

'Listen to me a moment,' Dad said. 'We both need to settle down.'

I heard panting, breath trying to find its normal rhythm.

'I think you need to see Dr Sandbrook again,' Dad said in his everyday quiet voice.

Mum didn't reply. I'd never heard of a Dr Sandbrook. Our doctor in Gyle was Dr Dukes, a balding man with pale skin who wore a suit with braces and a bowtie.

'You're not coping,' Dad said, 'so I think you need to go back on your medication. And it'd be a good idea for Eliza to go and stay with Helen a few days, maybe for the rest of the holidays.'

Mum started to cry, pathetic weeping like an overtired child.

'I can't take anymore,' she said. 'Rebecca going off with that teacher.'

'Come on, darling,' Dad said, 'let's get you back into bed.'

I hurried away before my bedroom door opened.

What teacher? I had no idea what they were talking about, until I remembered Bull asking me about Mr Soydan. Still, that made no sense.

Outside, I sat on the timber bench in front of the water tanks that were covered in ropey wisteria branches. The last wisps of purple flower draped above and behind me. I lifted my foot and examined the puncture hole. It was pulsing, a red circle around it.

From then on I exaggerated my limp. Surely someone would notice? When Dad was sitting in his chair watching the evening news, I hobbled in front of him. What more could I have done to bring attention to my predicament, that my foot was injured and probably needed medical attention?

The next morning when the throbbing was too much I told Dad that the heel of my foot was hurting me.

'I can't walk properly, it hurts,' I said.

He looked at me sideways, almost with suspicion. 'You'll be right.'

So I pulled in my breath, ignored the heat under my skin, took two Panadol that I found in the bathroom cupboard and waited until it was time for me to go to Auntie Helen's.

I didn't blame my parents for not paying me more attention. Rebecca had vanished. Maybe she was dead. Or perhaps she was alive. She was probably alive, of course she was going to turn up at any minute. Whatever. And there I was grandstanding about an injury I'd inflicted on myself.

SEVEN

On the morning of the Healys' burial a cool change passed across the mountain leaving Maryhill with colder temperatures and surprising bursts of rain. Ironic that Jacob and his victims were buried on a day that the drought broke. And an unhappy coincidence that Dad and I drove past the community hall as everyone was walking inside for the service, heads bowed. Tony and Jenny Russo and Andy Knightly's parents were standing together talking under the leafy elm beside the path that led to the entry. Lauren Reinhart and her new husband, Peter, were entering through the front door. She'd taken Peter's name and was now Lauren Wishart.

Dad slowed down, there was so much going on, and out in front Robyn and Gary were walking across the road from the shop. She was wearing a black dress, and sunglasses that were unnecessary in the weather, but essential for bloodshot, sad eyes. I'd worked in the shop the day before so Robyn could cut the roses from Sinead's garden for the coffins. It was a task too heartfelt and depressing for one person to do alone, but she did it anyway with permission from the police to enter the property. I don't know if Robyn saw me in the car with Dad or not, but in the seconds it took us to approach, she leaned more heavily against Gary, who had his arm firmly around her.

When I'd told her I was going to stay with my Auntie Helen in Melbourne for the duration of the school holidays she hugged me, said it was a good thing and that 'Whatever happens in the future I'm here for you.' And she also said, 'Call me whenever you want.' It seemed overly dramatic and I was left feeling defensive that things weren't all that bad at home. I wondered what she saw and really thought about my family. But then Robyn didn't have kids of her own, which perhaps accounted for her care of me and why she'd been so interested in the Healy kids.

The Healys' funeral was probably the biggest held on the mountain, then and now. Cars were parked all the way back to the shop, on the grassed median strip between the maples, and up the side road under the long-limbed conifers. I recognised Virginia Hurley, the reporter who'd stood at the top of Glen Lochan Road on the day the world heard about the shocking deaths. She was wearing a green dress, her hair long and loose around her face. There were other reporters, TV cameras on tripods on the grass nature strip opposite the hall. And when I saw the three black hearses filled with roses of all colours, I clenched my teeth so I didn't cry and decided right then that too much sadness could kill or disable a person. At least I had the distraction of my foot, which hummed every second of the day, red and inflamed. All I could do was breathe through the agony and be thankful that at least I was going to Auntie Helen's.

Dad was staring ahead, both arms firmly clasping the steering wheel as if we were setting off on a treacherous journey. If he took in what I saw, all the mourners, the hearses filled with roses, he didn't let on. Perhaps he was simply a strong person, or just past caring about anything beyond the heartbreak in our own family. When I turned to face him, I saw the deep creases on his face, lips tightly closed, glasses sitting too low on the bridge of his nose. I've always known that he loved me, but not once in my life has he ever said those words to me.

That morning when Mum was in bed, I bent down and kissed her goodbye. She reached up with trembling fingers, touched my face, and smiled at me. Her eyes were shrunken back and she had an unfamiliar clammy odour. Still, she was beautiful in a porcelain doll kind of way, the rise of her cheekbones, the pink of her lips, her hazel eyes. The way she'd changed since Rebecca had vanished frightened me. My mother had always been such a force, working on her cakes and running our house, everything in order. January was her busiest time with weddings and seeing her so distressed in bed there was no way she would be able to complete those orders. Her fingers shook almost all the time, so it would've been impossible for her to make the delicate flowers or lace.

'Mum, you need to get better. What about all your cake orders?'

'It's eight days today,' she said.

'What is?'

'Since Rebecca left us.' She closed her eyes and rolled onto her side. 'Bull knows where she is. I'm one hundred per cent certain of it.'

'He doesn't,' I said.

'Those two running around together in secret, meeting up at the cottage. Of course he damn well knows.'

My bags were in the boot. As Dad drove past all the mourners and down the mountain, I felt like I was deserting Rebecca, or leaving her behind.

'I should really stay home until Rebecca shows up,' I said.

'Don't worry,' Dad promised, 'I'll phone you when she does.'

*

For all the decades of experience Dad had driving his Ford cars, his two Fergie tractors, the Clark forklift, and his Bedford truck, he was nervous on Melbourne roads. Twice he pulled over to study the Melways, licking the tip of a finger to turn the pages and looking out the window at the street signs. Mum was always the navigator when we came to the city, sitting beside Dad in the passenger seat with the directory on her lap, telling him to turn left or right, using her hand as an added guide. I sat quietly so I didn't add to his worries and it was a relief when we finally pulled into Auntie Helen's bricked driveway.

Dad seemed unsure, perhaps nervous, the way he slowly, with great deliberation, carried my suitcase up the front steps, rang the doorbell and stood back waiting for his sister to come. It wasn't usually like that. On previous visits, we just walked inside yelling that we'd arrived and there were hugs and loud talking from then on. When Auntie Helen appeared and embraced me, I felt relieved, strangely safe. She smelled different to Mum and wasn't as bony. Just as we entered the hallway the 14.16 Alamein to Flinders Street train, via Camberwell, roared past the back fence, deafening to us, but not Auntie Helen. She kept talking because those trains were white noise to her; she no longer noticed them.

Auntie Helen was a straight talker. Unlike Dad and Mum when they were discussing adult topics, she didn't send me out of the room.

We sat at the kitchen table and ate sandwiches, a late lunch. Auntie Helen offered me coffee and I said, 'Yes please', because it felt like a compliment, even though the only other time I'd tasted coffee I didn't like it.

I noticed a glance between Dad and Auntie Helen.

'Maurie, Eliza needs to understand what's going on. Don't you?' she said to me, and without waiting for Dad to agree or disagree, she went on to ask him when Mum was going to see her Melbourne specialist. 'It's important she sees him as soon as possible.'

Dad cleared his throat. 'I can't get an appointment until mid-January.'

'And what's the latest on Rebecca? Where do you think she's gone?' she said, crossing her arms, as if expecting we had an answer.

That's when Dad started to cry. As if trying to hide from us, he lowered his chin as he reached into his trouser pocket for his handkerchief, then blew his nose. And when Auntie Helen put her arm around Dad's shoulders to comfort him, he stiffened and shook his head, so she pulled away and sat back in her chair.

We sat quietly, waiting for Dad to calm himself. Breathing heavily, he took his glasses off and wiped his eyes. Poor Dad, the huge effort he made to get himself under control.

He looked straight at me and paused before he spoke.

'Eliza, yesterday the police advised me that over a period of a few months, since about June this year, Rebecca sometimes went to a teacher's house at lunchtimes. It's not known yet if he picked her up after she left the showgrounds, but that's being looked into. It's her maths teacher, a Mr Soydan, Errol Soydan. The allegation is that she went there for maths tutoring, but it seems unlikely.' Dad shook his head, pinched the bridge of his nose. 'It was Jasmine who told the police about this. Well, Rebecca wasn't being tutored because your mother and I don't know anything about it. The thing is, if she needed tutoring it'd have to be at the school, or by a paid professional person. Never her teacher in his home where they were alone. Do you know anything about that?'

'No way,' I said, slapping my hand across my mouth.

I saw Mr Soydan with his good looks, which were more about his straight white teeth and big smile, because his features put together weren't all that attractive. He was popular and told his students to call him Errol as if they were his friends. I'd seen him wearing shorts and a t-shirt, covered in sweat, playing basketball with the Year 11 and 12 boys. I'd never had him as my teacher, but he had a reputation for making maths fun by organising competitions and giving out chocolates as prizes. Yes, and his hair was longer and styled a little like Michael Douglas in *Romancing the Stone*. And his clothes stood out, different to the other male teachers who mostly wore the same things every day, like they had a teacher uniform of grey trousers, white shirt and tie, and a home-knitted jumper or cardigan. Whereas Mr Soydan's clothes were modern. Perhaps he bought them in Melbourne because they were brighter, his trousers were flared, and sometimes he didn't wear a tie.

'Last I heard the police have taken him up to Benalla and are talking to him there. That's why your mother is so rundown and upset. And the business with Bull at the old cottage.'

I was shocked. Still, I thought this. That it was possible Rebecca had gone to Mr Soydan's place because he had a way about him that all his students responded to. And Rebecca was the best-looking girl in the school, so she stood out. She was also gutsy, so I could somehow see how they might've flirted with each other. I don't know if they did or not. As I've said, he never taught me, but whenever I saw him in the corridor, or somewhere on the school grounds, I always wanted him to notice me. I don't think he ever did.

'My God,' Auntie Helen said, 'what's this teacher done? Does he know where she is?'

'Bull asked me about Mr Soydan,' I said. 'He said he gave her a book to read.'

Dad reached into his shirt pocket and pulled out a small notepad and biro.

'What did Bull tell you?'

When I repeated that Bull had asked me what I knew about Rebecca's maths teacher, Dad wrote it down. The page was full of his handwriting, neat, cursive, small, line after line, and there were many written pages before the one he had open.

'Maurie,' Auntie Helen said, 'I thought it'd been decided she'd had another blow-up with Diane and taken off to Queensland with some wedding cake money she'd stolen.'

'Maybe she has,' Dad said, 'but we don't know anything for sure. She's not contacted us to say where she is. I can't make sense of why she'd be away this long without one word.'

'But she's seventeen and it's just over a week,' Auntie Helen said.

Dad stared back at his sister. 'That's the point. She's only seventeen and been gone eight days and no one knows where she is.'

'So what are the police saying?' she asked.

'She's listed as missing and they've got a photograph of her. They're doing their job, bits and pieces, talking to different people. Although it doesn't seem urgent to them and they've been busy with the Healy situation. But they've now got this Soydan fella in Benalla and they've spoken to Bull Tennant as well. And the other consideration is that Rebecca was the Healys' babysitter.'

Auntie Helen jolted upright. 'It's a coincidence, right? Rebecca babysitting for them.'

Dad shook his head. 'It probably is, but the police are looking into it.'

'And there's that strange man I saw at the showgrounds. The man with the black dog,' I said.

'What strange man?' Auntie Helen asked.

I recounted how I'd seen him watching Mum and Rebecca fighting, that he seemed overly curious, and he would've seen where Rebecca went. I noticed that the more I told the story about him, the more I exaggerated the details. I said he was quite close to the

Moreton Bay fig trees, not at a distance. And that from the first time I saw him, I'd thought how odd it was that he seemed so interested in us.

'What on earth?' Auntie Helen said, looking at Dad for a response.

Dad appeared to shrink, his shoulders narrower. 'I've told the police about him. Gave his description. I don't know what else I can do.'

'This could be very serious,' Auntie Helen said, reaching out to hold my hand.

I knew wicked things happened to girls and women. At the shop it was impossible to avoid the front-page headlines, stories, and photos of the victims. At any age, but to a fourteen-year-old girl, sometimes the stories were so distressing they made me fearful, convinced I'd be next. I looked to Dad for some kind of reassurance, because surely we weren't really suggesting Rebecca had been sexually assaulted and killed. Not that. But right from the start it had been me who kept talking about the man I'd seen at the showgrounds.

'Who else have the police spoken to?' Auntie Helen asked.

'Just people around the place. Me, and Diane, of course. Bryce Jones, our workman. There's the Healys connection, like I just said. But Diane thinks Bull Tennant knows something.'

'Why him?' Auntie Helen asked.

'Because Rebecca has been seeing him without telling us. We'd warned her off him, but she's always been strong-willed.'

'What's wrong with him?'

'Nothing,' I said. 'Bull is a good guy.'

'He's had a couple of run-ins with the police,' Dad went on. 'Not the type of fella we want her spending any time with.'

'And Rebecca is his girlfriend?' Auntie Helen said, eyes wide.

'Seems that way,' Dad replied, standing up, saying he had a long drive home.

'Maurie,' Auntie Helen asked, 'is there anything I can do?'

'Just look after this one.' He turned to me.

When I went to hug Dad goodbye he raised his forearms and gently held my arms so I couldn't get close. His lips were dry on my cheek and he smelled of Palmolive soap. So quickly he was gone, the front door closed behind him.

*

'So tell me,' Auntie Helen said, 'why are you limping?'

'I stood on a rusty nail.'

'When?'

'A few days ago.'

That afternoon she took me to a doctor who prescribed antibiotics. Because I had no idea when I'd had my last tetanus injection, Auntie Helen phoned Mum from the doctor's surgery, but she didn't pick up, which was strange. I knew she was home because we'd agreed that someone had to be there at all times in case Rebecca called – which meant for every minute of every day since she'd been missing we were on edge, waiting, hoping.

And whenever our phone did ring our hearts skipped, and whoever was closest snatched the handset and pressed the receiver hard against their ear, while holding their breath, waiting, waiting, for Rebecca to say something like, *Hi, it's me.*

EIGHT

It took a full week for me to stop hearing the trains. At first I anticipated them, heard their faraway reverberation on the track, increasing in volume, then the quick rush and it was gone. The Alamein Line wasn't all that busy. I learned the last train passed through at 11.13 pm and the first one the opposite way at 5.41 am. I knew that because I couldn't sleep. I'd developed a sudden and frustrating insomnia, long hours lying on my back staring upwards in a strange room. It was my cousin Sam's room, who early in 1984 had moved to Canberra to study at ANU. I didn't know him that well so it troubled me to be sleeping in his room, his private space for all of his life until he moved away. Tom and Sam were eight and six years older than me. They were big city boys, and we were the small country girls.

And so, lying on my back, I thought of many things. Why was I there, in that room? Why had Rebecca left without a word to me or our parents? Where was she? I came up with different scenarios and played them out in my mind like short, vivid movies. Sometimes Rebecca was laughing and dancing on a beautiful beach. I always imagined her wearing a long white flowing dress, which I thought was interesting. Perhaps a bride or an angel, something pure and innocent, yet I knew by then she was neither of those things. Other times she was tied up, bruised and bloodied with red and swollen eyes, duct-tape covering her mouth so she couldn't scream for help. My imagination surprised me, and there were worse things I thought of, graphic, extreme, appalling. I was sending myself mad. Which made me think of my mother, that perhaps I was more like her than I knew. The point was, nothing made any sense.

As for Errol Soydan and Bull. Two grown men. They were both interesting and handsome in their different ways. Not so much now, but back then, the notion that Rebecca was having sex with different men in the same period of time was shocking to me. I was certain that's what was being implied. I'd asked Auntie Helen about it and she said she didn't know. But why was Rebecca going alone to his house at lunchtimes? Maybe Jasmine was lying? And why had the police asked questions about Rebecca babysitting for the Healys? Whenever I tried to make sense of it, I got lost in my thinking and froze because there was too much to consider.

As exhausting as it was lying there with my eyes wide open staring into the shadows, I came up with a conviction, something to hold on to. I would one day leave everyone behind and become independent. It seemed that's what Rebecca had done. Or maybe not. And so, the wheel slowly turned once more. The urge to imagine what had happened to Rebecca was irresistible, and off I would go on another terrifying ride. Nothing added up. She might be dead. Or kept captive somewhere. I begged her. Begged her. *Answer me,* I said, with some stupid, hopeful notion that telepathy worked and she would somehow give me the answer to any question I asked. But she never did. So I lay there, staring upwards to the light fitting hanging from a ceiling rose, which in the dark I imagined was a skull.

*

During that twelve-day visit with Auntie Helen, she seemed wary, cheerful in a false way, always watching me sideways with worry in her eyes. She kept asking me if I was all right and my answer was always the same: 'I'm fine.'

'Are you sure?'

'Yes.'

I mean, what else was there to say?

At every opportunity she pushed food in front of me. 'You need to eat more,' she said.

But I was stressed and could only nibble on the edges of buttered toast, and sometimes I kept food inside my mouth for the duration of a meal, until I could go to the toilet and spit it out. Once Auntie Helen heard me vomiting in the bathroom. And there she was kneeling beside me lifting my hair away, a cold facewasher on my forehead. Her soft touch on my back felt nice. Still I couldn't look at her because it was shameful to be caught doing that. Those were such dark days.

Auntie Helen insisted I go to bed. She brought me a mug of tea and fussed around, opened the window to let a breeze come in, the lace curtains lifting. A train raced by. She pulled up a chair and spoke frankly to me, telling me how she felt about Rebecca's disappearance, that she was worried for Dad because he'd gone unusually quiet and seemed unsure of himself.

'What's wrong with Mum?' I asked her. 'She's got wedding cakes to make. A whole January full of bookings.'

'Your mum won't be doing that this month. Not until Rebecca is located and brought home,' she said.

'Mum's been acting strange.'

Auntie Helen looked at me, deciding something. 'Any mother in her situation would be sick with worry,' she said.

'Even before Rebecca left she was acting weird, going nuts all the time.'

Auntie Helen took a long breath.

'Who's Dr Sandbrook?' I asked.

She pulled at her bottom lip the way I'd seen Dad do.

'What?' I said.

So Auntie Helen disclosed things about my mother that I'd never heard before. That she'd been seeing Dr Sandbrook on and off for years, starting within weeks after Rebecca was born when she was first diagnosed with psychosis with childbirth caused by rapid hormonal changes. That Mum had been hospitalised on about three occasions and in some ways had never fully recovered. 'But then Diane has always been a bit highly strung.' I held my face perfectly still, acted grown up and didn't let on how upset I was. My mother wasn't normal, her hysterics and passions were on the edge of something that made me feel our family was in danger. I craved for normal, whatever that was. Yet again, the thought came that I needed to escape, like Rebecca had.

Auntie Helen told me something else that had never been explained to me before, something I've held close ever since because it partly helped me understand what was to come in the following years.

'Eliza, when your Mum and Dad got together, they were the happiest couple in the world. Maurie had always been so shy, introverted, worked on the orchard all the time. But when Diane came along they were so in love. We were all so happy for them. They brought the best out in each other. That is, until Rebecca was born and your mother's nerves went haywire for a while. Like I said, though, she was probably always on the fragile side of things.'

I had always enjoyed my visits to Auntie Helen's house, but on that occasion I was overwhelmed and weary from her constant attention, which had become smothering. So perhaps it was a relief, for both Auntie Helen and me, when Dad phoned one evening to say Mum had an appointment with Dr Sandbrook and that I would return home to Maryhill with them.

NINE

1985

I'd been home in Maryhill about a week. It was a Friday, late afternoon, and Dad had just left in the truck to make his weekly delivery of peaches to the distributor in Coldstream. A mild day, warm. Birdsong in the garden. Mum and I were taking the washing off the clothesline, dropping pegs into the tin. We turned to the sound of tyres on gravel to see a police car pull up beside the backyard gate.

The plain-clothed police officer seemed to take his time getting out of the car, walking towards us. We left the laundry basket and walked up the grassed incline to meet him. He wore a dark suit, white shirt, a tie. He didn't smile, and I couldn't read his eyes because of his dark sunglasses. Perhaps he was behaving so sombrely because it was insensitive to appear overly friendly in our presence. After all, we were a family suffering intolerable grief. We just wanted news about Rebecca, a sighting, a strong lead, perhaps someone coming forward with information.

And so, a policeman had come to see us. My heart raced.

He reached out and shook our hands. Mum first, barely a touch because she was so weak. The medication Dr Sandbrook had put Mum on had flattened her eyes, made her thinking slow.

In some ways I felt sorry for her because she was so opposite to before. But I didn't like who she was then either.

'Afternoon, Diane. Detective Sergeant Jeff Butler,' he said. And when Mum put her hand to her throat, confused, he said, 'We've met before.'

Mum glanced at me for help.

Sergeant Butler turned to me. 'You're Eliza?'

'Yes.'

'Is your dad around?'

'He's taken a delivery of peaches to Coldstream.'

'Diane,' he said, 'can you ask Maurie to phone me when he gets home?'

'Why?' Mum asked.

He shuffled his feet, glanced back at his car, undecided about something.

Mum reached out and squeezed the sergeant's arm. 'You've found her body, haven't you?'

'No. No. Nothing like that,' Jeff Butler said. 'There's been a sighting of a girl hitchhiking on the Gold Coast Highway. It mightn't be her, but she had a slim build with red hair. About Rebecca's age.'

I gaped at him, such wonderful news.

'It's not her. Rebecca knows not to hitchhike,' Mum said, turning around as if someone had tapped her on the shoulder.

Jeff Butler glanced at me, unsure.

'We don't know if it was Rebecca,' he said. 'It's just that the description sounded pretty good and I thought Maurie would want to know about it. I was up this way, so thought I'd come and see him.'

'Have you spoken to her? The girl?' I asked.

'It was just a sighting, someone called the police, that's all.'

I was in the presence of a drugged mother and a policeman and was uncertain when to speak or what to ask.

'Eliza, please ask your dad to phone me. Jeff Butler. He's got my number.'

'Yes.'

'Diane, please don't worry. I'll speak to Maurie and sort this out.'

Tears filled Mum's eyes then spilled down her cheeks. Her lips trembled.

'I don't know how much more of this I can take,' she whispered.

'I'm very sorry I haven't come here with better news,' Jeff Butler said.

When he got in his car, I took Mum by the hand and led her back to the clothesline so we could finish unpegging and folding the washing. But she wandered off to the white metal swing that Dad had made for Rebecca and me. She pushed herself gently and moved backwards and forwards, hardly moving, more like the slow rocking that comforts a baby. She was wearing the white patent leather sandals she'd worn that day at the showgrounds.

That evening Dad tried to phone Sergeant Butler and couldn't get hold of him. That feeling of bursting with impatience. I watched Dad circle the room, try the number again even though he knew Jeff Butler had finished for the day and wouldn't be in to work until the next morning. And when he finally did get hold of him I watched him carefully write a few more lines in his notepad.

'It's not her,' he said to Mum and me.

'Told you,' Mum said.

'But it *might* be Rebecca,' I said.

'The local police up there now don't think so.'

'But how do they know?'

I didn't get an answer, just a long stare from Dad, who'd run out of things to say.

TEN

Towards the end of January, before school started, I worked a few days at the shop. If I'd known that the *Herald Sun*, *The Age*, *The Australian*, the *Gyle Gazette*, plus all the radio and TV news stations were going to break the story of Rebecca's disappearance I wouldn't have gone. Up until then, at least in the minds of everyone on the mountain, Rebecca's disappearance had been overshadowed by the Healy murder-suicide.

It was the scandal surrounding Errol Soydan's involvement with Rebecca that made the headlines. It's true, sex sells. Interesting when you think about it, why we so quickly become voyeurs, fascinated by the secret lives of others. Perhaps it's because there's something lacking in our own lives? Or is it just human nature?

I still don't know how the media found out about Rebecca and Errol Soydan. Or how they got hold of his photo, but there he was on page five, handsome, young, smiling, his perfect white teeth. And alongside his photo was Rebecca's, also smiling, captivating. Looking back, I now see Rebecca's good looks differently, perhaps more objectively, but there was something beguiling about her, a type of innate sexuality that some lucky, maybe unlucky, women have. Think Marilyn Monroe, or a modern-day equivalent,

Scarlett Johansson. Rebecca's smiling pout, unabashed flirty gaze. Errol Soydan and Rebecca's photos were positioned as if they were looking at each other, making it easy to imagine a tryst between them. The media, only by association, were linking him with her disappearance. 'Teacher Suspended After Secret Tutoring with Missing Student.' If it wasn't for major bushfires in central Victoria – three deaths, 180 houses, and 500 farms destroyed – I'm certain the story would've made the front page. Anyway, the reporting of Rebecca's disappearance was finally out in the world, implying Errol Soydan was guilty, even though he'd pleaded his innocence of all allegations and said he knew nothing of her whereabouts. I also read that the police had searched Mr Soydan's house and car. Looking for what? Of course, Rebecca's absence meant she couldn't confirm or deny anything.

And so, there I was, a young teenage girl, standing behind the shop's counter hardly able to raise my eyes to look into any customer's eyes. There was nowhere to hide. Everyone knew, a scandal unleashed. I didn't really know what was being said about Rebecca and our family, but in my mind I imagined the excited whispering, the wide-eyed and revelling gasps, as word spread like a highly contagious virus across the mountain and down into Gyle, that Rebecca Bundy had been fucking her maths teacher.

*

It was about ten-thirty in the morning. The shop was unusually quiet. As Robyn had instructed, I'd swept the floor, dusted shelves, wiped out the fridges, unpacked boxes of Kit-Kats, Turkish Delights, other chocolate bars, onto the shelves beside the counter. I heard a car pull up out the front, didn't look up but waited for the buzzer. Even then I was slow to react. A sense of something, the quiet footfall approaching the counter, not heavy work boots or the usual brisk familiarity.

I turned. It was the reporter who was at the top of Glen Lochan Road covering the Healy murder-suicide and their funerals. The wind had blown hair across her eye. I recognised her straight away. My heart raced.

'Are you Eliza Bundy? I'm Virginia Hurley from Channel Nine News,' she said, smiling like we were good friends.

'Yes.'

'Is it okay if we have a chat?'

'I don't know. I don't think so.'

'It's fine. Just a few questions.'

'What?'

She looked over her shoulder, glanced at a man in the carpark holding a large TV camera at hip level. 'Can you come outside?' she asked.

'I'm working.'

'It'll only take a couple of minutes. It doesn't look like you're busy.'

For most of the week, Robyn had been out the back in the spare bedroom sorting all the items she'd bought at the Healys' recent clearing sale. Filing cabinets, crockery, cutlery, bric-a-brac, boxes of books, a sewing machine, pots, pans, things that seemed of no use. 'Not having Sinead's stuff going off to any old person,' she'd said.

'I need to ask Robyn,' I said to Virginia, stepping back, and without waiting for her to speak, I opened the door and flew down the hallway, heart pounding, and burst through the bedroom door.

Robyn was sitting on a single bed, holding a yellow envelope of Kodak photos. It took a moment to notice she was pale, mouth open, upset.

'There's a reporter out the front who wants to speak to me. About Rebecca. The woman who did the Healy story. Channel Nine.'

'Christ,' she said, standing up, slipping the photos back in the yellow envelope and into her apron pocket.

I followed her back to the shop. And without introducing herself, Robyn launched in. 'How dare you ask a fourteen-year-old to answer your questions without an adult's permission?'

Virginia Hurley smiled. 'It's about Rebecca. Any news we get out there will help locate her. Isn't that a good thing?'

'Then go and speak to the parents,' Robyn said.

Virginia licked her lips, took a breath, glanced over her shoulder as if to tell the cameraman something. 'I've been to the Bundys' house and they've declined. But can't you understand that the publicity we can offer will assist in locating Rebecca? Isn't that what everyone wants? To find her?'

The buzzer went, the cameraman entered and stood beside her. The space around us was suddenly smaller, the air thicker, intense.

'Don't you come in here thinking you can con me. I know your game,' Robyn said. 'You're doing a salacious story about a young girl who got mixed up with a teacher. So, go and speak to him.'

'Please, I'm sorry. I'm obviously not expressing myself clearly,' Virginia said. 'If you, or Eliza here, answer just a couple of questions, we can broadcast it and ask people who may have seen Rebecca to let the police know. Why on earth wouldn't you agree to that?'

Virginia must've seen in my face that I thought it was a good idea.

'Eliza, you want your sister to come home, don't you?'

'Yes.'

'She needs her parents' permission,' Robyn said.

'Actually, she doesn't,' Virginia said, 'but seriously, I'm on your side. I just want to help.'

'Eliza, I'm not comfortable with this,' Robyn said. 'I'm phoning your father.'

Good one, Robyn. She grabbed my arm, held on to me as if Virginia might drag me away, picked up the phone and rang home.

Dad answered, and I held my breath while Robyn explained what was going on. She went quiet while Dad spoke to her. It didn't take long, thirty seconds.

'Okay,' Robyn said to Virginia, who stood pokerfaced waiting to hear what she had to say. 'Maurie Bundy just told me that the police are managing all the communication in relation to their daughter's disappearance. That you are to liaise with them. And you're not to interview Eliza here, or anywhere else.'

'I don't understand,' Virginia said. 'The way the media works is, our broadcasts go into people's loungerooms all over the country. Hundreds of thousands of homes. People don't watch sterile, boring reporting. They want human interest, people talking. Eliza would be the perfect interviewee because she wants her sister to come home. Simple. She should just talk into the camera and ask for help.'

It sounded good to me. Right then, I wanted to do it.

'Robyn', I said, 'if I just say "Rebecca, please come home", I can't see what's wrong with that?'

'Your father said no.' Then looking at Virginia she said, 'I'm asking you to please leave.'

Virginia put her hands up in surrender. 'I'm sorry to have bothered you. We'll be off then.'

At the time, I didn't notice that the cameraman was holding the camera at waist height, aimed at us, a little red light on the top as he filmed everything we'd said. How naive Robyn and I had been. They'd got their grab. Robyn saying, *A young girl who got mixed up with a teacher*. Me saying, *Rebecca, please come home*. All of it tightly edited into a bigger story on the news that night, fronted by Virginia saying that two days before the Healy murder-suicide, Rebecca Bundy, their babysitter, had disappeared. The same girl who had also been named as the student who allegedly went to her teacher's house during school hours. The story made Rebecca's disappearance appear sinister, with the added hint of a sexual scandal.

Having no idea we'd just been tricked, Robyn pulled the yellow envelope out of her apron pocket, started shuffling through the photos to show me. We shared a Kit-Kat while gazing at photos of Sinead's lovely blonde kids, smiling. A couple of Audrey posing in first position wearing a pale blue tutu. Some with Jacob playfighting on the floor with Elliot.

'Those little darlings,' Robyn said, her fingers gently touching their faces.

And unexpectedly, wonderfully, there was a shot of Rebecca feeding Mason in his highchair, a spoon in her hand, grinning widely, eyes bright, into the photographer's face. Audrey, in the ballet dress, was in the background.

'Jacob must've taken that one,' Robyn said. 'Sinead would've been at work.'

Rebecca was grinning into Jacob Healy's face.

'You can keep it if you want,' she said, handing the photo to me.

'Thanks.'

'And perhaps you should take a break from here, love, until we have some certainty about where Rebecca is. We don't want any more journalists bothering us.'

I knew Robyn was right, but if I didn't have the shop to go to, all I had was home, which was stressful and boring. Mum with her cups of tea and glasses of white wine in front of the TV soaps.

If Mum wasn't already distressed enough, the *Channel 9 News* story sent her off the Richter scale with bouts of uncontrollable crying, curled up in bed, lashing out at Dad to *do something*.

She became obsessed about what people were saying about us. *They should throw away the key on that Errol Soydan. How dare that reporter imply my daughter had something to do with what happened to the Healys! Bull Tennant knows the truth. What did I ever do to deserve this?*

It felt like she was more concerned about the gossip than Rebecca's whereabouts. And if she felt responsible for her daughter's disappearance I never heard her say so.

As it turned out, the *Channel 9 News* story just fuelled salacious speculation. Rebecca had been murdered. She'd run away with an unnamed lover. She was seen hitchhiking on the Pacific Highway near Newcastle. And then, so quickly, Rebecca's disappearance was just another story. We were media fodder, used, then forgotten.

*

In some ways, Dad had disappeared too. Harvest had started so there were twelve or more pickers to organise among the trees. Plus other workers in the shed who graded the apples for size, packed and stored them before loading the truck for Dad to take to the distributor, who sold the apples at the Footscray Market.

During that busy time Bryce Jones was around constantly. His too-long dark hair resting on his shoulders as he drove the tractor and trailer with three bins of apples to the shed, returning with empty bins for the pickers to fill again. In the warm weather he wore a navy singlet that showed off his tattoos on both arms, one a curved triangle that looked like plaited rope, and the other one was something blurry that I never got close enough to see. Every second day he came to the back door to drop off a cardboard box of groceries, and Mum's white wine cask, all purchased in Benalla close to where he lived.

Everything around Dad, Mum and me felt high-pitched, brittle, intense. The only respite from feeling so exposed was in routine, being private, staying close to home. I took charge of the kitchen. Set the table, put salad on the plates with cold meat, or sausages, sometimes fried egg with baked beans and toast. Without being asked I did the dishes and swept the floor, took the rubbish out to the incinerator. I fed the chooks and brought in the eggs. I took down all the Christmas cards, carried the dead tree outside, and packed the decorations away. If either of my parents noticed I was being so responsible neither mentioned it to me. All I wanted was a small compliment, acknowledgement that I was being so well behaved. I was being the daughter they had always wanted me to be, yet it made no difference.

After another trip to see Dr Sandbrook in Melbourne, Mum's medications were changed. There were different bottles of tablets in the bathroom cupboard, and she didn't appear so sleepy or drugged. Still, she seemed distracted. And strangely, she started to wear makeup again, and her Chanel No. 5 – a perfume that for the rest of my life took me back to those traumatic days immediately after Rebecca went missing. It was an odd thing to notice, Mum's red lips and made-up eyes, when nothing else about her was like before.

*

On the day before I started back at school, Ripper died. In the end it wasn't really a surprise the way his breathing had turned to panting, his sad eyes staring like he was begging for help. I sat with him and stroked his head, talked to him and just waited. Because Dad was a practical person we'd never taken our pets to the vet; most country people were like that. 'He's an old dog,' he said. And I heard him tell Mum that if Ripper didn't improve overnight he'd take him down to

110

the mulberry tree with his gun and bury him there. But Ripper died alone sometime during the night. I was with Dad when he put heavy rocks on his grave to stop the foxes digging him up. And when I laid a bunch of roses on top, I cried for the whole mess of my family and because Rebecca didn't know that our dog had died.

ELEVEN

On the first day of school, I stood under the blue gum waiting for the bus. The dead leaves under my feet were thick, like standing on a cushion. A little further along, towards the Community Hall, a skinny cat poked its head out from a clump of grass and eyed me off, a feral creature with low-hanging teats. I was trying to decide if I should return later in the day to feed it when Jenny Russo, from Glen Lochan Road, drove past in a silver Nissan Patrol that looked the same colour and shape as Sinead's car. Maybe it was Sinead's car because it would've been sold at the clearing sale, held a couple of weeks earlier at the Healys' property. And when Jenny waved, I turned away because I wasn't up to being friendly with anyone, except maybe with the cat, who had disappeared behind the hall.

Then Andy's father, Ted Knightly, drove by in his Toyota ute, and if he saw me I didn't know because I pretended to look at my feet, which got me thinking that the last time I'd stood in that spot Rebecca had been with me, like she had been every other day I'd gone to school. It was the same feeling I had at home. Her silence made me feel lonely, yet I didn't want anyone else around me. I took a deep breath and knew I was very tired. Something was wrong with me, a secret illness, or perhaps it was a secret power, because the night before I'd sliced my thigh with Dad's razor, just a quick stab to release something from my body, and ever since then when the cut hurt, I breathed easier.

I took my seat on the bus, always the same one, seven seats down on the left. Years earlier we'd somehow established who sat where and stuck to it. The usual kids were already seated, plus a couple of little kids starting Year 7 with their neat uniforms and anxious faces. Andy Knightly was two seats behind me on the right. When he leaned forward to speak to me, I slunk down and looked out the window. I felt self-conscious, a strange buzz in my ears. Most of those kids on the bus had witnessed Mum and Rebecca's fight at the showgrounds. And after all the weeks since, which had involved the Healy tragedy and their funerals, Christmas, for some holidays away from the mountain, there we were again starting a new school year. And in all that time – aside from the buzzing rumours about Errol Soydan and Rebecca – there had only been a couple of false sightings of her.

At school I read the timetable and somehow managed to find my way from one class to the next. I couldn't concentrate. I was aware of the teachers out the front, walking around, writing on the blackboard. Kids sitting in rows of desks. Words being spoken. Kids flicking the pages of textbooks. Whenever the bell rang it was too loud, too shrill and vibrated through me. I blinked at the sound of laughter because it'd been so long since I'd heard any. I could feel everyone staring at me, looking at me sideways, talking about me. More like talking about Rebecca, that she'd gone with Mr Soydan to his house.

I was diligent in avoiding Jasmine because she'd always intimidated me, but on that first day back at school we came face to face in the girls' toilets. She was Rebecca's best friend, but looking at her,

114

the piercings, thin black hair, heavily made-up eyes, a certain haughtiness, it made no sense to me why Rebecca liked her.

We stood in front of each other, and it was me who looked away first.

'Sorry about Rebecca,' she said.

'Thanks.'

'Any news?'

'Not really.'

'It's really horrible,' Jasmine said.

Perhaps because she was showing me kindness, empathy, I found my voice. 'Is it true about Mr Soydan? You know, Rebecca going to his place?'

'Yeah.'

'Why did she go?'

'Why do you think?' she said, leaning forward, staring into my eyes for emphasis, communicating that she thought I was too immature, or guileless, to understand, which at the time was probably right.

'How do you know that's true and not just a rumour?' I asked.

'Because she told me.'

I blushed, felt small, hot. With the ammonia stench of the toilets, I thought I might drop onto the concrete floor.

'Keep me posted,' she said, walking away.

Aside from seeing her at a distance at school, in the corridor, or the quadrangle, it was almost four decades before we spoke again.

On those first couple of days my friends, Rachel and Andrea, stood around me with exaggerated energy. I hated their prying questions about Rebecca and they soon started avoiding me because I was acting so strangely. I used to love school. The smell of new text books, the feel of new pens and pencils, writing neat lines.

The loneliest place in the world was the schoolyard, probably still is. On the third day, I found a quiet place around the back of the school, a no-man's-land that wasn't on the way to anywhere. So that's where I was when I wasn't in class, sitting on a concrete step staring at the clouds. Or I'd pick up a stick and draw patterns in the garden bed beside me. Sometimes a bird with brown and yellow feathers darted into a grevillea. I loved it when that little bird sat on one of those fine branches and gazed around as if expecting to find something. I counted the seconds it stayed, sometimes for thirty or more.

*

At lunchtime on the fourth day, I walked out of the school gate and headed for the showgrounds. I didn't know why, except my chest was heavy and I simply couldn't stay at school. I didn't want to go home. All I wanted was for Rebecca to come and find me and take me to wherever she was. As I walked along the pathway beside the Deveron River, I spoke to her, earnest words, begging words, tears wetting my face. I wiped my nose on my arm. Whenever a car passed me I turned away, acting like I was looking at something in the distance.

Through the granite pillars, across to the row of Moreton Bay figs and into their long casting shadows. I sat on the same concrete bench as the last time I was there. I counted back. It was almost seven and a half weeks since that terrible day. I liked being away from people, yet I wanted to be held by someone. But I couldn't think who by. Mum hadn't hugged me in a long time, she wasn't the type. Last time I'd tried to hug Dad he held my arms so I couldn't get close, which offended me. Auntie Helen hugged me, but she was away on an overseas holiday, somewhere in Europe. Robyn at the shop hugged me sometimes, but only when she was fooling around being playful. Other faces came and went. People I'd known on the mountain all my life. There was no one else. So, I sat there and wished I had a cigarette to smoke, only because it was something Rebecca and Bull did. Instead, I picked the scab on my thigh until it oozed a warm red thread down my leg. And when that secret comfort stopped bleeding I wiped it up with a tissue.

Perhaps I dozed. Time drifted. At school everything was controlled by bells, the routine of classes and breaks, but sitting on that concrete seat, I had no idea how long I'd been there. I studied the angle of the sun, still couldn't make a good guess. I thought I should go and catch the bus home, but still I didn't move. I watched the clouds slowly morph from a giant baby's profile to a map of Africa then into Dad's Massey Ferguson tractor that we called 'Fergie'. A car came into the showgrounds, parked at the pavilion, stayed a few minutes and left. I kept glancing around in case the blue-shirted man with the black dog was lurking around. Later a woman walked onto the oval with her golden retriever and played fetch with a tennis ball. I heard her laughter and the dog bark. Somewhere behind the toilets a dove cooed.

I had the feeling someone was close. I looked up. Andy Knightly was walking towards me, a can of Coke in his hand.

'What're you doing here?' he asked.

'Nothing.'

He sat beside me, took a sip. I glanced at him, baby whiskers above his lip, grey shadows on his front teeth. He was in his school uniform, tie loose, the top button of his shirt undone.

He scrummaged inside his schoolbag, took out a packet of Winfields and a lighter, then lit up as if he was on his own, not sharing. He must have seen my pleading eyes.

'Want one?'

117

I nodded.

We smoked, staring ahead.

He offered me a sip of his Coke and I took it.

'It's shit about Rebecca,' he said. 'Where do you reckon she is?'

'Dunno.'

'Saw you on TV.'

'It wasn't a real interview. Robyn and I didn't know we were being filmed.'

'Yeah, heard that. So, Bull's in trouble with the cops again.'

'He doesn't know anything.'

'You reckon?'

'He has no idea where she is. I know that for a fact.'

'And Mr Soydan. Jesus. That can't be true.'

'It's just a stupid rumour.'

'Really?'

I glared at him.

'Fair enough. So how are you doing then with all this going on?'

No one else had asked, not so directly, and when I tried to answer no words came, and I squeezed my eyes shut.

'You okay?' he said.

Still, I couldn't speak.

His arm went across my back as he hugged me into the side of his body. The feeling of his grip and the heat coming from him made me feel strange. I leaned forward as his other arm swung in front to keep me from falling.

'Hey,' Andy said, 'it's all right.'

'No, it's not.'

His fingers were up and down my arm, unexpectedly tender for a boy.

'What's going on at your place?' he asked.

Careful, I thought.

118

'Dad's flat out with harvest. And Mum isn't coping. She's really upset.'

'Yeah, fair enough. So have you heard anything?'

'Not really.'

'What, so that's it? Rebecca takes a walk and everyone just guesses where she went?'

I told Andy about the missing travel bag, the summer clothes she'd taken. And yet as I heard my voice I remembered that her new bra had been in the laundry. Her favourite white shorts were in her bedroom drawer. That for certain she would've taken those things with her. And she must've come home wearing her school uniform and left wearing it. Why didn't she change out of it?

'Does that mean she's taken off then?' Andy said.

'But she's not phoned to say where she is and tell us she's okay. I can't believe she'd do that. Not even on Christmas Day. She used to babysit the Healy kids and she's not even called us to talk about what happened to them. And our dog died, and she doesn't know.'

'Rebecca doesn't want your parents dragging her back home,' he said, pausing, gathering up his words. 'Because your mother is a bit, you know, over the top. But you already know that.'

Andy was still holding me, so I was caught between his opinion of my mother and my feelings about him, especially his warm breath on my neck. It was an impulse when I turned, surprised how close our faces were. In a moment his lips were on mine, soft and slow, weird, but exciting.

In the dark shade of those ancient trees, Andy and I walked further back to a hidden bench. My memory of what happened next was like I wasn't in my body, but watching the two of us from above. A fourteen-year-old girl too willing to lie back and open her legs. Andy pushing inside me. My eyes squeezed shut. Jaws clenched as the weight of him rammed me into the concrete table. It only took seconds before he grunted into my ear. Then straight away he lifted himself off me, zipped his school trousers as I put my undies back on.

'How'd you do that?' he asked, pointing to my thigh.

'Accident.'

'Needs stitches, I reckon.'

'It'll be okay.'

We lit up, and didn't talk. I blew smoke through my nostrils. There was a rightness between us and the first time since Rebecca had left I felt my chest loosen. I could breathe.

Andy looked at his watch. 'Shit,' he said, 'we need to get going.'

So we ran, Andy in front because he was faster. We talked with panting breath.

'You want to catch up sometime?' he called over his shoulder.

'Okay.'

Across the railway line, down the concrete path beside the Deveron River.

The bus was up ahead.

Along the aisle, and without a backward glance, Andy strode ahead and sat in his usual seat beside Shaun Taylor. I risked a fleeting look and saw his face was blank and his arms were crossed on his chest as if he might fall asleep. I sat alone, imitating his posture. But all my attention was on the wet feeling between my legs. That's when I counted the days from my last period and when I worked it out a shudder of alarm washed through me.

When the bus came to my stop opposite the shop, I stood up and glanced back towards Andy, wanting a signal. I knew a smile was too much in front of everyone else, but a simple nod would have done. He just looked at his shoes, as if something down there needed his attention.

TWELVE

When Dad was inside the house, and not in bed or eating at the kitchen table, he sat in his office doing the orchard bookwork. His desk was made of dark timber and it was always neat, the pens perfectly aligned above a white ink blotter. Since school had started, I doubted he'd spoken to me beyond cursory greetings or instructions.

He was sitting in his tan leather swivel chair, bent forward, glasses low on his nose, blue pen in his right hand. I was the only left-hander in our family so I noticed those small differences that set me apart. Dad was writing in a bound ledger filled with numbers.

'What are you doing?' I asked.

'Bookwork.'

'What's the latest with the police?'

'No news,' he said.

'Have they checked out that man from the showgrounds?'

Dad turned to me. His mouth had somehow shifted from a natural upward curve to a downward shape, as if it would be impossible for him to ever smile again.

'They've worked out that he's an electrician from Echuca who was in town for a couple of days doing some work at the footy club,'

Dad said, glancing at his notebook. 'His name is Jeremy McCourty and he was staying at the caravan park.'

'How did they locate him?'

'I don't know.'

'Did you ask?'

'Off you go, Eliza. I'm busy here.'

'But are they still investigating him?'

'I believe so.'

'What's happening with Mr Soydan?'

'The latest I heard he's now in Melbourne.'

'Is he in jail?'

'I don't know. Now, off you go,' he said in his quiet voice.

'I spoke to Jasmine at school. She said Rebecca went to his house. So it's true.'

'Perhaps it is, but it's her word against his. Now, leave me please.'

Looking back it's obvious how overwhelmed and burdened he was. The harvest was on. Mum was on medication. Rebecca's reputation was in tatters, and by default our family's was too. Everything seemed a mess with no obvious solution, except to slog it out, day after day. It wasn't surprising then that Dad was unable to meet my needs, even if he was aware I had any.

I'd become as much of a ghost in my own home as my parents. Each of us merely existing, silently circling, our three hearts still beating. Mum's drinking was new, or at least I'd never noticed her drink wine during the day before. On the coffee table, and the kitchen sink, were her wine glasses, red lipstick stains on the rims. In the past she had been busy, taking orders, baking, decorating, organising the house, preoccupied with her grooming. The change in her was dramatic. And she'd stopped sleeping in bed with Dad. Every evening she draped a sheet and blanket over the couch, and slept there.

I remember one time I went looking for Dad in the orchard. I'd found Bryce Jones in the tractor shed and he told me where he was, down in a part of the orchard we called Kirks. Dad was with the other pickers, among the Red Delicious tree branches, up a ladder, a canvas bag strapped across his shoulders hanging in front so he could pick with both hands. I had this idea that I'd stay and work with him, to help out.

'Can I pick too?'

'Go back to the house with your mother,' he said sharply, in front of everyone else who was there.

*

A couple of times I returned to the cottage hoping that Bull would turn up again, although I knew he'd be working at Glencoe Station and wouldn't come. One Sunday morning, I just wandered away from the house, letting my feet make the destination decision for me. I went down to the corner of Fosters Lane and Marion Road, climbed over a stile that spanned a barbed wire fence with timber posts, walked along the narrow and partially hidden track that would eventually come out at Cheryl and Bull's old timber house. As I walked, I mulled over troubling things that I couldn't quite comprehend. I laid out everything I knew. It was definite that Rebecca was Bull's girlfriend. It seemed possible that she went to Errol Soydan's house during some lunchtimes. And there was this other nagging thing. In that photo Robyn had given me, the way Rebecca was beaming into Jacob Healy's face, the glint in her hazel eyes. There mightn't have been anything wrong with that, an innocent moment caught in a photo. Perhaps I was a prude, uptight? Rebecca might've been right to treat me like a kid. But still, I was bothered by it, unsure.

At Earls Creek Road I followed a narrow track that led down to Earls Creek. Green willows draped in flowing water. Sheep grazed, lambs skipped and played. Up a grassy bank, past Cheryl's workroom. My spirits lifted when I saw Bull's ute parked beside Cheryl's Cortina, both in the driveway under the shade of a red-leafed maple.

Woody, their staffy, barked loudly alerting them that someone was approaching. 'Woody, calm down,' I said. But he kept up his noise, only faster and louder. His collar was clipped to a long chain so he couldn't reach me, and the closer I got to the porch the more he strained against it.

When I turned to the back door I saw the outline of Cheryl's cold stare through the flywire screen.

'Hi,' I called out, suddenly unsure.

She pushed the door open, stood on the top step, looked as angry as the dog. She was wearing a clay-splattered black t-shirt and blue sarong tied in a knot at her tiny waist, thongs on her feet. A smouldering cigarette cupped in her left hand, swollen fingers.

'What're you doing here?' she said.

'Came to see Bull.'

'The cops have got him. Took him away again early this morning. So you can just piss off right now.'

'I've done nothing wrong,' I protested.

'Get the hell off my property, you stupid girl. My God, I've had enough of you Bundys. My Bull is a good lad by anyone's measure, and you've named him and got him into serious trouble with the coppers. He doesn't deserve it.'

'I haven't said anything about Bull. I've only defended him. I agree with you.'

She paused, thinking, took a slow drag on the cigarette, followed by a stream of smoke through her nostrils. 'You think I've not heard about Bec and that schoolteacher? And that the cops have now got divers in the Healys' dam? Just get out of here and go home. And tell your parents from me that they're getting what they deserve for mixing my boy up in their troubles.'

I stood there dumb, couldn't think of anything to say.

'Go on, get out of here, you little bitch.'

And with the burning cigarette squeezed between her lips Cheryl turned away. The wire door banged behind her, leaving me alone in the backyard, heavy in my body and confused. Woody was lying in the dirt watching me. And when I walked away in the direction I'd come, he stood up and let out a low growl as if to warn me to never return. I wished I'd followed Woody's warning, because years later I did return, innocently, and straight into danger.

As I walked along that partially hidden track towards Earls Creek, I thought about Bull being at the police station. I saw him, like in *Hill Street Blues*, sitting at a table answering questions and it struck me that Bull wouldn't be afraid of the police. He'd sit there with his shoulders back, tell the truth, and for sure he was an honest person who would be believed and be back with Cheryl in no time. That was how it was going to go.

I went home with my head full of everything Cheryl had just said. She'd called me a *little bitch*. And why were divers in the Healys' dam?

I found Dad at the Granny Smiths, standing in a row with other pickers. He was in his own quiet zone, a kind of meditation, reaching out, twisting the stems – his large hands could carry two or three apples at a time – then placing them into the canvas bag that hung across his chest. I needed to speak to him, it felt urgent. Still he didn't stop working.

As I waited for Dad to notice me, I looked up and saw a wedge-tailed eagle rising higher and higher into the thermals, gliding with its wings spread wide and free. I wanted to be that bird, liberated from all my troubles and worries. I thought of my beautiful, strange mother. My sad, hardworking father. My wild, brave sister.

'Dad,' I called.

When his picking bag was full, he emptied it into one of the bins on the trailer. Always unhurried. I don't think Dad could do anything at high speed, not like Mum.

'Eliza,' he said.

'Why are police divers searching in the Healy dam?'

He stared at me, and I could see I'd just told him something he didn't know.

'How did you hear that?'

'I was just over at the Tennants. Cheryl told me.'

'What were you doing there?'

'Just somewhere to go.'

Poor Dad. Without a word, he unclipped the leather straps on the picking bag, and started walking back to the house. I knew to leave him alone, so I just stood there watching him go, a tall man, who got smaller and smaller the further he walked away from me.

When I got home, I pulled out the photo of Rebecca feeding Mason in his highchair. I didn't like the photo, had put it in the middle drawer of my desk and not paid any attention to it since Robyn had given it to me. The photographer was close because there was more of Rebecca in the shot than Mason, something playful going on between her and whoever took the photo. Robyn said it would've been Jacob, probably was. Audrey was standing behind. These days, seeing a candid shot like that wouldn't faze me, we're used to selfies. But back then, taking photos wasn't so spontaneous. It cost money to have them developed, so we were more circumspect in what we chose to photograph.

I put the picture aside and went looking for Dad, who was in his office. I stood at the door, waiting for him to glance up. He was writing cheques, I guessed the wages for all the workman, pickers and packers.

'Dad,' I said quietly.

He looked up.

'Did you find out about the divers at the Healys?'

'It's nothing. Just the police doing their job.'

'What were they looking for?'

'Never mind.'

'Rebecca's body?'

'Rebecca's not in the Healy dam. Nothing was found. So please don't go worrying about things like that.'

'Is there any other news?'

'Eliza, I've got a lot of work here.'

'But no one tells me anything.'

A pause. I waited.

'No one tells me much either,' he said. 'Now off you go.'

'But why? We're Rebecca's family.'

'I think it's a case of the police waiting until they've got something firm to tell us.'

'Do you think we'll get some good news?'

'I hope so.'

*

It's a terrible thing to be lonely and sad. At least I had Andy. He was all right. Not handsome like Bull, but good-looking enough, although his teeth were bad, perhaps he was a bit on the chubby side with lily-white skin. That's what I'd seen when he had his pants down and he lifted his shirt out of the way. His father was a sheep farmer, and since Andy only had older sisters, he was going to inherit the family property. He had his career as a sheep farmer all sorted out, so he just went through the motions of school, attending the classes he liked and wagging the ones he didn't. That's why he appeared at the showgrounds that first time I left school. Not because he had any idea I was there, but because it was the place to hang out before it was time to catch the bus.

In those first few weeks of the new school year, Andy made my life happier. School was hard for me. All the whispering gossip and sympathy mixed with awkward smiles, glances and silences made it impossible for me to know who to trust or how to act. I may have become paranoid, making things worse than they really were, I knew that too. Even so, sitting in class trying to concentrate and learn anything was impossible. I couldn't breathe, or sit still, and when the bell went for lunch or morning or afternoon break, I was relieved because I could go to that quiet place I'd found at the back of the school.

It didn't take long before I started wagging school all the time with Andy. It seemed he had nothing to lose and was very casual about it. If his teachers knew he wasn't attending his classes there didn't seem to be any repercussions, at least not that I knew of. He never came to school for the full five days of a week. Sometimes only three days, mostly four. On the days he was absent, he stayed home to help his father with the sheep, mulesing or shearing, sometimes feeding out grain or whatever else was going on. On the days he turned up he left when he wanted, mostly to avoid English and History. That suited me because I didn't want to be in any of my classes. When he gave me the signal – in the corridor or when he found me sitting on my step – that he was nicking off, I just opened my locker, stuffed my books in, and walked out the front gate.

At the showgrounds, Andy and I had established a kind of routine. First, we shared a can of Coke. Then we smoked a cigarette, sometimes two. We sat on the same concrete table, our feet on the bench seat. We talked, mostly me telling him about what was going on at home and what I was thinking. I trusted him. When I told him that I was always alert to Rebecca, that she might somehow contact me or simply appear, he said that sounded fair enough. He didn't judge me. The signal that it was time to have sex happened when Andy rubbed the back of my neck, a soft double-pat, and had a serious look in his eyes. That's when I knew it was time to kiss him on the lips, then take my undies off. I lay on the bench seat on the far side so that anyone coming into the showgrounds couldn't see us.

Sometimes, on the days I was working at the shop, Andy rode his bike there to tell me to meet him at the waterhole on my way home. So we started catching up at the end of the long dirt track that wound along the Earls Creek to a sprawling river red gum that had a swing rope hanging from a branch.

My period finally came, and I started taking Rebecca's contraceptive pills. I'd found them where she'd hidden them, inside a cloth zipped purse behind some books in the bottom drawer of her desk. Another odd thing to notice, that she'd not taken them with her.

THIRTEEN

Towards the end of March, when the bulk of the apple harvest was over, Dad told me he was planning a trip to Queensland to investigate for himself another sighting of Rebecca. I remember that moment vividly. We were sitting at the kitchen table eating canned spaghetti on toast. Mum was feline-stretched out on the couch watching *Sale of the Century* on Channel 9. The volume was up too high and a glass of white wine was on the coffee table a hand reach away.

'She's been seen,' Dad said.

My heart leaped. 'Where?

'I'm not one hundred per cent clear on that. It's just someone who saw Rebecca's picture on the TV and went to the police station on the Gold Coast saying they were served in a café by a girl with her description.'

I realised then that conversations and plans had been going on around me without me knowing. Not even a hint of anything had come my way, which confirmed what I already felt, that I was unimportant. There was applause coming from the television; someone had won something. I wanted Mum to turn the thing off. I glanced down at my lap, saw the raw cuticles on my fingers that I'd nipped at with my teeth. Then as if I could see through my jeans,

I imagined my undies and under them my pubic hair and private parts. I crossed my legs, thinking of Andy. That the previous afternoon when we'd been together he put his hand on the top of my head and pushed me onto my knees. I hated myself because I didn't resist. To be honest, I was so surprised, I just opened my mouth.

Perhaps Dad noticed my tight face and wounded look because he leaned across and told me his plans. He seemed to have more energy; more light shone from his eyes. He said that the Gyle printers were making A4 posters with Rebecca's latest school photo in the centre. The words MISSING would be at the top. Sergeant Butler had arranged for the Crimestoppers phone number to go on the bottom for anyone to ring if they'd seen her. He showed me a mock-up and I looked into Rebecca's beautiful hazel eyes and I couldn't give my feelings words except to notice a deep-down pain, like never-ending humming.

'How many people have seen her?' I asked.

'A couple. One seems more definite than the other. It sounds like her.'

'Why? What did they say?'

'That she was about seventeen, a pretty girl with hair like Rebecca's.'

'Who told you?'

'Jeff Butler called me.'

'Is he going with you?'

'No. But he said the local police have been to the café to talk to her and she wasn't there.' Dad turned the pages of his notebook over. 'If we count the other sighting from a few weeks back, then that's twice she's possibly been seen in roughly the same location.'

Dad wasn't exactly smiling, but close enough.

'But what about all the other things going on? You know, with Mr Soydan and that man I saw at the showgrounds?'

I'd deflated him. He sighed. 'The police are still looking into that part of things.'

'So who are you going with?' I asked, glancing at Mum, thinking it'd be normal for her to go with him, but then I'd be in the house alone.

'I'm going on my own.'

'I want to come too,' I said.

That's when Mum raised herself up into a sitting position and turned to us. 'No you're not. That's a definite decision and I won't have any discussion about it.'

'I agree with your mother,' Dad said.

I hated the way he let Mum dominate and control everything, that he didn't resist or push back. She'd stopped cooking meals or doing any housework or food shopping. I'd been changing the sheets on my bed and washing my own clothes. She'd cancelled all her wedding cake orders. At least every morning she got off the couch, folded the sheet and blanket and put them away, ready for the next night. Whatever was going on between my parents I didn't know. To me, my father had become weak. His quiet voice that once had so much authority had mostly lost its power.

'Hey, Eliza,' my mother said, 'I've had a phone call from the school about you missing some classes. What's that all about?'

Dad looked at me, asking for an answer with his eyes.

'It's okay,' I said, giving the lie I'd already practised. 'They've changed our timetable, so a lot of us have been in the wrong place waiting. Don't worry.'

That seemed a good enough answer. Mum refilled her glass. And Dad went to his office.

*

It was early morning, an opal sky, when Dad drove out of the driveway. Watching him heave his suitcase into the backseat, and push the door closed, I thought he was too old, bent shoulders and new jowls, to be taking on such a long drive to the Gold Coast. Sixteen hundred kilometres that he planned to do in three days. He was only forty-eight years old, but to me, when I was fourteen, he looked much older than that. But then, we'd all changed since Rebecca had stopped living with us so allowances needed to be made for the stress. Even so, the outline of Dad's skeleton, mostly his bony joints showing through his clothes, made him look frail. Perhaps because his way of doing things had always been in small, deliberate and silent moves – almost as if everything was an effort – it made him appear burdened, a man with many worries. And of course, he had many worries.

Mum was standing back beside the clipped hedge, slippers on her feet and her white dressing gown tied at her waist. Her hair hung around her shoulders and when she glanced at me she smiled as if she liked me, or as if we'd just shared a joke, which we hadn't. I wondered if she was happy Dad was leaving us for a few weeks.

'You make sure you're in the right classroom,' Dad said to me as I moved closer for a hug, but all I got was his large hands on my arms preventing me from getting in close. His dry lips on my cheek. 'And look after Mum.'

Perhaps Dad and Mum had already said their goodbyes in the house because they didn't embrace, but levelled their eyes on each other, which must have communicated something that only they understood.

'I'm off then,' Dad said.

'Bye Dad,' I replied, and in my belly was a flowering of happiness that maybe Rebecca would be in the cabin of the ute when he returned. He would find her for sure and she'd want to come home.

Rebecca was just waiting for him to tell her that Mum wouldn't yell or slap her anymore, that things would be different. Of course, Rebecca would have to make some changes as well. And there I was talking to myself, concocting a story about how our family would suddenly be changed and that wasn't ever going to happen.

I kept my eyes steady on Dad's head as he backed out, turned into the driveway and accelerated away. He didn't wave, just abruptly left, and after he was gone there was an unfamiliar silence that made me anxious. When I turned around Mum had already disappeared inside.

*

Dad phoned every night at seven o'clock. His first stop was somewhere on the outskirts of Sydney where he stayed in a cabin at a caravan park. When he asked to speak to Mum she'd forewarned me to say she had a migraine and would speak to him the next night. On it went, night after night. All her excuses why she couldn't come to the phone and Dad's quiet voice asking me questions about where she was and what she was doing. I didn't say that she was sitting on the couch with a full glass of white wine. And that as soon as the phone rang at seven o'clock she turned the TV sound to mute and put a pink polished finger across her lips to remind me not to say a word about her.

'How's your mother?'

'Okay,' I said.

'Where is she?'

'Asleep in bed.'

'How are you both managing?'

'Good,' I replied, although I wasn't sure if that was true. For dinner Mum and I had eaten toasted cheese sandwiches that

I'd made from the last slices of frozen bread in the freezer. Everything we ate was simple, easy-to-make meals. I'd cleaned up the kitchen and swept and washed the floor. Strangely, I didn't mind doing jobs around the house because no one was expecting it of me.

As for Mum, we somehow got along in a companionable way with unspoken rules. We didn't talk except for transactional things like when I asked, 'Do you want Vegemite on your toast?' or 'Would you like a cup of tea?' Since Dad had left she'd returned to their bed. When I'd asked her why she'd slept on the couch for those last weeks she flicked her hand at me as if it was nothing. But when I persisted, she said with slurred speech, 'Stop nagging me. You're just like your father,' which I knew was meant as an insult. I didn't understand what made her think that about me.

It took Dad three days to arrive at the Gold Coast, where he checked into the La Costa Motel. On that nightly call, he asked me if I was going to school.

'Yes,' I replied, which was half a lie.

Nothing was different at school. But as the days passed, I understood that it was me who had changed. I couldn't relax, couldn't lift my head and look around. I could hardly breathe, let alone learn anything. It was Andy who kept me afloat. But he didn't really know what was going on inside me. Still, what he knew, or thought, wasn't my concern. I was numb. Hurting. Alone. Doing my best, and there was no one who cared very much about me, except him.

I had cut myself again, that time on my lower abdomen, a short, thin line, inexplicable and terrifying. Of course, I knew it was a bad thing to do, but the release seemed worth it. To explain, maybe it was like taking drugs, a kind of pain that made me rise upwards and open my mouth so I knew I was alive. I could breathe. When Andy saw it and asked how it happened I told him that I'd gashed myself by tripping on a roll of barbed wire. The barbed wire was obviously non-existent, but it was the first thing that came to mind. Anyway, that's all it took; a story with a smile and he believed me.

FOURTEEN

Dad had been away about a week when I found Mum in the garden, deadheading roses. That was unusual. But what was even more odd: she was working alongside Bryce Jones. As far as I knew, she only ever saw him at the back door when she gave him her shopping list and money, and again when he returned the next morning with our groceries and her wine. He was wearing a faded white cloth hat, and Mum had her wide-brimmed straw one on. She also wore gardening gloves, and they both held secateurs as they worked side by side on the same bush. Perhaps it was nothing, a normal part of maintaining a garden, yet it startled me seeing them standing so close together, that's all. And when I appeared they stopped talking and stood frozen because I'd interrupted something.

'What are you doing here?' Mum asked.

'What do you think? I just got home from school.'

'I mean, how long have you been standing there?' She was breathing deeply as her face reshaped into a frown, which was her way of informing me I'd somehow offended her, or done something wrong.

'Why does it matter how long I've been standing here?' I said. 'I'm just in our garden.'

I didn't wait for an answer but turned towards the hedged and concreted small courtyard and into the house. There were dishes in the sink, the fan whirring, the floor sticky under my shoes. The house smelt airless with trapped cooking smells.

A good daughter would clean up the kitchen, open windows, wash the floor. But I didn't do any of that. Instead I dropped face down onto my bed and pretended to be Rebecca, planning my escape from this family. How did she do it? Where did she go? I concentrated, thinking, imagining, waiting for her voice to come to me. Nothing happened, which left me feeling dumb, like I didn't understand something that should be simple.

And why was my mother outside being so friendly with Bryce Jones? Surely she couldn't stand his unusual blue eyes, the same colour I'd seen in small tropical fish. The best way to explain my reaction to his eyes was this. A person looking at Bryce Jones's face had to make a quick choice. Either let his eyes bore into you, like one of the replicants in *Blade Runner*, or to look elsewhere, focus on the side of his head, or his neck, never his face. For me it was instinctive. I always avoided looking at him, or having anything to do with him for that matter. I had assumed Rebecca felt the same way. What I'm saying is, I was beginning to doubt how well I knew my sister.

*

I had started working again at the shop, only two afternoons after school, which I didn't mind. Robyn was herself, appearing cheerful and always giving me little hugs, but to be honest, she also seemed older, beaten down. There were streaks of grey in her hair. Everyone on the mountain looked like they needed to join Rebecca on the Gold Coast and have a decent holiday.

Gary had gone off on one of his hay carting jobs, so perhaps Robyn asked me back because she wanted the company. Either way, it was good. 3SR was coming through the speakers. Good music. Foreigner. Springsteen. Van Halen. U2. My fingers hadn't forgotten the cash register, the way they knew where to tap without me looking. The only thing that was different: I'd stopped waiting for the customers' praise. I could barely lift my eyes to see if they noticed.

It was Robyn who bailed me up and wouldn't let me step away.

'What's going on at home?'

'Nothing.'

'Tell me.'

'I told you, nothing.'

'When's your dad coming home?'

'A couple of weeks.'

'How's your mum?'

'She's all right.'

Robyn stepped closer and looked at me differently.

'You think Gary is off somewhere carting hay? Well, he's not. Sometimes he is, but other times not. Right now he's back in his ward in Melbourne because he's a Vietnam vet who's got an illness called post-traumatic stress. At times he's good. He tries, there's no doubt about that. But other times he drinks to rid himself of his memories. He takes medication to help him cope with everyday living, but still the ghosts come for him.' She sighed. 'So I'm telling you, Eliza, be honest with me. I want to help you because I can see your family is falling apart.'

I couldn't put any words together.

'Eliza. What's your mum doing with herself? I know she's not baking or decorating.'

I thought of Gary, the few times I'd seen him down the back in the house. A row of tinnies on the floor beside his armchair.

A smouldering cigarette burning between his lips, or resting on the edge of the silver ashtray half-filled with butts. Whenever he saw me he smiled weakly, like it was an effort. His fingers often trembled in a jerky way. His teeth were stained. There was one time, when I opened the door to their living room, I saw his eyes were red, face wet, and his mouth open in silent crying. I'd hurried away, back up the dark hallway to the shop, and there was Robyn laughing with Sinead, her pregnant best friend, who didn't have long to live. I wondered how Robyn put all the parts of her life together and remained so strong and positive. If she could do it, I probably could too.

'Mum lies on the couch all the time. And before Dad left she slept all night there too.'

'Watching the telly?'

I nodded. 'And drinking white wine.'

A flicker of something in Robyn's eyes, surprise, concern. 'Well, she's had a shocking time, poor love, not knowing where Rebecca is.'

I waited for her to say something that would make everything better. But the buzzer went and Jenny Russo came in, quickly followed by Andy's mother, Bea Knightly, who looked into my eyes and smiled in that cheerless way all the locals had started doing, or perhaps had always done. I blushed at the thought she might know, or could somehow guess, that her son and I had been having sex. What would she say if she knew he'd pushed me onto my knees and forced me to give him a blowjob? And how afterwards, when I spat it out, he sulked and turned his back on me until I told him I was sorry. Actually, that experience made me decide I'd had enough of Andy. I didn't like having to wait on his signals, the lift of his eyebrows in the corridor to indicate that he was leaving school for the showgrounds. The double tap on my neck when I was to lie down, his particular stare when it was time to leave.

'Any news on your sister?' Bea asked me, Jenny Russo standing beside her looking on.

'No,' I said.

'When's your dad getting home?'

'Before pruning starts.'

'What are the police doing?'

'I don't know.'

I took Bea and Jenny in, their round shiny tired faces. Bea's hair pulled back in a thin ponytail. Jenny's cropped short. They were typical hard-working farmers' wives – who should've called themselves farmers too with all the farm work they did. They both wore too-big jeans, oversized shirts, and worn leather boots with smatterings of mud and cow shit on them. They blended in with all the other mountain women and I guess that's why my mother's appearance and conceit screamed wherever she went like a wailing siren.

The point I want to make is this. When Jenny Russo and Bea Knightly left the shop together, they huddled up out the front for almost an hour talking. What on earth could they have been discussing, standing there clutching all their purchases for so long? They made me feel self-conscious and ashamed, because for certain it was my family they were talking about. More to the point, they would've been kicking around all the juicy rumours surrounding Rebecca's disappearance. Errol Soydan. Bull Tennant. Jacob Healy. Never before, or since, has there been such a scandal in Maryhill that had everyone so enthralled.

'Bloody gossips,' Robyn said, and she would know.

We were busy until close and by then it seemed Robyn had forgotten what I'd told her about Mum's drinking. But as I gathered up my things to leave, she quickly packed a cardboard box with bread, milk, a packet of cream biscuits, cheese and sliced ham, a couple of Kit-Kats.

'Do you need eggs?' she asked.

'We've got chooks,' I said, realising that I'd not attended to them in the past couple of days and I was sure Mum hadn't. Perhaps Bryce Jones had.

'And Eliza,' Robyn said. I turned.

'What I told you about Gary is our private business. Okay?' She drew a line across her mouth like she was zipping it. 'I only ever told Sinead about my worries. I miss her, you know.'

'Did you know that the police had divers searching their dam?' I said.

'No secrets up here,' she replied.

'Do you think it was a coincidence Rebecca went missing two days before Jacob killed his family and himself?'

To my dismay, all Robyn did was sigh and shake her head, as if to say that she didn't know, which meant it could be a possibility.

'Robyn,' I said, 'what?'

'I think I need to speak to your father. How can I get in touch with him?'

'What about?'

'Come here, love,' Robyn said, reaching out, pulling me in an awkward hug. 'You're a good kid, you really are. Next time your dad phones, can you ask him to call me? And because your mum is going through such a rough patch right now, perhaps don't mention to her that I want to speak to Maurie.'

'Okay,' I replied, pulling away.

'None of this is your fault, you know that, don't you?'

'I guess,' I replied.

*

I walked home along the track, carrying the box of groceries, thinking that perhaps there was no cure for my family. That the way we were these days was how it would be forever. That we'd never see or hear Mum swaying along with her music as she decorated her cakes. Or the lamb roasts she used to make. Her special apple crumble with whipped cream. Those familiar kitchen smells and the way we'd sit together at dinner and be a family. It might never be like that again. I hated Rebecca then for ruining my life. And whatever Robyn wanted to speak to Dad about I couldn't imagine, not one clue.

A car horn. I jumped and turned.

Bull.

He slowed down, pulled to the side of the road. Gravel split. Dust rose. The driver's window lowered. I walked across to him as he was lighting up.

'Hi,' he said.

'Hi.'

'What's happening?'

I told him that Dad had gone on a trip to the Gold Coast to look for Rebecca. That there'd been a couple of sightings and he was going to hang up posters with her photo in all the backpacker places and anywhere else he thought of. And he was going into every police station to introduce himself.

As I was speaking Bull's brow tightened as he sucked hard on his smoke.

'He phones every night at seven,' I said.

'Is everyone fucking deaf? She's not gone to Queensland.'

'But someone has seen her up there.'

'Bullshit they have.'

'Why do you say that? No one would make it up,' I said, shifting the weight of the cardboard box.

Bull looked at me, three or four days unshaven, clear brown eyes, strong whiff of a workman's sweat and cigarettes.

'You can all think what you like, but she was meeting me on that Saturday morning. She wouldn't leave without telling me.'

'What do you think about Mr Soydan?' I asked.

'That's bullshit too. Just people telling stories.'

I was relieved, took a breath.

'It was Jasmine who told the police about him,' I said. 'Why would she do that?'

'Maybe because it was her who was going to his place. I don't know or care.'

'Really?'

'See how easy it is to make shit up? Spread a rumour? I've got no bloody idea what's going on in Jasmine's fucked-up brain. But I know what I know.' He sat back. 'See ya,' he said, 'and best if you don't come to our place for the time being. Cheryl can't handle it.'

'Why are you in trouble with the police?'

'Soft target. Bastards got it in for me.'

'That's not fair.'

'You go tell 'em,' he said, facing the steering wheel.

As he accelerated away, I felt there were many things left unspoken, more questions than either of us had answers to. I walked the rest of the way home considering Bull's certainty that Rebecca didn't go to Queensland. She'd always said she'd go with Jasmine, so why would she suddenly go on her own? I thought of Jeremy McCourty, the man I'd seen at the showgrounds with his dog. There was still something niggling in my mind about him, the brazen look he'd given me as Mum drove away.

Back then, I didn't see Rebecca like I do now. I'd never considered her a flirt, an attractive young woman exploring her sexual powers. I'm convinced she loved Bull. Surely he was enough for her?

So it didn't make sense that she would've cheated on him with her maths teacher. Or a married farmer with a pregnant wife, father to three kids?

All that speculation just went around and around in dizzying circles. But I've since recalled an incident, like a gradual dawning, that occurred sometime in early November 1984, a few weeks before Rebecca disappeared. Jacob had driven Rebecca home after she'd been babysitting the Healy kids. Perhaps it was about eight pm when she came inside. I met her in the kitchen and noticed the front buttons of her school uniform were undone. When I pointed it out, she looked down, and said, 'Shit, thanks,' as she quickly did them up.

At the time it meant nothing to me. I was too naive, too inexperienced, to consider that Jacob Healy might've had his hands inside her bra. And now my mind goes rife with pornographic thoughts of what two people could do in a parked car, on the side of a deserted road, between the Healys' and our place.

Memory can be a sly thing. I know the buttons on Rebecca's school uniform were undone. I can see her fingers quickly pushing the buttons through the holes before she hurried to her bedroom. But it might've been Bull who had dropped her off at the bottom of our driveway, not Jacob Healy. I couldn't swear on it one way or another. I just know that her buttons were undone on her school uniform.

*

Walking up the driveway, the cardboard box had become heavy. On my right, the beginning of autumn, red and yellow leaves on the Red Delicious and Jonathan trees, a few on the ground. Two rosellas chased each other between the rows. Around the corner, up the incline, and out in front was our house with Dunny Hill rising up in the distance against a pale sky. I stopped and took it in. A stranger looking at our home could easily make positive assumptions about us as a family, and they'd be wrong. Inside, Mum was probably on the couch, half-drunk, possibly asleep. Dad was interstate, probably wasting his time. Even Ripper was dead.

Through the back gate and into the concrete courtyard.

Laughter inside the house. A man's voice, recognisable, but I couldn't find the name.

Up the step, into the porch and straight into the kitchen. And there was Bryce Jones in Dad's chair sitting opposite Mum at the table. A bottle of wine, half-filled glasses. A plate with cheese and biscuits. That wasn't right. Actually, everything was wrong. The way Mum was sitting forward, the strap of her dress off her shoulder giving a peek of a black lacy bra. Her hair was tied up with strands falling around her face. And her legs were apart, her dress was in between. She would've slapped Rebecca and me if we'd ever sat like that.

I'd never seen Bryce inside the house before. It was an unspoken thing. He was Dad's workman, who I'd only ever seen at the back door waiting for an instruction about his day's work. It's difficult to explain that rule, the demarcation between any workman coming inside our big house, but it was a real thing, almost as if Bryce was trespassing. Usually Dad met him, and other casual workers, every workday morning at the shed at exactly eight, even on Bryce's gardening days. Since Rebecca had gone away, our family routines had collapsed, but even then Bryce only ever came to the back door, never inside. And none of that accounted for this new and startling familiarity between him and my mother. All I knew was he shouldn't have been inside our house. Dad wouldn't have liked it, and I was certain if he was home Bryce wouldn't be sitting there drinking wine with Mum.

Bryce smiled at me, open mouth, pink wet tongue. He was studying me to gauge my mood, any clue that I might go along with his audacity. But it wasn't okay that he was sitting in my father's chair. Him, of all people, sitting at our table like he was a family friend. It was beyond confusing to me because Mum was always so conscious of propriety, how things would appear to others. But she must've invited him in. Perhaps I was seeing everything the wrong way?

Leaning forward, he pushed his dark hair behind his ears, and cut a thick slice of cheese, fumbling as he put it on a dry biscuit. And when he bit into it crumbs fell down the front of his navy work singlet, which he casually brushed onto the floor. Another thing Mum would've gone nuts over if Rebecca or I had done that. We would've had the broom in our hands sweeping up before we found the words to argue about it. I glanced at Mum, but she averted her gaze, picked up her glass and drank. Then sitting back she straightened the front of her dress and sniffed as if she resented my presence.

'How are you today? School going okay?' Bryce asked me.

'Fine,' I said without looking at him. I put the cardboard box on the table.

'What's that?' Mum asked.

'Robyn gave it to me.'

She peered inside. 'Take it all back.' She sniffed. 'We're not a charity case.'

I hesitated, startled.

'God, she's got a nerve,' Mum said.

'What are you on about? She's worried about us. We've run out of bread and you do nothing except lie on the couch.'

'How dare you speak to me like that,' she snapped.

'You're drunk.' I stepped back. 'You need to go to bed. Or do something. And he shouldn't be in the house.'

149

Mum stood up, one hand on the table for balance.

Then Bryce stood too and moved towards Mum, hands out in front, gently moving like he was trying to settle a stirred-up animal.

'Hey, hey, Diane,' he said. 'It's all good, love.'

He called my mother *love*.

'Please go, Bryce,' she said. 'I'll deal with this and see you tomorrow.'

Then Mum lightly patted her hair as if neatening it and stepped forward and touched his arm, as if offering him an apology for my rudeness. Her smile was strange, forced and almost crooked like her lips were dry and couldn't slide properly over her teeth. And once again I didn't know who she was, or I felt that she was more than one person. I wanted my old mother to come back, to have her energetic and happy in the kitchen, beating up cake mixture, her music on, chatting to a bride who'd come to the house to select a cake out of one of her display albums.

'You'll be right,' Bryce said to me and I had no idea what he meant. Of course I would be all right.

'There's a quiche in the fridge for tonight. And a couple of chops and some veggies,' he said to both of us as he backed away. 'And more bread and milk,' he said looking at me, winking. The back door slapped, and he was gone.

I glared at Mum.

'We need him, Eliza,' she said, 'so don't you go upsetting him. With your father away we need to keep him happy, because if Bryce doesn't turn up we're on our own and I can't deal with the orchard. I wouldn't know where to start and have no interest anyway.'

I supposed there was something in that, sort of. Still, the way she was sitting, her bra showing, drinking wine with him in the middle of the afternoon.

'Can you please clean all this up?' Mum said, emptying the last of the wine into her glass. 'And when your father calls tonight, tell him I'm exhausted and am asleep. I don't want to be disturbed.'

'What about dinner?' I said.

'I'm not hungry. And don't forget,' she pointed to the box, 'I want all of that returned to the shop. We don't need anyone's charity in this house.'

Then she opened the hallway door and disappeared.

FIFTEEN

A couple of days later I woke up feeling unwell. Stomach cramps, tired limbs. I could hardly lift my head from the pillow. It was a Thursday, overcast with squally winds that rattled the window. I had double maths and hated it, couldn't tolerate Mr Olsen's belief that I should understand what he was talking about, and that it had any relevance to my life. So it didn't take much for me to decide I wasn't going to school. I moved deeper into my warm bed and drowsily slept. At some point I went to the toilet but didn't flush; I didn't want to disturb Mum. From the bathroom I crept to the kitchen, closed the hallway door, and quietly made toast with cheese and a cup of tea, which I took back to bed to eat and drink. Then read a few pages of a book, *The Color Purple*, that I'd taken from Rebecca's room. After a while I dozed again.

Since Mum was back sleeping in her and Dad's bed, I often didn't see her until mid-afternoon when I got home from school. Or even later if I had been working at the shop. It didn't really bother me. For years Rebecca and I had been cutting our own school lunches and organising ourselves, so it wasn't a huge deal if she didn't appear before I went to catch the bus. And besides, before Rebecca went missing, it wasn't uncommon for Mum to work on one of her cakes half the night, so it was usually Dad who farewelled us as we walked out the back door.

I heard Mum in the shower, followed by the long drone of the hairdryer. When she walked down the hallway she quietly sang that new song, 'Sweet Dreams (Are Made of This)'. I thought that was a good sign, that my mother might becoming more herself again. Hearing her melodic voice had made me smile. But at no time did I call out and reveal that I was holed up in my bedroom. I just couldn't be bothered with any potential drama.

I'm guessing it was late morning. Gentle rain. Wind still rattling my bedroom window. I was sitting up in bed pin-pricking an ink tattoo into my right forearm, dabbing the blood with a tissue, when I heard a man's voice coming up from the kitchen calling out Mum's name.

Bryce Jones. He was inside the house again.

'Hey, Diane, love,' he called.

'Up here,' she replied.

I glared at my bedroom door.

Footsteps up the hallway, a door opening. He didn't knock.

My mouth wide open. Heart thumping.

'Where have you been?' Mum asked.

And whatever he said I couldn't make out because he, or perhaps Mum, closed the bedroom door.

From then on I could only hear muffled voices. My bedroom was further down the hallway, but we shared a wall where my wardrobe was. I couldn't quite move, or breathe. Ringing inside my head like a siren had gone off. Bryce, with those strange eyes, was in my parents' bedroom. I put my hands over my mouth, thinking. Out of bed, I stood on the mat trying to decide how to get out of the house without being caught. I started to shiver and couldn't make up my mind what to do.

A burst of Mum's laughter, followed by Bryce speaking. I crept to the wall, put my ear against it and heard him say something about *arse*. Then a noise, like a dog panting on a hot day, and Mum calling out something that mightn't have been an actual word. I thought then of the sounds Andy made when we had sex, that I always stayed silent mostly holding my breath until he finished. But Mum seemed to like what was happening to her.

And then I thought of Dad, that if he knew about this he would close his eyes and maybe never open them again. It would make him cry, and I'd only ever seen him break down once before, that time at Auntie Helen's house. But this surely was the thing that would break him, as if he wasn't already broken enough.

I felt hot standing there, waiting to see what would happen next. Perhaps it was my chance to silently put my school uniform on, take off and come home later pretending I'd been to school. But I didn't move. I was shaking, tremors in my legs, and I couldn't get a full measure of air into my lungs. I sat on the brown shaggy mat, stared at myself in the wardrobe mirror wondering who I was, and if I was real. Perhaps I'd been selected as part of a bizarre universal experiment. Maybe everyone in the whole world could see me right then and was laughing at my predicament. I told myself that was rubbish, to calm down because I did really exist. I was Eliza Bundy who lived in a fucked-up family. I moved forward to look at myself more closely. There I was, a girl with straight mousy brown hair that came to her shoulders. I lifted my chin to recognise myself. It was true that I didn't look anything like my mother or Rebecca, who were both really good-looking. I had Dad's aquiline nose, oval face, ordinary mouth and smile, nothing that stood out that told anyone I was special or beautiful. I grinned into the mirror and stared at my teeth, hating how the incisors were slightly crooked.

Again, I put my ear against the wall and wondered about the silence in my parents' bedroom. Mum and our workman were still in there. Perhaps they'd gone to sleep. I hugged my knees and started rocking, strangely soothing, until the half-finished pin-prick star tattoo on my forearm started to bleed. I stretched out for a tissue, snatched too hard, pulling the box forward and toppling it, along with a photo of Ripper and me, to the floor.

I held my breath.

Mum's voice. 'What was that?'

Silence.

Then Bryce said something that I couldn't hear.

Dad and Mum's bedroom door opened. My mother's light footfall down the hallway. I was quick, snatched up the tissue box and the photo, stepped behind the door, back pressed hard against the wall, teeth clenched tight. Her hand on the doorknob to my room. The door swung open. I didn't breathe. Three heartbeats, then it closed.

I squeezed my eyes shut, unsure and afraid. I wanted Dad, who shouldn't have gone away and left me. I took a deep silent breath and tried to settle down. In my mind I saw where Mum and Bryce were. The gold satin curtains, the cream silky bedspread, white sheets. Mum's dressing table with embroidered doilies and crystal jars and pots. A rectangular bottle of Chanel No. 5. I didn't understand who my mother was and started to count how many different people she was. Angry. Sad. Baby. Violent. Weak. Proud. Selfish. And right then, she was Whore or Slut, I wasn't sure of the difference. And through the wall the moaning and sighing started again. I heard my mother say something about *cock*, I'm sure that's what she said, and other words that I couldn't quite grasp. It seemed to go on forever, repeating noises and movements.

I'd lost track of the time and wasn't sure when I was supposed to make my entry, making out I'd just got home from school. Very slowly I slid down the wall and carefully hunched against the side of the wardrobe. I closed my eyes and lightly dozed. And snapped awake when the toilet flushed.

As they walked down the hallway, Mum said, 'Hungry?'

'Got any of that quiche left?'

'Pretty sure. Unless Eliza ate it.'

I stayed where I was, waiting for my chance to escape. Perhaps out the front door. I glanced at my window but wasn't confident I could pull the flywire screen off without making a sound. I needed to go to the toilet, busting, but I held on. I stretched out my legs because they had become stiff. I rolled my neck. Opened and closed my mouth. I waited. And waited.

Whatever was going on in the kitchen, it was taking forever. I heard the whistle of the kettle. Chairs scraping on the vinyl. Finally, the distant whack of the back door.

Still, I didn't move.

I heard Mum walk to the bathroom, turn on the shower. That was my chance. I quickly dressed in my school uniform, shoes and socks on. Then at my door, scared, hesitant, I carefully turned the handle, a little pull and opened it. I could tell then it wasn't the shower but the bath that was running. Quick. Quick. Out into the hallway and down to the kitchen.

Mum.

She was at the fridge, filling a wine glass from the cask.

She flinched.

My heart stopped.

We gazed at each other, guessing, making sense. She was wearing a pink cotton dressing gown, the buttons down the front mostly undone. Her large breasts were exposed until she tugged the gown tighter. Her hair was a wild upswept beehive, eyeliner smudged. Even then she looked extraordinarily beautiful, perhaps so striking as to be frightening.

'Where did you come from?' she asked.

'School.'

'But you're early.'

I shrugged, no answer. I glanced at the wall clock. 2.48. I was way too early.

'Right,' she said, 'I'm off to the bath.'

I stepped aside for her to pass, the full glass of wine slopping as she went.

When I returned from the outside toilet, I went to the fridge, opened cupboards and drawers and made myself a peanut butter sandwich. I drank a glass of milk. And when I opened the rubbish bin to put the crusts in, I peered down to try and work out what I was seeing.

Strands of brown hair. Lots of it. I picked some up between my fingers and straight away dropped it back into the bin. The hair was curly. I turned to the hallway door. Bryce's hair was long and curly. Mum had always cut Dad's hair. She had all the gear, even a black cape to prevent hair falling on his clothes. Usually she cut his hair in the courtyard, but on cooler days she did it in the kitchen. I could so easily see it. Dad sipping a cup of tea as she cut away.

I glanced at the phone, thought of his next call and what I would say.

*

Fifty minutes soaking in the bath was enough time for Mum to come up with her questions for my interrogation. She took her

158

time. There was no hurry and perhaps she knew I'd be wary and nervous so deliberately gave me plenty of time to stew. I had tried to read my book, and flicked through the TV channels looking for something to watch, but nothing helped. I couldn't concentrate. A vein in my neck was tapping. I wanted to cry and run away and thought about packing a bag and leaving home forever, but that would just make things worse for Dad. I was confused as to why I felt so guilty about not going to school, and why I was so upset about what had happened with Mum and Bryce in the house. It was Mum who had more to be worried about than me. All I could do was stick to my story, stare her in the eye. Although I didn't have a good story.

'So, Eliza, how was school today?'

She was fully dressed, blue skirt with a cowl-neck cream knit jumper. For some reason she'd gone to a lot of trouble with her after-bath appearance. Her hair was neatly brushed and twisted up and held with combs. She'd put on make-up, dangly earrings. It unnerved me that she was so calculating; moving cat-like, looking at me sideways as if searching for weakness. It was as if she'd dressed up to perform, put her mask on, foundation, mascara, eyeliner, blusher, the whole works. Yes, she intimidated me when she looked like that because somehow she was stronger, more powerful.

'Double maths, and I hate it.'

She got straight into it. 'So you got home before three. How'd you manage that?'

I turned my back so she couldn't read my face.

'Eliza,' she said.

'Got a lift.'

'Who from?'

'Why are you asking all these questions?'

'Because I'm your mother and I have a right to know how you got home from school today. And if you don't speak up right now, I'm going to call the school and make a few inquiries.'

There was nothing for it.

I turned to face her, lifted my chin. 'I felt sick when I woke up this morning. I didn't go to school.'

A flicker of something in her eyes, surprise, fear. 'So where have you been all day?'

'Asleep in bed.'

'Really?'

'Yes.'

'Why didn't you tell me you weren't feeling well?'

'Because you were asleep.'

She stepped closer, too close. Warm breath. Chanel No. 5.

I stared back, held her gaze, took in the curve of her black eyeliner, the shine of her dark pink lips.

'I don't believe you,' she said, a tremor in her voice.

'What don't you believe?'

'That you were asleep all day.'

'What does it matter whether I was asleep or not?'

'No one sleeps all day,' she said. Her voice had become quiet, almost a whisper.

Silence.

Her mouth twitched.

I swallowed.

'I heard things in your bedroom. A man's voice. I know it was Bryce. And you had sex with him.'

'That's ridiculous. Why on earth would you say that?'

'I know he came into your bedroom and stayed there for a long time. I heard you.'

'Stop these lies, Eliza. For God's sake,' she said, stepping forward to touch me.

'Don't come near me,' I snapped. 'I know what I heard. What would Dad say if he knew?'

Mum covered her mouth with her hand, her eyes glaring back at me. Then she lowered herself onto a chair at the kitchen table, shoulders curved, her head low.

'No. No. No,' she said, turning to me with round pleading eyes. 'You can't ever tell your father, Eliza. He's got the whole weight of Rebecca running away on his shoulders, and if you tell him about today it'll be too much for him.'

'So why did you do it?' I said.

I flinched as she reached out to take my hand.

'You're too young to understand this. But let me try and explain, Eliza. Listen to me. I've been devastated with Rebecca leaving. You know that, right? And your father is so quiet and has been working all the time. I've been lonely and lost. Really lost. Do you understand?' Her eyes welled with tears and she made no attempt to wipe them away, black mascara rivulets down her cheeks. 'And Bryce has been the only person who's helped me. He's the only one who's asked me how I am. He was the one to offer to get our food. Not like some charity box from Robyn when she gets the bright idea that we might need help. Bryce has been reliable. Does that make any sense to you?'

'I heard you with him, Mum.'

She reached out again to touch me. I stepped back.

'Eliza, please.'

I closed my eyes, remembering the sounds.

'Promise me you won't tell your father.'

Still I had nothing to say.

'If you love him,' she said, 'you won't say a word about this, because it'll hurt him too much. Promise me.'

'Do you love Dad?'

She sighed as she pressed her fingers on her temples, rubbed like she had one of her migraines. 'You're too young and wouldn't have a clue about marriage. All the compromises and sacrifices. Yes, I love your father. But he's not perfect. Actually, to tell you the truth, he's hard to live with. You've got no idea what I have to put up with.'

'Are you going to tell him?' I asked.

Mum stared at me, surprised. 'Of course not.'

'So then. What about Bryce?'

Her chest rose and fell, lips tight, and suddenly she became stronger, alert.

'I'll tell you what,' she said, 'if you promise me you'll never ever tell your father about this, I'll tell Bryce he's fired. I'll work something out. I'll find someone else to help out until Maurie comes home. It'll be all right.'

She smiled at me as if relieved to have found a solution.

'You're disgusting,' I said, edging closer to the back door.

Mum jumped to her feet. 'Stop thinking of yourself, Eliza. Think of your father.'

'I hate you.'

'Hate me all you like. I probably deserve that. But I'm begging you. Think of Dad. Think how it'll affect him. We're already suffering as a family. Please, Eliza, don't make it worse. Please.'

I didn't know what to do. The idea came that I should run away. Maybe I could live in the workman's cottage until Dad came home. But I couldn't stand ever seeing Bryce again. Him walking around the orchard. My father. His sad face.

'Eliza,' Mum said, 'I'm begging you. Please think about Dad. Let's not do this to him. I'll tell Bryce to leave and never come back. I'll take care of all that. Trust me. Everything will be as normal. I'll fix it. I promise.'

'Nothing in this family will ever be normal again,' I yelled, 'and it's all your fault.'

'Please. I'll give you whatever you want,' she begged. 'I'll make it happen.' She locked me with her eyes, waiting for me to say something.

I already knew I'd never tell Dad what had happened that day. So perhaps Mum did have the answer, that Bryce should be told to go away. But even then, it'd be too weird living with her knowing she and Bryce had been fucking in Dad's bed for half the day. Those muffled sounds.

'What do you want, Eliza? I know school has been hard for you this year. Maybe we could look at another school. I've been wondering about it, but was waiting for your father to get home. Think about it. A fresh start. What do you say?'

Still, I couldn't make it so easy for her. I turned my back and ran out of the house.

'Eliza!' she yelled.

But I didn't stop. The wire door hit the frame in that familiar way. Out through the courtyard gate. It was good to be getting away from the house. Somewhere beyond the water tanks magpies warbled. Without a proper decision, I headed up the track to the workman's cottage. I trudged forward on the wet ground, past the row of tall pines, around the dogleg turn at the dam. I paused to look at the ballerina waterlilies. When Rebecca and I were younger, perhaps eight and eleven years old, when Dad and Mum considered us good swimmers, we played in that murky dam with the lilies, tadpoles, frogs, and eels that sometimes slithered between our legs.

Dad made us a raft by fastening four empty 15-gallon oil drums to a forklift pallet with rope. It was our diving board, boat, island, whatever we wanted it to be.

Cool air shrank my skin and I didn't have a jumper. Even so, I didn't mind feeling the cold; it made me walk faster and faster and I was running by the time I turned the corner to the cottage, heaving for breath. I sat on the verandah steps, busy ants at my feet. I felt better somehow knowing I'd come to the right place. I waited until my breath calmed, inhaled the eucalyptus-drenched air, took in the yellow leaves of the liquidambar, and the ryegrass that had come with the change of season.

If I could have cried I would've felt better. I wanted Dad to come home. I wanted my mother to die. I hated everything about her. I could still hear her moaning, how Bryce had said something about her *arse*, then a smacking sound. Both of them, repulsive.

'Mum's crazier than ever,' I whispered to Rebecca, and in my internal video, I showed her everything that had happened that day.

I looked up to the clouds and asked questions about being human, being a girl, being trapped, hating my life. One thing became clear, something I'd known all along but pretended otherwise: Andy was embarrassing. It was his discoloured crooked teeth I loathed the most, couldn't stand his smile, kisses, breath. Why did I tell myself he was good-looking when he wasn't? And he demanded things from me that I didn't like, yet went along with so he didn't sulk and stop being kind to me. I was done with that. Completely finished, especially then because my mother's sounds that came through the wall were repeating in my head. I would never have sex ever again.

I sat there for a long time. I wanted a smoke, a jumper, someone to talk to. In the end it was the cold that got me onto my feet, walking back towards the house. Along that row of pines, their peppery resin smell mixed with wet earth and apples. Past Dad's diesel tank, the garage where Mum parked her Volvo. I was crossing the gravelled backyard, headed for the courtyard gate when I heard the fast revs of a car behind me. I turned. Bryce's blue sedan was coming up from the sheds in the direction of the driveway. My heart thumped and I looked away so I didn't have to see him.

His car horn, long and loud, close. I jerked around, saw him speed past with his arm outstretched through the driver's window, middle finger pointing up at me as he disappeared along the side of the house and down the driveway to Josephs Road. Yes, I got a glimpse of his shorter hair.

In the kitchen, Mum was at the sink, rinsing dishes. I glanced at the clock. Almost six.

'There you are,' she said. 'I'm about to cook some chops and veggies. Do you want tomato sauce or gravy with the chops?'

'I don't care.'

'I'll do gravy then.'

And there was Mum behaving all efficient, multi-tasking. Rapidly peeling potatoes and carrots. Frozen peas from the freezer. The electric frypan on the bench, a splash of oil, then sizzling chops. She didn't ask me to set the table but did it herself. Two placemats, a knife and fork each. Then to the steamer: she tossed the veggies in. A saucepan, a good splash of water, a spoon of plain flour, some fat from the frying chops, a pinch of salt, fast whisking, and the gravy was made.

Soon we were sitting opposite each other.

I wasn't going to talk, because there was no point.

'I spoke to Bryce,' she said. 'He's finished up here with us. He won't be coming back.'

We looked at each other. I had no words, but I did wonder how she was going to explain to Dad about him leaving.

'And when your father rings tonight, I'll tell him that he has to come home straight away. I'm sure we can manage here without any outside help for a couple of days,' she said lightly as if she was happy with herself for sorting things out.

Silence.

'Eliza,' she said.

Still, I had nothing to say to her. Or rather, not speaking gave me unusual advantage, kept her guessing.

'I just want you to know that I'm sorry. Desperately sorry. And if I could turn back the clock I'd change so many things. I know I get too cross at times and need to be more patient.'

I kept my face perfectly still, but I was listening.

'You don't know this about me. It's not something I've wanted anyone to know, except your father, that is. And regrettably, we have had to confide in Helen, and Leon when he was alive, because sometimes they helped out minding you kids. I was hospitalised a couple of times after Rebecca was born. And ever since then I've had problems with my nerves. A few times I've seen a Melbourne doctor who prescribes tablets that make me feel more in control and calmer somehow. What I want to say is this. It's not completely my fault that things have gone so bad for me lately. I've got a medical condition that relates to my mood swings.' She paused. 'But you must never tell anyone about this because it's my private business.'

I could've told her that Auntie Helen had already filled me in on all that. Still, I had an important question I couldn't hold back.

'What's having sex with Dad's workman got to do with any of that?'

She studied me, her eyes sparkling with tears. 'I can see that you're angry with me. That's fair enough. And I'm just going to have to accept that you're only fourteen and way too young to under-stand the complications of adult life.'

'If you like Bryce so much, and have sex with him, what was wrong with Rebecca having Bull as her boyfriend?'

'So you're going to punish me. Is that it?' she said, putting on a half-happy twitchy face that looked more frightened than anything else. 'But I want you to understand that when Dad calls tonight I'm going to ask him to return home as soon as he can.'

I cut into the chop, dabbed it into the gravy and mashed potato. Best meal I'd had in weeks.

'So how are you feeling?' she asked.

I kept chewing, not looking at her.

'Have you had any thoughts about another school?'

I glanced at her then. There were no other schools close to where we lived.

'No.'

'It'd be a good thing, Eliza, if we could talk to each other properly, you know, without all this worry about the future. What I mean is, your father is obsessed with looking for Rebecca. But I'm certain she would've contacted us by now if she wanted to be found.' She studied my face. 'So, with that in mind, it's just you and me sitting here trying to work out what's best for what's left of our family. Tell me, what do you want? Would you like, for example, to go to a boarding school? Or to live with Helen and go to a Melbourne school? All these things can be sorted out, I just need to know what you'd like to do.'

Another blow to my already bruised and bleeding heart. Mum was offering me a free pass to move away and live somewhere else. I wanted it, yet to leave my home seemed an absurd and completely unexpected notion. Even so, I could see myself alone in a strange place, my arms raised high with my face to the sun. I'd cope if no one knew what my mother was like and that my sister hadn't been seen in almost three months. That she might have been screwing a teacher, and Bull. I didn't want to believe she'd ever let Jacob Healy touch her. I wanted to be anonymous, a person nobody looked at and wondered about. Wherever this new place was, I knew it would be quiet and private.

The scrape of knives on plates. As I swallowed the last peas and gravy I glanced at the clock, almost seven. Mum followed my eyes, saw the time too.

'Well,' Mum asked, 'do we have an agreement that it's in Maurie's best interests to not be told what happened today? It would crush him, Eliza. Think about that. And we need to float the idea of you going somewhere else to complete your education because of the pressure you're enduring at Gyle High. Agreed?' She didn't wait for my response. 'And one final thing. If you do speak to your father about what happened today, I'll deny it. I'll say that Bryce was inappropriate with me and I had to send him packing. He'll believe me. Do you understand?'

We stared at each other; neither blinked.

The phone rang, loud, jarringly.

Mum stood, answered it, kept her eyes on me.

'Maurie,' she said.

I took in the way she leaned against the doorframe, hand on hip, so natural, feline-casual. My mother was an actress, playing a role, which meant she wasn't a real person and therefore it was impossible to know what to think, how to react to her.

The call started with a five-minute, one-way conversation. Mum held the handset against her ear while Dad did the talking. She didn't speak until the end when she told him I'd not gone to school that day and drastic measures needed to be taken. She announced to Dad that I'd agreed to go to another school. I supposed I had.

'And, darling,' she said, 'one final thing, there's been a problem with Bryce.'

I walked away then, out the back door into the yard. A small flock of cockatoos were flying low to their nests all the distance to Dunny Hill. The light had subdued to mauve. It was peaceful.

So that's how it was going to play out. Dad was coming home and I was going away.

SIXTEEN

I can't fully express how breathtaking this was at the time. Bull the vigilante. A couple of months after I left the mountain, Bull hunted down Errol Soydan, Bryce Jones, and Jeremy McCourty. At the time I had no idea how he'd discovered their whereabouts and it was many years before I found that out. I was living in Melbourne with Auntie Helen, only picking up what was in the news, and bits of gossip from Robyn on the rare occasions we spoke on the phone. Dad had always been a man of few words so he didn't have much to say about it. And Mum was biased and unreliable with any information.

It seemed that Bull's intention was to find out what those men knew, to satisfy himself they weren't in any way responsible for Rebecca's disappearance. I could understand his motive because all the leads in the investigation were inconclusive, leaving the spotlight on him. For months the police had been surprising him at his work or home, taking him to Melbourne or Benalla for more questions, never making an appointment; all that serious staring into his face.

So to get the target off his back, to get rid of any suspicion against him, he took the law into his own hands. I should also mention, he'd lost his job at Glencoe Station. Some story about how his boss, who lived on the property, didn't want Bull in close proximity to his three daughters.

The regional media, TV, radio and print news, were so enamoured with the story of Bull going after those men, they attempted to make it personal to the district. As bizarre as this sounds, the *Gyle Gazette* had a caricature of Bull dressed like Ned Kelly on the front page. In the late 1800s, Kelly had carried out raids around the north-east not far from where we lived. Kelly and his gang had killed three policemen, robbed banks. Any similarity in crimes between Bull and Kelly was entirely mangled. But anyone who knew Bull understood how the association could be made: both outlaws, and something to do with stature and attitude.

Bull had found Errol Soydan in outer Melbourne teaching maths in a state secondary school. I was surprised to read that he was still employed by the education department. But then, he'd always denied Rebecca had ever gone to his house, and always maintained his innocence. No evidence was found after his car and house were searched, meaning his involvement in Rebecca's disappearance remained an allegation and no charges were laid against him.

Bull targeted his prey and hit on them in two consecutive days. According to Robyn, 'He beat the crap out of that teacher to see what he knew about Rebecca's whereabouts, and probably one extra boot in his ribs for good measure.' It seemed Bull followed Errol Soydan on an early evening run, caught up with him in a park.

Bryce Jones got the same treatment. Bull found him at his mother's place in Benalla, left him lying on the ground inside a shearing shed. Jeremy McCourty had been located in a car park behind his workplace in Echuca, also left bashed and bloodied.

Breathtaking in his audacity, courage and stupidity.

Then he handed himself in.

Bull was given a two-year prison sentence for aggravated assault. He would've known the consequences that were coming his way, and at the time I thought what he'd done was heroic, sacrificing his liberty in search of a perpetrator, if there was one.

I didn't miss much about Maryhill after I moved to Melbourne. But I often thought of Bull and remembered those times we'd talked about Rebecca, where she might be, especially on that Christmas Day when we coincidently met up at the workman's cottage.

I'd written to Bull in Beechworth Prison a couple of times, though he'd never replied. I can see why now. Me, a silly fifteen-year-old girl, who penned a letter telling him how impressed I was with what he'd done.

He would've also been conscious of the situation he'd left Cheryl in. Her arthritis was disabling by then. She was unable to craft any pottery, and presumably carry out other domestic tasks that she'd relied on him to do.

Anyway, the washup of Bull's personal interrogation of those three men meant we were left with nothing much. If Bull didn't get a confession out of them, and the police hadn't, then what did we have? An unsubstantiated link between Rebecca's disappearance and the Healys' deaths. And the odd sighting in Queensland that Sergeant Butler told Dad about.

At least that's what I believed at the time.

SEVENTEEN

1991

I glanced sideways at Dad. He was staring ahead, glasses pressing into the bridge of his nose. His eyes were small and squinting into the midday glare. Why didn't he wear sunglasses? Two hands on the wheel. His forearms were brown from all the years he'd spent in the sun with his sleeves rolled up. I knew my father was a quiet man, someone who liked his own company, thinking his own thoughts. But I didn't realise he could drive for so many hours saying so few words.

We were heading to the Gold Coast to continue the search for Rebecca. Since she'd disappeared seven years earlier this was Dad's seventh trip up the Newell Highway. He always travelled between picking and pruning and followed the same route until he got to Queensland. He stayed for about six weeks, to retrace his previous visits and to find new places to ask around. He handed out the A4-size posters, stapled them on power poles, taped them on bus shelters, anywhere, always at the eye level of an average-height person. In 1988 he drove as far north as Port Douglas and was gone for almost two months. That was my first time. Mum had never been.

After Dad's first trip, in March 1985, when he drove away at short notice to follow up a sighting of Rebecca, he bought a small cream-coloured caravan with a green strip along both the sides. It was behind us, being towed by Dad's four-door Toyota Hilux. Earlier that morning we'd stopped at Benalla and bought supplies, canned food, salad things, general groceries. He stored them methodically in the caravan's cupboards and the small fridge. In the short time we'd been on the journey, I'd observed his silent routine. Perhaps a better description was that he practised a series of his monk-like private rituals. All his actions were deliberate, and familiar only to himself. I felt he got satisfaction out of the order he created.

Across the border into New South Wales, at Narrandera, without appearing to hesitate, he pulled over to a parking bay. In the caravan he boiled the kettle, then we sat under a park shelter and drank tea with a slice of fruit cake. That was something else to notice: we ate fruit cake bought from a shop. Mum hadn't baked or decorated a cake in seven years and I wasn't expecting that she ever would.

'Do you always stop here?' I asked.

'Yes.'

'Why?'

He glanced at me and shrugged. 'Because I do.'

When he was away Mum stayed at home on her own. She continued to believe Bull Tennant knew where Rebecca was, or at least what had happened to her. And she didn't hesitate telling Dad he was wasting his time. I'd seen him stare back at her and say, 'Until we know something different, I'm looking for our daughter.'

His quiet voice still had a lot of power to it, a kind of authority that didn't invite an argument. I'm convinced he travelled every year not just to search for Rebecca, but to have a break from my mother.

In 1986 there had been a breakthrough, of sorts. Sixteen months after Rebecca vanished, a homeless young woman on the Sunshine Coast, fitting Rebecca's age and description, told a social worker her name was Rebecca Bundy, an orchardist's daughter from Maryhill in Victoria. She gave details about how she'd worked at the Healys' as their babysitter. She knew the names and ages of the kids. That she'd been a student at Gyle Secondary school. She gave vague details about her association with her maths teacher, Errol Soydan. There were other bits and pieces of information, all of it thrilling to us. I could hear the joy and lightness in Dad's voice when he phoned to tell me. It was a happy coincidence that he was only days away from heading north. He left immediately, arriving two days later in Maroochydore, only to be told the girl couldn't be located. She'd run away.

It left us bereft. The police said she was likely to be an attention seeker, possibly an addict with psychological problems. At that time, not so much later on, we found it difficult to believe that anyone would make up a story like that. It was true that all the information she shared had been in the public domain from various media reports around the time Rebecca went missing. Even so, it left us worse off, especially Dad, because every sighting afterwards that Jeff Butler told him about, he linked to that one girl who said she was Rebecca Bundy. He kept thinking, hoping, she was our Rebecca, just not found yet. In the face of having no other clear leads, it's what motivated him to keep going back, year after year. Still, Mum never took her sights off Bull.

'He knows something,' she'd say.

*

I didn't have a clear picture of what it'd been like for my parents in the years since Rebecca left us. When I first moved away in the Easter of 1985 – a couple of days after my fifteenth birthday – I lived with Auntie Helen until I finished secondary school at Camberwell High. I didn't go home to Maryhill for about eighteen months, and when I finally did it was only for a couple of days during the school holidays. Then I moved into a share house in Fitzroy when I started university. I found it difficult being around Mum, mostly because of that secret between us about her affair with Bryce Jones.

On those few visits, Dad was kind and attentive towards me, and still Mum's faithful servant, taking her tea and toast in bed each morning. And when she finally got out of bed, she fake-smiled at me, sat too close on the couch, paid me compliments that I knew she didn't believe. She made a big fuss about cooking my favourite foods, expecting me to be grateful for her efforts. She confused me. I couldn't relax in her presence. Was she testing me or teasing me? Were we playing acting roles? Actually, I had no idea what she was doing. I knew that I was supposed to love her, but I couldn't. All I knew was I kept hurting myself, secret cuts on my forearms and the soft skin on my inner thighs.

At least I was finally getting away. I'd secured a job in London and was leaving in the first week of May. At Melbourne University, I'd studied Public Relations and Communications, got an internship at West & Hutton in Melbourne. And when I applied for a junior account manager position in their London office, I got lucky.

*

We were back on the freeway, the caravan rolling behind. Along the never-ending road, I chatted to Dad about my plans to find a share house when I arrived in London, the sort of work I would be doing, meeting clients, writing press releases. I heard my voice as I spoke, telling him about my ambition, pausing at the right moments for him to respond, like normal people do when talking to each other. He had no questions, so there was nothing for it but to go straight to the problem.

'Dad, do you think you're depressed?' I asked.

He scratched his neck.

'I know where you're coming from,' he said, 'because a missing child is a kind of grief that can't be recovered from. But I don't think I'm depressed. I just don't have much to say.'

'So what do you think of when you're not talking?'

'Nothing much. Just looking out.'

My chest ached with sadness for him.

'What do you think of my new job, me moving to London?'

'I don't understand things like that. But I see you're happy about it.'

'Haven't you ever wanted a bigger life?' I asked.

'A bigger life? Until Rebecca went away I had everything I ever wanted. Two beautiful daughters. And Diane, of course.'

We drove on. In front, various road signs, a railway crossing, another small town. On the left, in a paddock, was a large muddy dam. I thought of the Healys, and wondered what Jacob might've been thinking about when he waded into the middle of his dam, before he lifted his rifle and blew his brains out.

*

Late the next morning we crossed the border into Queensland, drove into Burleigh Heads and pulled into a long parking bay. Out of the car, stretching, feeling my legs, we walked up to the main street. Dad didn't say where we were going and I'd stopped asking questions because he seemed too tired or reluctant to answer. I was trying not to be a nuisance.

Dad pushed back the red plastic flyscreen strips and I followed him into Connie's Fish & Chips.

'Have you been here before?' I asked.

'Yes.'

It wasn't the first time I'd thought that my father had a private life away from the orchard. All those roads, caravan parks, shops, service centres, so very different to living at Maryhill.

Dad ordered without asking me what I wanted. So I spoke up and said I'd like some scallops and potato cakes as well the fish and chips. What I would've preferred was one of Nico The Greek's falafels, and a cold beer.

He looked at me in dismay, like I'd asked for something he didn't understand. The way he slowly opened his wallet and pulled out another note made me feel I'd done something wrong.

I held the hot sweaty package to my chest as we walked to a picnic bench with a view across a choppy sea. We sat side by side. And when Dad told me it was the Pacific Ocean in front of us, I acted surprised as if I didn't already know that. I unwrapped the paper and lay our meal on the table. The warm salty smell was wonderful.

Seagulls circled and squealed.

'Don't feed them,' Dad said, 'until we're finished.'

'Okay.'

I thought back to when I used to work for Robyn in the Maryhill shop, those popular fish and chip nights. Six and a half years ago, yet it seemed much longer. That Friday night, when Rebecca went missing, it was the last time I'd worked late. I remembered Cheryl coming to pick up her order. Her arthritic hands, and the friendly way she'd spoken to me when paying. All my memories of her fused together, the gap between her front teeth, her wrinkled but lovely face, the way she could talk with a cigarette wedged in the corner of her mouth. That time she turned on me and said I was a *little bitch*.

There's bad news about Cheryl. In 1987, a few weeks after Bull got out of prison, she died. Bull found her in their woodshed half frozen. The talk was she'd been gathering up logs to take inside, had a heart attack and collapsed. Bull wasn't home and didn't discover her until after dark. Mum had said, 'Fifty years of chain smoking, what did she think was going to happen?' For sure all the smokes would've been a factor, but it couldn't be denied she'd undergone enormous stress with Bull in the police crosshairs, followed by his time in prison.

And so, with Cheryl buried in the Maryhill cemetery, and Bull's reputation forever ruined, he left the mountain. I'd asked around but no one seemed to know where he went. On one of my short visits to Maryhill, I'd caught up on all the rumours, how he'd just shut the door on the old house, whistled Woody onto the back of his ute, and drove away.

With everything I knew, it was foolish of me to harbour a romantic idea that when Bull moved away he went to Rebecca, that maybe they'd been together in those intervening years.

Dad was squeezing the juice from a wedge of lemon onto his battered flake.

'When Bull left the mountain, do you think he went to Rebecca?' I asked.

He looked at me, surprised or annoyed, maybe both.

'Why do you say that?' he said.

'No reason. Just a thought I've had.'

Dad stared ahead, thinking.

'The police would know if he knew where she was. They interviewed him enough times to uncover something like that. And he wouldn't have roughed up those other fellas to find out what they knew if he already knew where she was.'

We kept picking at the chips. I offered Dad a scallop and he shook his head, no.

'What did Robyn say to you? You know, that time she wanted you to call her when you were up here on that first trip.'

Dad put a chip in his mouth, chewed, but I could tell he was weighing something up. I'd asked him a couple of times before, but he'd always avoided answering me directly.

'I guess you're older now, so I'll tell you,' he said, sitting up straighter, looking ahead, pausing to consider his words. 'Maybe at the Healy clearing sale, I don't know, but Robyn got hold of a lot of Sinead's private things, books, photo albums, and such. She found a journal that Sinead had been keeping, like she was writing long letters to herself. Maybe there was more than one journal, Robyn didn't say. The point is, it seemed there was lots of arguing between Jacob and Sinead over money. I remember at the time there was talk about financial strife, that Sinead paid for things they couldn't afford on a credit card. But the other thing was, as I remember it, Sinead didn't like Rebecca being in the house alone with Jacob, even when there were littlies with them. Robyn was upset about it and thought I should be told.'

Strange how random memories push forward. There I was at the shop, standing in my usual spot behind the counter, Robyn beside me. Sinead had just driven away, all the kids in the car. I'd watched Elliot strap Mason into his car seat, thinking how responsible he was, the eldest child. Robyn quietly spoke, as if to herself, 'Why does she spend more than she can afford? Perhaps she's unhappy.'

I recounted that memory to Dad, but all he said was, 'No one really knows what goes on inside the walls of other people's houses.'

We sat there together, side by side, a treasured memory. Briny air, a slight breeze.

It was then I told Dad about the photo I had of Rebecca taken at the Healys' house, described it in detail.

'You should've told me about that,' he said.

I felt unfairly accused. Back in those first months after Rebecca disappeared, our family was broken, making it near impossible to add to the already wild accusations going around.

'So, what does all that mean?' I asked. 'Do you think Rebecca going missing had something to do with Jacob killing his family and himself?'

'I told Robyn to take the journal to the police. But because Jacob was dead, there was no one to interrogate. Still, there's a question there.'

'I think so too,' I said.

The quiet whoosh of waves rolling on sand. Impatient gulls overhead, squawking.

'Does Mum know about Sinead's journal?'

'She's not a strong person, so I've not told her.'

It was all too hard. I wanted to relax, be in the moment, yet all I felt was an urgent need to separate, to split off.

'Rebecca has become a stranger to me,' I said.

'She's not a stranger. She's your sister and a victim of rumours and misunderstandings. Don't ever forget that.'

I was happy he'd said that.

*

Mid-afternoon, after we arrived at the caravan park and Dad unhitched his ute, we drove to all the bus shelters and phone boxes, the noticeboard at the local library, supermarkets and the pubs. It was obvious he'd done that many times before, the way he didn't hesitate as he stapled or taped Rebecca's face at eye level. And always, before he stepped away, he pressed the palm of his hand on Rebecca's beautiful face and held it there, like he was saying a prayer, or maybe he was making a wish for that particular poster to be the one that brought her home. A few times an old poster remained from a previous trip. He didn't take it away, but positioned the new one on top. I understood something then. Dad was on a pilgrimage. The solitude and routine had become central to his wellbeing. It was how he coped.

I asked if I could help, have my own bundle of posters.

He pinched his lips and looked worried. 'I've only got one of these staple guns,' he said, 'and I only have one roll of tape on the go at a time.'

So, I followed him around trying to keep out of his way. Sometimes I sat in the car and waited, or read a book. I felt detached from the experience of being on the trip. Why was I there? I didn't want to do what Dad was doing. I was impatient to start my new life in London.

In the evenings I watched Dad sitting at the table folding a large road map into manageable sections. He had one of his exercise pads close by and also a pen. Sometimes during the day, and every evening, he transcribed his notes from a small notepad he carried around with him into a larger exercise book. Details of where he'd been during the day, the posters he'd put out, the names, contact details and relevant comments from people he had spoken to.

'Can you remember the sound of Rebecca's voice?' I asked.

He didn't answer.

'Dad?'

I waited.

'I don't think so.'

Silence.

'You're quiet all the time,' I said. 'What do you think about?'

He shrugged, didn't look up.

'I'm sorry you have to carry the burden of Rebecca all on your own,' I said.

'She's not a burden.'

'You know what I mean. That you do all the work looking for her.'

'We're all affected in our different ways.'

'How's Mum going, do you think?'

When he shrugged again without speaking, a couple of things became clear. First, that I had to accept my father for who he was. That he was not going to be any different to what he was then, a quiet man who was doing the best he could to cope. Second, that I couldn't hang around with him for another five weeks. I would think of a reason to leave so his feelings wouldn't be hurt. But I was going to catch a bus back to Melbourne as soon as I could. And besides, I'd decided he wasn't lonely. More like the opposite: he needed the solitude.

*

Four days later Dad dropped me off at the Coolangatta bus terminal. I'd told him that I'd phoned my boss at West & Hutton's Melbourne office and he wanted me to return to work on an important job. Even though it was a lie, I was disappointed he didn't ask me any questions about what I'd be doing, a job significant enough to force me to return early.

We stood in front of each other, and like he'd been doing since Rebecca vanished, when I stepped forward to hug him, he set his arms out in front and held me at a distance, then leaned in and pecked me on the cheek. I loved his familiar smell. His lips quivered before he bowed his head and closed his eyes. He wouldn't see me again for at least a year, or more, because when I left for London in four weeks, he'd still be in Queensland looking for Rebecca.

'Bye, Dad.'

He pushed his hand into his trouser pocket and pulled out an envelope. 'To help cover some of your expenses when you're away.'

I didn't look, but could feel the thickness of cash inside.

'You don't have to, Dad. I'm on a wage at West & Hutton, and I've saved up my airfare already.'

'Take it. And be careful, won't you?' he said, reaching out, putting his hand on my shoulder.

'Are you sure you're okay about the money?' I asked.

He nodded.

'And you be careful too,' I said.

'Will you go and see your mother before you leave?'

'I'll try.' Thinking that was unlikely.

The bus driver was loading suitcases under the bus. Passengers were boarding.

'I love you, Dad.'

'I want you to call your mother when you get to London, so we know you've arrived safely. And then maybe, if you can manage it, call us every week. I'm planning on getting home around the end of May, in time for Rebecca's birthday.'

'Okay.'

'And please let us know your phone number and address so we can contact you.'

'Yes,' I promised.

He smiled weakly, hesitated as if he had something else to say, but changing his mind he turned away, not waiting for the bus to leave.

I settled into a window seat midway down the aisle and searched for Dad in the distance. I saw his ute poised to turn right into traffic, the caravan behind. My body felt heavy, a kind of loneliness. The bus's engine started, a humming vibration that momentarily distracted me from keeping my eyes on Dad driving away. And when I looked out the window again, all I saw was a flash of the caravan before it was gone. I closed my eyes and held my breath, begging myself to be strong so I didn't start bawling in front of the other passengers.

EIGHTEEN

I didn't want to visit my mother. I really didn't. Yet, the memory of Dad at the Coolangatta bus terminal, urging me to see her, kept returning, prodding me. It was his humility, the way he reached into his pocket and handed me the thick envelope filled with cash. Later, when I counted it, there was five hundred dollars in fifty- and twenty-dollar notes. It was Dad's generosity, and the effort he was making to find Rebecca, that changed my mind. So, yes. I went to see Mum before I left for London.

I phoned her to let her know I was coming to up to say goodbye. 'Why wouldn't you?' she replied.

There were too many answers to that question, so I just told her I'd see her the next day.

One of my house mates, Liam Evans, lent me his car on the promise I'd return it with a full tank of petrol. So off I drove, fearful, like I was headed towards danger.

*

Autumn in Maryhill was especially beautiful that year. The rows of maples in the main street were vivid gold. It had rained earlier in the day; the ground was wet, not muddy. I unwound the window to breathe in the cold air infused with eucalyptus and chimney smoke. On the left was the old blue gum, where for years I had stood with Rebecca and Bull waiting for the school bus. I was struck by the passage of time, that there I was so casually driving by, just turned twenty-one. I gave a little wave to our younger selves. Bull and Rebecca, wherever they were, would be twenty-six and twenty-four. Stupid, I knew, but I sometimes still fantasised that they were together, that they'd found each other somehow.

Smoke drifted from Cora Engelman's chimney. I remembered her regular Saturday order. Standing at the counter, a big woman wearing her dead husband's clothes, sometimes even his slippers. *The Age* newspaper and a packet of Werther's toffees. And that day, soon after Rebecca went missing, how she'd dropped off a lasagne for us; as it turned out, our Christmas lunch.

I pulled up out the front of the shop, went inside to say hello to Robyn. Fearful of prying questions, if there had been cars out the front, other customers, I wouldn't have stopped. The grapevine draping across the verandah railings was dark red, at its most beautiful. Some leaves at my feet. Small birds flitted in the canopy.

The buzzer rang. I stepped inside, and there she was, bending over, staring into the *Women's Weekly*.

'Hey,' I called.

I'd not seen Robyn in a long time, my trips to Maryhill weren't that often.

'Look at you,' she said, arms wide, 'all grown up and about to fly away.'

I'd not told her, but didn't bother to ask how she knew.

We smiled into each other's faces. She looked older, but Robyn was probably only in her late thirties.

'Off to see your mum?'

I nodded, saw something in her face.

'What's up?' I asked.

'Oh, nothing new. Just your mother up there rattling around in that big house on her own with your dad away.'

'Does she come into the shop?'

'Not often, I think she goes into Benalla.'

'Most likely Gyle,' I said.

'No, Jenny Russo told me she's seen your mum in Benalla a couple of times.'

I shrugged, thinking that was where Bryce Jones lived.

'Any news on Rebecca? I've not heard anything for a while,' she asked.

'Just different sightings. Lots of nutcases making up stories.'

'Want a cuppa or something?' she offered, urging me to sit at a table with two chairs beside the large front window. 'I'm thinking of turning this space into a café. Start serving proper cappuccinos, muffins, toasted sandwiches, simple food.'

We drank tea while she shared her plans, where all the tables would go, the upgrade to the kitchen.

'So what have you been doing?' she asked.

'I was with Dad a fortnight ago, in Queensland, watching him staple or tape Rebecca's face at every bus stop, noticeboard, you name it.'

'Do you think he's wasting his time?'

'I don't know.' I shrugged. 'Maybe. Mum thinks so.'

A flicker across her face.

'What?' I asked.

She shook her head, no.

'When I was with Dad he told me about the journals Sinead kept. That she wasn't happy about Rebecca being in the house with Jacob.'

Robyn's lips tightened, her eyes narrowed. 'Eliza, I don't want to discuss any of that. It was a long time ago. There's no point.'

I kept going. 'Do you think there was any connection between Rebecca not coming home and what Jacob did to his family and himself?'

'I'm not going there.'

'Do you know something?'

'Honey, I thought you came in to see me, not dig up all that old stuff.'

I tried to keep things light, smiling, too cheerful. 'I don't need to be protected anymore.'

'Look, Eliza. I'm not going to say bad things about your sister. Okay? I want you to go off to London and have a ball. Live your life. I'm so proud of you, always have been.'

What wasn't she saying? But before I could press her, she stood and said, 'Honey, I'm in the middle of something, got to keep moving.'

As we hugged goodbye, she made me promise to write to her.

'Yes, of course.'

At the time I thought I would. Why not? But I never did, until years later when we made contact on Facebook. How strange life can be. On that day, the last time I saw her, neither of us would've ever predicted what was ahead of her. I won't go into the details, but Gary died – another tragedy reported in the *Gyle Gazette*. And the following year, Robyn remarried, sold the shop and moved to a property on Bruny Island. And when she was forty-two she gave birth to a son. Called him Fletcher, the name Sinead had chosen for her baby.

*

190

Down the dip, across the bridge.

On the right was the long narrow track that wound along Earls Creek to the waterhole, and the swing rope that hung from that majestic river red gum. I felt sorry for the girl who'd walked down there after working at the shop to meet Andy Knightly. Flash memories. Fresh shame. How awful it had been for me back then. I'd heard that Andy was engaged to be married. He was only twenty-three. It's hard to make sense of things sometimes. He would stay on the mountain forever, and I was leaving forever.

I indicated, turned left, and drove up the driveway.

Mum was outside, broom in her hand, sweeping the back concrete porch. She'd watered the geraniums; the concrete was wet around the pots. The washing machine in the laundry was agitating. She looked all right, dressed in navy slacks and a pale blue jumper with a V-neckline. Her hair was tied back in a ponytail, small gold earrings. She seemed normal, like a regular mother. Her face was different too, not as much makeup, lighter lipstick, no eyeshadow. Perhaps she appeared older, but not in a bad way.

On the way up from Melbourne, I'd played Crowded House, Queen, U2, too loud, a distraction from my anxiety about visiting. But seeing her then, I thought the visit might go okay. Yet I'd never been back home when Dad wasn't around.

I stepped forward as she pulled me into an embrace, Chanel No. 5, her arms around me, patting my back. 'So good to see you,' she said.

Mum had never, in my whole life, embraced me like that before. I pulled away, steadied myself and followed her inside.

'I made a frittata,' she said, looking at the clock. 'It's a bit early, but let's eat now. I'm starving. Are you?'

I shrugged. It was only just past eleven. But I did as she asked, and sat. The table was set with the Royal Albert crockery and

191

cutlery that had always been reserved for special visitors. I couldn't remember being that close to it before, it was usually locked in the buffet behind glass doors. Two wine glasses were also on the table.

'Want some wine?' she offered.

'No,' I said, judgement in my voice, 'I'm driving, and besides it's too early.'

'Good for you.' She poured herself a full glass of red wine. A flicker of memory seeing her sitting at that table with Bryce Jones.

She served the frittata, sipped the wine, dabbed her lips with a paper serviette. It took me from when I first arrived, to that moment, to realise what was going on. I saw it. Mum was playing a role, and I was suddenly uneasy.

'So tell me about your time with Dad?' She smiled broadly, strangely.

'It was okay. He's very organised, keeping records of everywhere he's been.'

'So why didn't you stay the whole time?'

'My boss at West & Hutton needed me back in the office.'

Mum was studying me, thinking something.

'That's the PR company where I work,' I said. 'The same company I'll be working for in London.'

That was her cue for her to ask about my job, what I did, my preparations to relocate. I hesitated, waiting. Nothing.

'I wondered with all that time alone with Maurie, whether you might've had some conversations, you know, private ones.'

'Like what?'

She shifted in her seat, put her elbows on the table. 'I don't know. You tell me?'

'What are you on about?'

Mum cut into her portion of frittata, used her fork like a shovel, chewed like she was ravenous.

'When was the last time you ate?' I asked.

She waved my question away.

I was thinking of something to say, when Mum looked at me, swallowing. 'You've put on weight since I last saw you.'

'So what if I have?'

'You'll live to regret it. Men don't like fat women.'

'I'm not fat, or overweight for that matter.'

She leaned back, gazed at me, making her own judgement.

I shrank in my chair, hating her.

'I popped in to see Robyn on my way through,' I said.

'What's that husband of hers up to these days? He's never carted hay, you know. Goes to Melbourne when he's not up here.'

I stared at her, my complicated mother. 'Robyn's putting in some tables and chairs so she can offer customers proper coffees, muffins and cakes.'

'I don't go there anymore. Haven't been for a long time.'

'Why?'

'I don't like being in the presence of people who talk about our family. Everyone has an opinion. It's very distressing.'

I thought, *Fair enough*. 'So where do you do your shopping?'

'Mostly Benalla. There's more shops, and I don't often see anyone I know.'

It wasn't a conscious thought; the words just escaped my mouth, hung in the air between us. 'Do you still see Bryce Jones?'

Mum picked up her wine glass, raised it, didn't drink, but eyed me off, a hint of a smile. 'I was wondering if you'd ever have the guts to ask me about him.'

I blushed, stupidly.

'Oh, look. You've gone all red,' Mum said.

Ringing in my ears, I was small, once again a little girl in the presence of her powerful mother.

'Have you ever told your father? Come on, you must've been tempted.'

'I wouldn't want to hurt him.'

The mood had shifted, weighted against me.

'Do you ever hear from Bull Tennant?'

'No,' I said.

'What do you know that you've never told us?'

'Nothing.'

'What about Jacob Healy? What was going on there with your sister?'

'No idea.'

'I don't believe you,' she said, looking at me, staring me down.

'I came up here to see you today because Dad asked me to. But I don't know why I've bothered.'

'Oh, come on, Eliza. Always so serious. You need to learn to relax.'

'Yeah, well, I can see how you do it,' I said, 'on the booze all the time.'

'He knows something,' she said.

'Who does? Bull? Mum, get over it.'

'It's easy for you, isn't it?'

I moved in my seat, suppressed an urge to stand and walk out.

'Jesus, Mum. It's impossible for us to have a normal conversation, let alone a normal relationship. You need to do something with your time, instead of going over all the possibilities.'

'Come on. Don't be naive. Everyone knows the rumours about him and Rebecca.'

'What are you going on about now?'

She stood up, went to the buffet, opened a drawer.

Back at the table, she dropped the photo of Rebecca taken at the Healys' house. The photo that Robyn gave me before I went to live with Auntie Helen.

'See those two kids there? Sinead would've been at work. So who is Rebecca making eyes at? One guess.'

'Where'd you get that photo?'

'In your bedroom, of course, hidden away. See, I am productive, a sleuth in my own home.' A cunning grin.

Mum was crazier than ever; I could see it in her eyes and crooked mouth.

'Your sister was a slut,' she said, counting on her fingers. 'Bull Tennant. Errol Soydan. Jacob Healy. Three men. And she was only seventeen.'

'You shouldn't buy into the rumours, Mum. She was only with Bull. And Dad would be upset if he heard you talk like that.'

'Oh, God. You're so like him,' she said.

I stood. 'I'm going, Mum. I'll send you and Dad my address.'

'Running away, are you? Goodness, you are over-sensitive.'

'Goodbye, Mum.'

'Hang on a minute,' she said. 'I've got something for you.'

I was about to tell her about the money Dad had given me, but I wasn't sure if he'd told her, or how she'd react.

She wheeled a large grey Samsonite suitcase towards me, a purple ribbon tied to the handle. 'I didn't wrap it because it's too big, but see how easy it is to move? You don't need to carry it, just roll it along. I thought it would be a good going-away gift for you.'

It was the perfect present, but I felt restrained, self-conscious, unable to express myself. 'Thanks,' I said.

'You like it?'

'Yes. It's really good.'

'Good. Well, off you go then,' she said, ready for me to leave.

She followed me outside, stood with her back to the hedge, arms crossed, a solitary figure. How peculiar to notice that both of my parents were loners, isolated, doing their best to cope. Had they always been like that? Why had she bought me such a thoughtful gift when she was so disapproving of me?

I put the suitcase on the backseat, sat behind the wheel and rolled down the window. Part of me wanted to hug her, cling on, sob into her shoulder because our family was in ruins. Not for a moment had I forgotten my part in it. I knew to withhold my emotions, wait, wait, stay strong, do not blubber in front of her.

In the rear-view mirror, Dunny Hill stood proud, beckoning me. I'd hoped to walk up there, for no other reason than to sit on the cottage steps, say goodbye. I didn't know when I'd return.

I waved at Mum, as she lifted her hand and let it drop – not a wave, more of a slow flick, like shooing a fly. Such an inadequate, blunt parting. I waited, as best I could, until I was out of her sight. Then let my face loosen as tears wet my cheeks.

*

Up Josephs Road, a right turn into Fosters Lane. I drove slowly – wallabies, kangaroos and wombats could sometimes surprise a driver, even in full daylight. Perhaps because I'd left Mum's place earlier than I expected, I had some time. Right into Marion Road, then onto Earls Creek Road, probably my favourite road on the mountain. It followed Earls Creek's meandering bends through a valley. Low wispy clouds, shallows with white water spilling over rocks, grazing sheep, golden willows in the distance, rising green hills.

It was impulsive, nothing but curiosity. Across a cattle grid and down Cheryl and Bull's driveway, over a grassed hump, slowly around deep potholes. Vivid colours. Orange, red, yellow. Maples, oaks, elms. I'd never approached their house from that direction before, I'd always walked up from Earls Creek.

I pulled up, opened my window and took the house in. Yes, it was rundown, grass in the gutters, front blinds pulled down, dark in those rooms. It was deserted. On the left was the corrugated iron woodshed. It was where Bull found Cheryl. It felt unreal to be so close to where she had died. In the distance was Cheryl's pottery shed, grander than the house with its gabled roof and casement windows. I thought about going for a wander, some idea about reminiscing, saying goodbye to Bull, wherever he was.

Then from the side something moved, a flash of blue.

'What're you doing here?' a bearded man demanded. Big, muscled, fat face, small eyes.

'Nothing,' I said, starting the motor, heart racing.

'Bullshit.'

'I used to know the Tennants. Bull and Cheryl.'

'Cheryl's dead. Ashton doesn't live here anymore.'

'Where is he?' I asked, for a split second thinking he might tell me, this could be all right.

'Wouldn't you like to know?' he said smiling, broken front tooth, stepping back, taking in Liam's Ford Falcon.

Then another man, tall, long hair, bald on top, was walking slowly towards us, scratching his groin.

I reversed hard on the accelerator. Blindly, panicky. I swung the steering wheel so I could straighten up, tyres skidding on wet grass. Metal crunched. Shit. Shit. I'd hit a tree. Heart pounding. Hands jittery. Into first gear, second, third, fast back down the driveway, sliding and thumping in and out of potholes. I didn't slow down, or catch my breath, until I was on Earls Creek Road.

I didn't know what to make of that encounter. Was I seriously in danger? Who were those men? How did that man know that Bull's real name was Ashton?

It was a stupid, impulsive thing I'd done, going to the Tennants' old house. If only I hadn't gone. Aside from the serious fright I'd given myself, all the money Dad gave me I handed over to Liam for the damage to his car.

NINETEEN

1998

In front and behind there were hundreds of moving people. Off the escalator I stepped forward as the mass dispersed, splitting off in all directions, rushing, flat-faced, focused. A London Underground inspector glanced at my ticket as I surged with the crowd out of Victoria Station and into the cold morning chill.

It was the short days that took getting used to, not the cold. I'd grown up in a cold place, Maryhill, which was more than six hundred metres above sea level, and icy during the winter months. When the traffic lights changed, I crossed Vauxhall Bridge Road with the throng and walked down Victoria Street. The double glass doors opened and I entered the West & Hutton office ground floor reception. Into the lift, my security card against the pad, I was sped up to the sixth floor. That building was my second home. In those days, the other place I called home was a one-bedroom flat in Islington, an old brick house on Wheelright Street that had been converted into four flats.

Out onto the carpeted floor, soft underfoot. The faint hum of white noise, photocopiers, air-conditioning, fluorescent lights. The smell of ink and coffee, although that was probably an association I made. It happened every time I entered that office, a sensation of lightness because I was in the centre of things. I felt important. A right turn along a corridor that separated workstations, each shielded from all eyes by blue partitions.

Mine was fourth on the left. Such a familiar space. If I close my eyes I can still place the exact position of the rubbish bin, the landline phone, my computer monitor and keyboard in front. Drawers on the right. Overhead shelving. A prickly cactus in a red pot on top of my filing cabinet, a birthday gift from my boss, Alison Hardwick.

There was a flashing light on my phone. I pressed for the message, turned my computer on, reached for my coffee mug.

It was Alison telling me she was too sick to come into the office. 'Can't do the brief with the CEO from Bell-Grant,' she said, pausing to blow her nose, hacking a cough, all to good effect. 'You'll have to step up, love. Sorry. You've got the file and I know you can do it. Call me if you have any questions. Oh, I should've said, his name is Duncan Ramsey. Do your best to make a good impression. Bye, hon.'

I had prepared for the meeting, read the file, written some questions. I was already scheduled to sit in on the meeting with Alison so she could do all the talking. My job was to write up the notes and prepare a document summarising everything discussed, actions to follow up with the name of the person tasked to do that.

I looked at my watch. An hour until Duncan Ramsey was due to arrive. In the staff kitchen I made coffee, chatted to Bryce Millar, West & Hutton's new executive health consultant for the whole of Europe. Of course, his name reminded me of that other Bryce, that weird guy with the piercing blue eyes who used to work on Dad's orchard, and in the garden. The pale man who stood before me also had blue eyes, but soft, almost grey. And as the London Bryce spoke to me, something about a trip he was taking that afternoon to Geneva to the WHO offices for various meetings, my concentration shifted. I was impressed, more like awestruck, as I so easily was in those days – that I was worthy enough to be told the details of his meetings. And as I watched his mouth move, I became conscious of an imagined pulse surrounding the fading star tattoo that I'd needle-pricked on my forearm on that unforgettable day. I clenched my fingers into a fist. That day I'd heard Bryce Jones walk up the hallway of my old home and enter my parents' bedroom.

I could still fall into a rabbit hole, remembering my childhood home, that I had a sister called Rebecca who was missing and I'd not heard from her in thirteen years. Sometimes I forgot about her. Rebecca was someone I once knew, vaguely, in the past. But when I did remember, it was a startling shock that flooded through me, like a hot flush without the red blotches.

I had returned to Maryhill earlier in the year, timed for Dad's return from his annual pilgrimage up north and Rebecca's birthday. Being with my parents for a fortnight was like entering a time warp, as if some evil superpower had pressed the pause button on Dad and Mum's lives as they waited for news of their eldest daughter.

Rebecca's disappearance had officially been classified a cold case since 1988. It felt hopeless. There was no national missing persons register, no formal coordination between state police forces when searching for someone who had disappeared. It was easy to become depressed with the constant temptation to stare into the past. What had we missed? Of course, after all that time I assumed she was dead. Even so, Dad still drove to Queensland every year, presumably following the same roads and routines that I'd witnessed, writing his notes alone at night in the caravan. Mum was herself, as unpredictable as the weather.

I blinked back into the tea room. Bryce was still talking, he'd asked me a question that I'd not heard.

'Sorry,' I said, smiling.

'Your summary report on lycopene was really first rate. I've been thinking, would you be interested in crossing over to my team as a senior consultant?'

Another promotion. Flattered wasn't the word. More like disbelieving, honoured. I put my shoulders back, stood taller, smiled wider. 'That sounds amazing,' I said.

Back at my desk, I reread the Bell-Grant file. They wanted us to support them with a public relations strategy to consolidate their factories. Bell-Grant had twenty-seven small to medium sized factories spread across multiple countries in the UK and Europe, each producing similar food products. The plan was to close those factories and build one super-sized factory in Portugal. The downside was thousands of workers in the existing factories would lose their jobs. That's what Bell-Grant wanted our expertise for, to protect the company's brand as they terminated their loyal workforce. I wondered if that made me a paid mercenary. If it did, I was completely okay about that. I had no conscience whatsoever, because I loved my job, my new friends, the local Ironmonger Row baths where I regularly swam. And my cosy top floor flat in Islington was perfect, everything so far, far, away from Maryhill.

*

Reception called to say Duncan Ramsey had arrived. 'Send him up,' I said, clutching the file.

I waited at the lifts, saw the yellow light move upwards through the floors. The doors opened and Duncan Ramsey stepped forward. A tall man with brown hair, clean-shaven, open face. Perhaps late thirties, early forties. Casually dressed in navy chinos and white shirt with no tie. A camel-coloured woollen coat hung loosely around his body. A blue scarf draped around his neck. Round tortoiseshell glasses that gave him an educated air, not sharp or corporate-looking like other men I'd met at work. I thought he looked a bit like Kenneth Branagh, with a Sean Connery accent.

He followed me down to the meeting room and we sat opposite each other.

'What's your accent? Australian?'

We got that out of the way. An employee from the Antipodes. How long had I lived in London? Did I miss the sunny weather? He came across as genuinely interested. His smile was easy.

I asked if he wanted tea or coffee.

So I returned to the staff room to make him tea. As it turned it out, that mug of tea with milk was the first of probably thousands I made for that beautiful man in the course of our twenty-three years together.

*

On a cold wet Wednesday in November, we married privately in the City Chambers in Edinburgh. The windows were misted from the fine, unceasing rain. Two vases of artificial white roses bordered the make-believe altar. Duncan's girls, Mary and Eve, from his first marriage, didn't come because Una, his first wife, wouldn't let them miss a day of school. If that disappointed Duncan, he didn't say and I didn't ask. Duncan wore a dark grey suit, a grey silk tie. I wore a long-sleeved cream lace dress several inches above my knees and slightly puckered at the waist. I was ten weeks pregnant with Kate.

I didn't feel nervous. Our wedding photo shows how happy we were. Duncan's two sisters came, Janet and Karen, along with their husbands and a collection of nieces and nephews who I'd met many times. They had welcomed me in such a natural and warm way, I felt I belonged. Perhaps because there were a bunch of redheads in Duncan's family – both his sisters, Mary his daughter, at least four nieces and nephews – that added an unexpected dimension to me feeling so at ease.

Auntie Helen was the only member of my Australian family who came. Dad was recovering from a bout of shingles, so severe he missed that year travelling to Queensland. And if Dad couldn't come, Mum wasn't coming on her own. I was relieved.

At least they'd met Duncan when we travelled to Maryhill with Mary and Eve earlier in the year. That trip was stressful, mostly for me. Duncan and Dad hit it off, perhaps because they were both quiet men who seemed to slip into each other's company, which didn't necessarily require conversation. For a large part of that trip – and on subsequent trips we deliberately scheduled so we were there during the pruning period – Duncan worked alongside Dad, secateurs in hand. As for Mum, she didn't pay Duncan any attention; quite the opposite, she ignored him. I don't know, perhaps she was jealous in some way? She was still drinking heavily at that time, and I'm certain she didn't like the interruption our visit caused to her routine. With us in the house with her for a few days, all her habits were on display. Mary and Eve were shy, a little frightened of Mum, so I spent the whole trip conscious of the tension, but unsure how to manage it.

A couple of days after we were married, we drove to the west coast of Scotland and honeymooned for four days on the Isle of Arran, in a rented cottage. We hiked up Goatfell Mountain, the first of many years trekking together. I remember thinking through that whole time that Rebecca didn't know where I was, or what I was doing. That I was just married. I was having a baby. Was she a mother? Had she married? That young woman in Maroochydore who said she was Rebecca Bundy, where was she? Was she my sister? And when I was standing beside Duncan in front of the celebrant, Rebecca should've been on my left side, my bridesmaid or matron of honour.

What I'm trying to say is, no matter where I was or what I was doing, happy, sad, getting on with things, Rebecca's absence was profound.

TWENTY

2009

Not quite six am and still dark outside. Upstairs in my study, the lamp shone a halo of light across my desk. A Scottish winter, cold enough for four layers, the sleeves of my red fleece pulled down to my fingers. The oil heater was on high and close enough for me to rest my right hand as I did a final proofread.

Kate was still asleep, a school day, so I would wake her in an hour or so. Duncan was in Portugal until Thursday, two days away. Being alone was precious time. I cherished the silence among the groans our old house made during the cold months. The platt staircase creaked at my tread. The plumbing pipes in the bathrooms, kitchen and laundry shuddered until the water flow became strong. Windows rattled in the wind. It had been my home for the past ten years and I loved it.

I hit enter, and the FIND REBECCA BUNDY Facebook page was launched. I planned to boost it for a month to get it as far and wide as possible. I hoped it was the right thing to do and that people would be kind. In front of me on the screen was Rebecca's face. The same photo the police released back in late 1984 and 1985, and that Dad had on the posters and flyers he still gave out up and down the east coast every year. He'd told me people he'd met recognised him from previous trips, expected to see him about the same time every year. Since Rebecca vanished in December of 1984, Dad had only missed his annual journey up the east coast twice. A couple of times he'd gone as far as Port Douglas. The first time he didn't travel was in 1999, as I've already mentioned; that time he had shingles on his chest, he couldn't bear the weight of the seatbelt across his body for any length of time. The other time was in 2003 when Mum had a hysterectomy and relied on Dad to help her convalesce.

I closed my eyes and imagined Rebecca's fading image stapled to hundreds of power poles and taped to bus stop shelters all along the Queensland coast. I'd always hated the thought of her face being exposed to the weather, not sheltered from the wind and rain. And I didn't like that her photo was in places I'd never been to or didn't know about. It made her absence feel even more sad and hopeless. And yet I'd just put her face on the internet so she was now all over the world.

I read the blurb once more and saw that I'd referred to Rebecca in the past tense as if she was dead. I wondered about that. Then decided it was the whole point, that we didn't know if she was alive or not. In moments of clarity I thought, of course she was dead. It had been too long, almost twenty-five years. Logic told me that. Sometimes I said goodbye to her and for a short time I felt okay about it. I needed it to be a permanent state of acceptance that she was dead. But no, a tiny voice told me that Rebecca had deliberately cut herself off from her family. She was alive and simply took off because Mum was impossible to live with. And after so much time it had become too hard for her to return, to explain herself. She was established and happy somewhere and simply didn't want to be found. Maybe that's what was going on?

All of that was rubbish thinking. Stay with the facts. We didn't know if she was alive or not.

I quickly edited and put Rebecca in the present tense.

Rebecca Bundy, aged 17, was last seen at the Gyle showgrounds on Friday, 20 December 1984 at approximately 2.50 pm. It was the last day of the school year and five days before Christmas. At the time of her disappearance there was speculation she was planning to travel to Queensland, although that has never been confirmed.

Rebecca is 5' 5" (165 cm). She has a slight build and when last seen weighed about 53 kg. Her hair is a light red or auburn. She has fair skin and her eyes are hazel.

Rebecca is now 42 years old.

The Bundy family asks for anyone with information about Rebecca's disappearance, or where she is living now, to contact us. Please send a private message. We respectfully ask that only honest and legitimate sightings or knowledge of Rebecca's whereabouts be given to us.

I closed the page, and opened a file of a novel I was editing for a publisher. Since I'd moved to Inveresk in 1999, that was my employment. It meant I could work from home and juggle my time with Kate more easily. I kept reading, checking the tenses. It was an act of will to give the story my full attention because I would've preferred to stare at Rebecca's Facebook page and drift away wondering about all the possibilities.

The window rattled. Splats of rain hit the glass. Through the window an ivy branch shook wildly. The writer's tenses were all screwed up. I worked until it was finished. Then straight back to Rebecca's Facebook page to see if there had been any activity. None. I glanced at the time and phoned Dad. He would be standing at the kitchen sink washing the evening dishes, or perhaps he was already sitting beside Mum in his recliner rocker ready for the news.

I've been as honest as I can be about the effect Rebecca's disappearance has had on my life. My mother's psychiatric diagnosis had never properly been explained to me other than what Auntie Helen had told me in those early days after Rebecca went missing. I'd read up on psychosis with childbirth and found the symptoms alarming, and yet that didn't entirely explain Mum's mercurial temperament. It was the whole ghastly mess of Mum's mental health and our collective raw grief that broke our family. It took me away from my home and everything that was familiar. I was never close with Mum, but I'd always loved my father. It upset me to feel partially estranged from him. I'd wondered if he felt the same way, but it wasn't something we could talk about.

Our relationship changed for the better after I married and moved to Inveresk. It was an apple tree that finally brought me closer to Dad. In Duncan's home, my home – Ramsey House, a three-century-old ancestral stone house surrounded by a large walled garden – there was a sickly apple tree in the far corner, beside the garden shed. Yellow leaves, knotty limbs. It hadn't been pruned in many years. For all I knew it was full of rot. So I'd phoned Dad, asked him questions, and took his advice. I bought a pair of secateurs, a pruning saw, fungicide spray, and potassium for the soil. Eventually, blossoms came, bees returned, apples grew. It was a Golden Spire – a common variety found in many Scottish gardens. It's similar to a Golden Delicious, but with a distinctive cidery flavour. I sent Dad photos, me standing beside a bucket of yellow apples.

Three rings, he picked up, cleared his throat and in his whispering voice said, 'Maurie Bundy.'

'Hi Dad, it's me.'

'Eliza?' he asked, as if anyone else called him Dad.

'Just phoning to say hello.'

'What's happening over there?'

'Duncan is away with work. And I'll be getting Kate up soon.'

'What's the weather like?'

'Twice as cold as a Maryhill winter.'

'That's pretty cold then,' he said, laughter in his voice.

'What's the weather like there?'

'Hot today. Thirty-five degrees, I think, or close to it. Got the split-system going.'

I imagined it, the unit high on the wall above the windows. Newspapers on the dining table fluttering, the quiet whooshing sound. Dad had it installed a few years ago. And there was one in their bedroom too.

'Hey, Dad,' I said. 'Remember I told you I was going to launch a Facebook page called FIND REBECCA BUNDY? Well, I've done it.'

'What happens now?'

'Too early to say, but I've put up her photo and asked for anyone with information to send me a message.'

'You know that stupid people will make things up.'

'Yeah, but you never know. Duncan said he'd keep an eye on it to help me.'

'I'll put your mother on.'

I heard him urge Mum to speak to me.

I waited.

'Diane here,' she said.

She knew it was me, yet chose to refer to herself as Diane. I didn't know why she did that, some kind of detachment from me.

'How are you?' I asked.

'How do you think I am?'

'I don't know. That's why I asked.'

'I'm just the same. Nothing much ever happens here. Your father drove me to the hairdresser in Gyle this afternoon. What's her name, the Reinhart girl, she came in this morning and did the floors and bathroom. I don't like her much, but she does a good job, saves me having to do it. How much do we pay her?'

'Her name is Lauren Wishart. And you and Dad pay her fifteen dollars an hour, which is the standard rate. She does extras, so you get value for money.'

'Well, I guess that's the main thing. I'll hand you back to Maurie.'

A pause. I heard whispering.

'I've got something to tell you,' Dad said. 'We've finally decided to subdivide the orchard. Have spoken to the town planning fellow in Gyle, and Will Trevor, the real estate agent. They're coming here later in the week. Friday, at ten.'

'That's good, Dad.'

He'd mentioned the possibility before and I'd encouraged it.

'Got to get it through the council first.'

'Will that be a problem?'

'Probably not.'

It was Dad who said he had to hang up, that the ABC television news was about to start. I could hear the anthem, the volume too loud. It was always a relief when Dad initiated the end of a phone call because it was usually me who did it. All our phone calls had similar patterns and often I lied about the reason I had to get going. After Dad and I finished with the day-to-day updates on practical things, like their medical appointments, and the food drop-offs that Lauren Wishart prepared for them, I heard the gears in his mind change, the quick inhale as he cleared his throat, the upbeat tone in his quiet voice. That's when I'd cut in and say I had to deal with Kate, leave for an appointment, something was in the oven, or Duncan had just arrived home. Otherwise, I'd be trapped, his

212

hostage, as he told me again, on and on, as if I'd never heard before, how exasperated he was with the police, who had stopped taking his calls.

In recent years, I'd initiated dealings with the police too. They were mostly good men and women, but busy with other things. Rebecca's disappearance had been a cold case for sixteen years when, in 2004, Dad's application to the Coroner's Court was rejected, confirming what the police already believed: that all leads of investigation had been satisfactorily followed through, and an inquest would prove nothing. Rebecca's disappearance was a mystery, a devastating family tragedy.

One of the hardest things for Dad was when the Victorian Police Missing Persons Unit was disbanded in 2005 and given to the local police to manage. By then he'd developed a strong relationship with Jeff Butler, who Dad had been dealing with since December 1984. Jeff knew the investigation inside and out, the leads, the false sightings, the various blackmailers, the psychics who said they knew where she was buried. He had retired soon after the unit was closed and sometimes he and Dad still spoke on the phone. The way Dad kept repeating the same old stories, unravelling the minutiae on every lead or possible sighting. This one and that one, as he tried to find linkages, as if the answer was right in front of him if only he could grasp it.

Listening to him now, you'd think Rebecca had disappeared in recent years, not twenty-five years earlier. Perhaps I wasn't much different to Dad, I just didn't say the words out loud and as often. Whereas for Mum, Rebecca's disappearance had always been simple. She had never stopped accusing Bull Tennant of being involved somehow.

'He's killed her, for sure,' she'd say, mostly towards the end of the day after she'd had a few. 'Why doesn't anyone listen to me?'

I wondered about Bull sometimes. I'd searched around on Facebook, LinkedIn and Google looking for him, but as far as I could work out he had no social media footprint. Ashton Tennant. Bull Tennant. AB Tennant. Ash Tennant. I had no idea how to find him, except to work out how to access the Australian electoral roll, but I never had.

Perhaps it was strange that I still held Bull up as a mighty human, an alpha male that was invincible somehow. When I imagined his life, wherever he was, he'd be the same as always, strong, in command, handsome, and hopefully happy.

TWENTY-ONE

2010

When it came time for the demolition of Dad's orchard, I returned to Maryhill to support him. A bulldozer was booked for late winter, before budburst in spring. The plan was to subdivide the property into four, twenty-acre lots, two on each side of the driveway, which was going to be widened and top-coated with crushed red rock. The remaining thirty-seven acres was Dad and Mum's, which included the old family home, the packing and tractor sheds, and the workman's cottage. They would also have the best view of Dunny Hill.

Kate travelled with me. She'd just turned ten years old. Duncan was busy with work so he didn't come. Over the years I'd developed a routine of sorts. Whether Duncan was with me or not, I picked up a hire car at the airport, then up the Hume Freeway, occasionally a detour into the showgrounds to remember the last time I saw Rebecca. Then up the main street to the IGA, and onwards up the mountain to Maryhill.

When Kate and I finally arrived at the house – after travelling for twenty-six hours – Mum was in the bathroom with the door closed. Soft music, a female vocalist I didn't recognise. A faint waft of Chanel No. 5, so familiar, so triggering.

I knocked on the door and waited.

'We're here, Mum,' I said.

Kate stood close, holding my hand, and for a moment I was her age, a child standing at the bathroom door waiting for Mum to come out.

And there she was, startling, wearing a silky green floral dressing gown. It'd been a couple of years since I'd visited. She was older than I remembered, new lines around her eyes, mouth, neck. Perhaps she was thinner around the shoulders and thicker around the waist. But still I blinked at the shock of her beauty, or was it that she was a couple of notches too good-looking, to the point she appeared slightly deformed, freakish, but eye-catching, a person who was hard to look away from.

Kate squeezed my hand tighter, pressed in closer.

'You're here already?' Mum said, smiling. 'I'll only be a few more minutes. Why don't you put the kettle on?' She stepped back and closed the door.

Dad already had the kettle on, so I sat on my old chair, pulled Kate onto my lap and we waited for the next thing to happen. How extraordinary to return to the family home and so quickly feel like a child again, not engaging my own will but aligning my thoughts and actions in a way to please or accommodate my parents.

A few months earlier, I'd told Kate that I had a sister who went missing. That it happened a long time ago, and it made her grand-parents very sad because they didn't know where she was. I thought telling her when she was young was a good idea, that she would grow up simply accepting the facts and not have them thrust on her when she was older and perhaps upset that this family heartbreak had been kept from her.

Kate cupped her hands around her mouth and whispered in my ear, 'Is this where your sister lived before she got lost?'

'Yes, but it was a really long time ago,' I said, whispering back.

216

'Is she ever going to come here?'

'I don't think so. But maybe she will.'

She stared across the room to the back door as if expecting her aunt to walk in. I held her tight, told her she didn't need to worry.

Then Mum entered. Yes, the grand entry, wearing grey trousers with a black polo jumper, her red hair loose around her shoulders. Pink lips, mascara, the works. Dangly silver earrings. She was seventy years old and as vain as ever. I didn't understand how she could be bothered with all the effort.

She sat in the seat she'd always had, diagonal to me.

As Dad took the cellophane off a packet of lamingtons and put them on a plate, he openly and silently looked at Kate.

'Not that plate, Maurie; the other one, you know, with the green and gold border,' Mum said.

Without a word, Dad went to the buffet, retrieved the plate and swapped the lamingtons from one to the other, then put it on the table.

'She looks like Rebecca,' Mum said, 'don't you think, Maurie? Every time I see her she's growing more and more like her.'

'Yes, she does,' said Dad.

'Which means you look like me,' Mum smiled widely at Kate. 'What do you think of that?'

'It's the hair,' I said.

'Oh, it's much more than that. The shape of her face, same nose and mouth.'

Kate pressed firmer into my body. Ten years old, she wouldn't normally sit on my lap that long. To change the subject I asked Mum how she felt about the bulldozer coming the next day.

'I don't think about it. The orchard has always been your father's thing. To be honest, I've never really liked apples.'

'Really?' I said.

'That's never been a secret. Has it, Maurie?'

I had no idea what was going on, the way Dad glanced at her, didn't answer.

'How do you have your tea?' he asked me.

'Same as always. With milk.'

'I thought you only drank coffee,' Mum said.

'Sometimes. But mostly tea.'

'So was it Rebecca who liked coffee?' she asked.

Dad and I acted like we didn't hear.

'What would Kate like to drink?' Dad said to me.

'I don't know. Why don't you ask her?'

It was strange, how Kate hadn't been properly spoken to. Their only grandchild was sitting in front of them and yet their sole acknowledgement of her was in relation to Rebecca.

He looked at Kate now. 'Do you want something to drink?'

Kate shook her head no.

'Has the cat got your tongue?' Mum teased.

And I thought, the ten days I was visiting were going to be hideously long. I'd been in the house less than half an hour, hadn't unpacked our suitcase, and already I felt myself floating away. I understood then, as I had at other times in my life, that my mother's changing moods, and the disappearance of Rebecca, had spun me far away. Right then, I wanted nothing more than to be back at home with Duncan in Inveresk.

I knew what to do. 'So, Mum, how are you?'

She turned to face me, an imperious expression that could've meant many things.

I waited for her answer.

'We manage, don't we, Maurie?' she said, picking up a lamington.

She shook the excess coconut off, and bit into it. Dad, Kate and I watched her chew and swallow, then put the half-eaten lamington back on the plate. She had this way of making herself the centre of attention. We watched her stand and go to the bottom shelves of the buffet and return to the table with the photo albums. She patted the seat beside her for Kate to join her.

'Come here,' she said, 'I'll show you some photos of your mum when she was little. And also photos of your Auntie Rebecca so you can see how much you look like her.'

Kate didn't move.

'What's wrong with her?' Mum said to me.

'Nothing. Just let her settle. Everything here is foreign to her.'

It was like Mum didn't hear me, or she'd forgotten we were even there. She opened the albums, one at a time, stared deeply into the photos, turned the pages. I couldn't see the pictures she was gazing at, but one of them she traced with the tip of her finger. I shifted Kate off my lap, half-stood to glance across to see what Mum was looking at. It was a photo of her standing alone in front of the yellow Volvo they used to have back in 1984.

I stood up, and Kate followed me down the hallway to my old bedroom. Years earlier, Duncan and I had bought a queen-sized bed and swapped it with my old single. We'd tried to transform the room so it didn't remind me so acutely of the childhood years I'd slept there, or being ordered to stay in my room and be quiet. That time when Mum was with Bryce Jones, their sounds through our shared wall. We packed away all my teenage stuff, painted the room in a colour called Tidewater, bought off-white linen, a doona cover, new pillows. It looked relatively inviting, at least it was different, gave the feeling of being in the present.

Mum came to the open bedroom door, stretched her arms to touch each side of the doorframe, filling the whole space as if blocking us in.

'I've made up Rebecca's bed for Kate,' she said.

I opened my mouth, speechless.

'Well, she's too old to be sleeping in that bed with you,' she said.

'She's sleeping in this bed with me. Not in Rebecca's bed.'

Mum looked down at Kate, studied her, disapproving of her shyness, which was really terror at being in her presence.

'Why would you even suggest that?' I asked.

'Because there's three bedrooms in this house and one of them isn't being used.'

'Has anyone ever slept in Rebecca's bed, you know, since she left?'

Without a word, Mum turned away and went into their bedroom, closed the door. Since my last visit a television had been mounted on the wall, a large screen. The sound of people's voices, some program she was watching.

*

At eight the next morning an excavator, chained onto the back of a flatbed truck, was slowly hauled up the driveway and offloaded at the turning circle down at the packing sheds. Todd, the bloke in charge, had a plan. He told Dad that he would start at the back, up near the workman's cottage, and work forward towards Josephs Road.

Dad, Kate and I stood together watching the landscape flatten. The merciless strength of the excavator, the roaring sound of the engine and squeal of unyielding tree roots until they snapped and were pushed forward into one of the waiting bonfire mounds.

I stole glances at Dad, looking for something on his face that would tell me what he was thinking. His expression was passive, unreadable. We'd packed a thermos of hot tea and blueberry muffins that I had baked the previous evening. The three of us sat on a flat granite boulder so we could watch the destruction continue on in front of us, but at a distance from the noise.

'How're you feeling, Dad? All those years you've been working out here?'

He sipped his tea, swallowed. 'It's a relief, actually. It needed to happen. Now it has.'

It took six days for the orchard to be ripped out of the earth, tree roots, branches and limbs pushed into fifty or more waiting pyres. It'd take the summer months for the dying trees to dry out, ready for matches to incinerate them.

On about the third day, after Todd had packed up for the day, I noticed Dad silently leave the house, put his boots back on and head out to the orchard. Where was he going? What was he doing?

Kate wouldn't stay in the house alone with Mum, so she came with me. Outside was quiet birdsong. A late afternoon breeze moved through the poplars and elms. The two of us walked up the dirt track to find him. Up past the dam with the pink waterlilies. And there were Rebecca and me in that muddy water on our raft, little girls playing, laughing, fighting. And beside me was Kate with her hair tied into a long bouncy ponytail. A pang in my heart because time kept moving forward. I was forty years old, and Rebecca was still seventeen.

Dad was in the distance, tall and thin, standing on his mutilated land, deep gouges, large clods of dirt. Still wearing his work clothes, he was carrying the long-handled gardening hoe, head down, walking slowly. He bent slightly forward and dug in one of the ruts, just a few short jabs, before squatting and looking down. Up again, and on he went. He was searching for something.

When he saw us coming he stiffened, and looked around as if he wanted to hide, or hide something.

'What're you looking for, Dad?'

'Nothing.'

We took each other in, then he deliberately glanced at Kate, something he wouldn't say in front of her. I nodded, and backed away.

I knew.

It was much later in the evening when Dad and I were alone and free to talk. I stood waiting for him on the back step. An immense black sky with salty stars. Insects swarmed the verandah light. Distant frogs croaked. Mum was in bed watching TV. Kate was asleep in my queen bed. Finally he came. I watched him open the gate and enter the back yard carrying a plastic bowl that had held veggie scraps he'd just fed to the chickens. Earlier in the day I'd attended to them with Kate.

'While I'm here, Dad, I'll take care of the chooks. Kate and I got the eggs this morning.'

'Saw that. Okay,' he said.

The temperature had dropped. I had my coat on, shrugged into it, put my hands in the pockets. 'Dad, can we talk?'

He seemed tired, so inward, like he'd lost the power of speech or didn't have the energy for it. An automaton, just going about things in one slow speed, keeping to himself. I followed him to the bench seat in front of the water tanks. The outside light caught the mauve wisteria, drooping clusters, a sweet perfume.

Dad put the plastic bowl on the ground at his feet.

We sat there, staring ahead.

'What were you doing up there with the hoe? You were looking for something.'

'Just covering all bases.'

'You think that Rebecca is buried somewhere on the orchard?'

He exhaled deeply, paused. 'No. I don't,' he said. 'But I don't know anything. Over the years, I've spent hours walking up and around Dunny Hill, just looking, not sure why or what I'm doing half the time, but it's something to do.'

I reached out and touched his arm. 'Dad,' I said softly, 'what do you think happened?'

'I don't know.'

'If she was buried somewhere in the orchard or up around Dunny Hill, who would've done that?'

'You need to stop asking me questions because I can't explain anything to you when I don't even know myself. It's just that Rebecca is somewhere. I've not found her in Queensland or any place else. I just need to keep looking for her and maybe one day we'll know what happened to her.'

'How long have you been looking for her around here?'

'On and off for years.'

'Does Mum know what you're doing, looking for Rebecca's body in the orchard?'

'Of course not. I need to protect her.'

'Protect her from what?'

He glanced at me, surprised. 'You know she's never got over Rebecca going away. She's had trouble with her nerves over the years so I don't want her to get any more upset than she already is. But you're aware of that already.'

I supposed I did know that, but he'd never put Mum's temperamental behaviour in such clear terms. And her eccentricities weren't only about Rebecca vanishing.

'But, Dad, if you're looking for Rebecca in the orchard, in the dug-up dirt, does that make any sense? Who would've buried her there?'

'I'm not saying she's buried here or anywhere. I'm just covering all bases, that's all, like I just told you.'

We sat in heavy silence. The faint buzz of insects. A rabbit scampered in front, pink eyes in the dark. The squeal of a fox somewhere beyond the sheds.

'I sometimes regret that I didn't sit down and have a proper talk with Bull Tennant,' Dad said.

'He doesn't know anything. Should we get a lawyer to help us push for an inquest?'

'I've been thinking about that. But can't see that there's anything more to be said or done. They rejected us last time and nothing has changed. It'll just be an open finding.'

'Isn't that better than nothing?'

'As far as I'm concerned, it's already an open finding. We don't know any more than we did back in 1984.'

I was about to counter his argument, that a clever detective with fresh eyes might see something that we'd always missed. I had written down all the inconsistencies, intuitive thoughts about what Rebecca did and didn't take with her when she left. The mystery of how she got home from the showgrounds only to leave again. Did Jacob Healy have something to do with that? Surely it was too much of a coincidence that he killed himself and family two days after Rebecca, their babysitter, disappeared? With all the years that had passed, I'd started to doubt the certainty of what I'd once felt I understood. Sometimes I even brought Bull back into the frame, wondered if he'd outsmarted us all. Maybe he had? And Bryce Jones, Mum's former lover, his alibi, was he the wildcard? I won't lie. I was the same as Dad, sick and tired of regurgitating all the theories.

'I think we're best to leave things alone,' Dad said. 'I don't have the energy for it anyway, all the questions and answers, going over everything again. And your mother certainly couldn't handle the pressure of the whole thing being opened up again.'

That was the end of it. Dad had spoken with that quiet, yet firm tone that said the discussion was over. Then he stood, told me he was going inside to have his shower, that he'd see me in the morning. He hardly looked back to say goodnight.

Sitting there alone, my thoughts were a mash of conflicting threads, flash memories that didn't quite connect. First of all, I was surprised Dad had been doing something so raw, private and astonishing – digging around in the dirt with a hoe looking for his daughter's bones. That for years he'd been wandering around Dunny Hill doing the same thing.

*

On that visit, like all my visits, I did my best to be a patient and kind daughter. I drove with Kate to take Mum to her weekly hairdresser appointment in Gyle, and when we got home the three of us sat together on the couch and watched the DVD of *My Little Pony*. One evening, including Dad, we all played Scrabble, and I remembered a sad and lonely evening in the caravan with him in Queensland back in the early nineties when we'd played. I cooked meals they would like. I offered to sort out Mum's clothes overflowing in her wardrobe and drawers – some that she hadn't worn since before I'd even left home – but she wouldn't allow it. As far as I could tell, for the duration of my visit, and presumably after I left, Dad kept combing the ground for any sign of Rebecca's body.

The day before I was due to leave, I left Kate with Dad and visited Lauren Wishart, the woman who had cleaned Dad and Mum's house for six years. I still remembered when she came to the house to go through Mum's wedding cake albums. The scrap of pink crepe her bridesmaid's dresses were made from so the icing flowers could be the same shade. She was Lauren Reinhart back then, much slimmer and with longer, darker hair. How our lives had intersected in unexpected ways. It was her wedding cake money that had started the whole crazy scene with Mum and Rebecca fighting at the showgrounds. Lauren wouldn't know any of that. Twenty-six years later, there I was sitting at her untidy kitchen table. An old labrador, his paws turned white, sat under the table close to my feet.

The tea Lauren served was too strong with not enough milk. I drank it as she told me, in confidential tones, stories about my mother. That she was concerned she didn't shower every day. That sometimes, even if she waited until the afternoon, she had to vacuum around my parents' bed with Mum still lying in it watching television. Nothing she did could coax Mum to do anything different. That her life revolved around the television or sleep.

Earlier in July, on a freezing day, Lauren arrived to find Mum dressed in one of her old ballgowns and refusing to change into warmer clothes. I remembered those Maryhill Golf Club gala balls, how my parents practised their footwork in the lounge room. The armchairs were pushed back against the walls, the waltz tape put on. Dad and Mum moved around the room while staring into each other's eyes. Dad with his right arm firm around Mum's waist, her left hand elegant on his shoulder, their other arms outstretched, hands clasped. They looked so in love. Rebecca and I used to join in, the two of us holding on to each other, giggling, and fighting between us about who would be the boy and who would be the girl.

Lauren told me about other times when Mum seemed hyperactive with bursts of cleaning or cooking. And that sometimes Mum did unusual things. 'Just last week, your mum went to the garden for flowers, but cut the stems too short, making it impossible to put them in a vase.'

Lauren's identical twin sons pushed through the back door. Scruffy, unshaven, cow shit on their jeans. Impressive big men who had recently turned twenty-one. They reminded me of Bull, two of him. Imagine.

'You know Mum's never been the same since Rebecca left?' I said to Lauren.

'Oh, of course. I couldn't imagine what that would be like. It's just that . . .' She looked away, finding her words, unsure.

I waited.

'Your Dad gives her tablets sometimes to make her sleep. It's his way of caring for her so he can leave the house without worrying about her. I'm just not sure about that.'

I didn't know that. 'Thank you for telling me. But all Mum's medication is prescribed by her doctor.'

'Yes, I guess,' she said, frowning.

I smiled widely, stupidly, told her how much Dad and Mum appreciated her. She didn't respond as I expected, but stared stiffly at me, uncertain.

'I'll email you if there's anything else you need to know about,' she said.

'Yes, please do that,' I replied, 'and thank you again for everything.'

Lauren's next email was her resignation.

*

On the day we left for the airport it rained. Dad was up first. When I entered the living room, breakfast was already on the way. The table was set. Bread in the toaster, a wonderful smell. The kettle rumbled as it approached boiling. Dad seemed a little lighter on his feet, possibly not so downtrodden. Perhaps it was my imagination, but I wondered if Kate and me leaving was eagerly anticipated by him, in the same way I was keen to go. They weren't used to having me around. Their little routines had been massively disrupted. But much more than that, I was a reminder of the past, that they had once had two daughters and only one ever came home.

The ABC radio news came on. The same radio in the same position on the mantelpiece for as long as I could remember. A story about a large bombing in Baghdad, ninety-five dead, then something else going on in Japan. Dad took Mum a cup of tea in bed, followed soon after with her porridge on the old green tray with the folding legs. I'd watched him do that every day of my visit and had decided it was weakness, not strength, that made him run after her the way he did. I could hear the television in their bedroom. The droning noise, phoney laughter, the never-ending reel of commercials. I'd had enough.

But then I thought, imagine if Kate disappeared, taken from me, not knowing where she was. I'd lost a sister, but losing a daughter would be another level of unbearable. I'd probably go mad too.

Since I'd lived in London and Inveresk, I'd found a way to manage the build-up of stress in my body, the overwhelming sense of a pending meltdown that had once manifested in self-harm. I swam. Strangely, funnily, just the smell of chlorine soothed me. Up and down between the lane ropes, following that black line, a tumble turn, ten, twenty, thirty, forty or more laps, arms pulling, legs kicking, lungs heaving. And when I lifted myself out of the pool, I could breathe, my mind and body had relaxed.

And so it was time to show love to my mother. When I was ready to leave, I bent down, gently moved her hair from her face and kissed her forehead. Her breath was warm. A hint of Chanel No. 5. Her eyes were closed, napping.

When I turned the TV off she looked up at me, her lovely hazel eyes. Rebecca's eyes.

'I love you, Mum,' I said.

She slow-blinked. 'Love you, too.'

But when Kate stepped forward to say goodbye, Mum gasped and recoiled, pushed deeper into the pillows.

Kate jumped back, wide-eyed, hand to her mouth, looking at me.

'What, Mum?' I asked.

'What's she doing here?' she said, stabbing the air towards her.

I held on to Kate who'd started to cry. 'Stop it, Mum. You're frightening her.'

Mum stared up at me, mouth quivering, hands trembling.

'Are you all right?' I asked.

Her eyes were sparkly with tears. She seemed lost or confused, trying to push herself away to the other side of the bed where she'd earlier placed the breakfast tray when she'd finished eating.

I reached out to touch her. 'Mum, what's wrong?'

'I'm not well. You need to go,' she said, still pushing herself along in the bed.

'What do you mean? Are you in pain?'

I could see she was getting too close to the tray on Dad's side, but I couldn't cross the room fast enough. Over it went. The tray with the crockery and cutlery fell with a clattering crash to the carpet.

Then Dad was in the room, striding around to his side of the bed. He ignored the mess at his feet, sat down and gathered Mum up in his arms like she was an adult baby. He rocked her slowly, dreadfully. Poor man.

He looked across to me. 'Give me a few minutes.'

'What's the matter?' I asked.

He shooed me away, so I retreated with Kate into the living room.

Rain slapped the kitchen window.

'You did nothing wrong,' I said to Kate. 'She's just not very well.'

'What's the matter with her?'

'Sometimes she gets very tired.'

'Why?'

'We'll talk about it later.'

'When are we leaving here?'

I looked at my phone for the time, heard Dad in the bathroom running water. 'Soon.'

Back up the hallway, I entered Dad and Mum's bedroom. She was propped up, pillows behind her back and head, her hand out like a supplicant for Dad to place two orange tablets onto her flat palm. He handed her a glass of water to swallow them.

'What are the tablets, Dad?'

He glanced at me, didn't answer.

Earlier in the week I'd searched around for some paracetamol and hadn't come across any of Mum's tablets. Nothing in the bathroom cabinet, or their bedside drawers. The notion that Dad sedated Mum as a way to care for her, it wasn't something I could ask him and expect a straight answer. A doctor was prescribing everything she was taking, so whatever he was giving her was okay, legitimised by Dr Wilcox, who'd been their doctor for at least fifteen years since Dr Dukes had retired.

One evening when I was alone with Dad, after a few days of seeing how Mum's hands frequently trembled, her obvious anxiety, how lethargic she often seemed, I'd asked him about her Melbourne psychiatrist, when she'd last had a consultation. 'She doesn't need a psychiatrist anymore,' he'd said. And I thought then, Dad was doing the best he could. And what was the alternative? I'll admit it was easier for me to look away and hope for the best.

It was on that trip that I realised how profoundly stuck he was. Of course he was. I'd just pretended otherwise, a kind of convenient denial. His wife's mental disorder, whatever was wrong with her, had trapped him. Both of them were tangled in a net. And what could he do? Leave her? Divorce her?

My only comfort was the account Auntie Helen had once shared with me, how they were so in love in the early years, how suited they were. Perhaps it was those memories that sustained Dad to remain so loyal and devoted to her.

'I need to get going, Dad.'

He stood straighter, his lovely sad face.

I didn't approach him for a hug.

'Love you, Dad,' I whispered, short breaths, trying not to bawl.

I touched Mum's beautiful face, soft as a petal.

'I'll phone from the airport,' I repeated, backing away. 'No need to come out, Dad. You'll get wet.'

*

In March the following year, as soon as the fire restrictions were lifted, Dad set alight the mounds of dead fruit trees that were once ninety-two acres of apples and six acres of peaches. I wasn't there but I saw it anyway because it was so easy to imagine. A solitary man carrying bundles of discarded newspapers and a box of matches, walking from one mound of tangled dead wood to the next, turning the whole place into a fruit tree crematorium, flames and white smoke rising. Dad said it took almost ten days for the smouldering to finally stop. Then the bulldozer returned to smooth out the ground and the sub-division of my family's land began.

Something else significant happened in 2011. In July Mum hit a car while making a turn onto Westland Street in Benalla. Both cars were written off and she hadn't driven since. When I heard about the crash I had asked Dad if she'd been breathalysed by the police who had attended. 'You don't need to worry about that,' he said.

After that accident, Dad decided to stop driving to Queensland on his annual search for Rebecca. He said that 'after more than twenty years of nothing concrete ever coming out of those trips, I now need to stay home with your mother because she needs me more than Rebecca does'. He meant what he said because he sold the caravan and never replaced Mum's car.

TWENTY-TWO

2018

Virginia Hurley sent me a private Facebook message with several unnecessary lines explaining who she was and why she was contacting me. I'd never forgotten her. She was the reporter standing at the top of Glen Lochan Road, covering the Healy murder-suicide. And also, at the Healys' funerals that day when Dad drove me to Melbourne to stay with Auntie Helen. But more significantly, she was the woman who came into the shop and tricked Robyn and me into making comments for her TV news story.

She wanted to speak to me about Rebecca's disappearance for a podcast she was writing and producing. At first, I hesitated because I didn't trust her. But Duncan encouraged me, saying it would draw attention to Rebecca's story. I wasn't convinced. A true crime podcast for the entertainment of armchair sleuths seemed wrong. Yet, it was a vehicle to perhaps uncover something new. It'd been a long time since anyone had deep-dived into the facts.

After a couple of emails between Virginia and me, I realised she was going to go ahead with or without me, so I finally agreed to be interviewed. Dad refused to be involved, saying he had nothing to say, that he wanted his privacy. That was his right. It was around that time Mum was diagnosed with dementia. The signs had been there for a few years, some days were worse than others, but another reason not to hassle Dad about the podcast. Even so, I didn't expect him to tell me to back out. When I explained my position, the value the podcast could have in discovering new information, he didn't change his mind.

'Let things alone,' he said, 'I've had enough. This whole business with Rebecca has worn me out. And your mother certainly can't talk to anyone.'

'It's okay, Dad. I can be the family representative.'

'What on earth can you say, or she say, that will make any difference?'

'With the publicity, we might find out what happened.'

'Rubbish. The whole idea of putting all the pieces of the puzzle together for everyone to listen to. I'm just not happy about it. In fact, I'm dead against it.'

'She's going to do it regardless of us,' I said.

'How can she do that?'

'Because it's her job. She's a journalist used to speaking with different people to get a story.'

'Rebecca isn't a story.'

'I know that, Dad. But she'll be in touch with Jeff Butler, probably Jasmine. And Bull if she can find him.'

'Jeff has retired.'

'He can still discuss the case.'

'I'm going to call him and ask him not to speak to her.'

Dad was determined. At first I didn't understand. But he was seventy-nine. Mum was seventy-eight and suffering dementia. Of course they wanted peace and quiet at their age. They'd earned it. For more than thirty years, my whole adult life, Rebecca's absence had defined us as a family.

I relayed Dad's position to Virginia, but she was as strong-minded as him. It seemed to me the more I procrastinated, the cagier she became. When I asked who else she was interviewing she didn't reply; I assumed because she didn't want Dad contacting them, imploring them not to cooperate.

In the end I gave her a statement of the facts as I remembered them, starting with that last day of school in 1984. I described how that day was. The oppressive heat. Why a group of schoolkids went to the showgrounds. I downplayed the public argument Mum and Rebecca had. I shared some details about how we managed as a family. All those trips that Dad took to Queensland. How Mum had a reputation as an award-winning baker and cake decorator, but from the day Rebecca vanished she had never baked or decorated again.

After Virginia received my statement she replied with a list of questions. She zeroed in on the stolen money. How much was it? Was it ever found? What was Rebecca wearing the last time she was seen? What was our family's relationship with the Tennants? At what point did Dad contact the police? Could I confirm if Rebecca had run away previously? Was it true that Rebecca went to her maths teacher's home during school hours? Did we think there was any connection between her disappearance and the Healy murder-suicide?

Her questions were so precise, I knew she must've been talking to someone with inside information. Jasmine? Bull? Andy? I hadn't had contact with any of them for decades and had no desire to reconnect with them to discover what they knew about it. I decided Dad was right, it was time to let go and move on.

I wished Virginia well, and stopped communicating with her.

*

The podcast came out a few months later, titled *Gone*. It turned out Lauren Wishart was Virginia's main source of information – more like repeated gossip. She was introduced as the last bride to ever buy one of Diane's blue-ribbon wedding cakes. That the catalyst for Rebecca running away was the payment for that cake. Lauren had eventually become the Bundys' part-time housekeeper, and over the course of six years, she saw firsthand the strain Rebecca's disappearance had placed on the family. She hinted at Mum's drinking. The medication Dad regularly gave her. Mum's car accident. My fly-in and fly-out relationship with my parents made me look uncaring. Andrea Goodman described in agonising detail the fight Mum and Rebecca had had at the showgrounds. Her recollection sounded exaggerated, but it wasn't.

Bea Knightly and Jenny Russo both shared the story about Mr Soydan, implying that Rebecca was loose, *a certain type, shall we say?* They confirmed that Rebecca was also in a relationship with a local farmhand called Bull Tennant, who had been a prime suspect for some months and who eventually went to prison for aggravated assault. Without giving any reasons, the podcast implied he should still be a person of interest.

The *Gone* podcast ran over eight episodes, and not one new piece of information was discovered. I've wondered if I'd cooperated with Virginia maybe the podcast would've been more sympathetic to us. I told Dad that he and Mum shouldn't listen to it. As far as I know, they haven't.

Ultimately, I was left with the question of betrayal. Lauren, Bea, Jenny, Andrea, those who lived among us on the mountain, all giving their opinions on our family tragedy. Duncan said it wasn't personal. 'They're just small people having their moment in the sun.'

I didn't agree, especially about Lauren, who'd entered my parents' home for so many years, who told the whole world how crazy my mother was. That time in the middle of winter when she found Mum wearing one of her ballgowns. She actually described it, the dark green satin sleeveless dress with beading on the bodice. When I was little, I thought Mum looked beautiful in that dress.

Sergeant Paul Keegan, a subordinate to Jeff Butler, gave his perspective, that after months of intensive investigation there were no suspects. And no known link between Rebecca's disappearance and the Healy case.

What he didn't say was that there were weeks and months when the police were missing in action. The Healy murder-suicide distracted them. The city cops came and went. I was never spoken to.

After I'd listened to the podcast, I wrote Virginia an email, telling her she'd let down my family. That she achieved nothing, except perhaps to titillate and entertain listeners on the back of our suffering.

She didn't reply.

TWENTY-THREE

2020

I don't want to dwell on this, but Duncan died on the 25th of July. It happened in the early evening, after a pleasant day. I was in the kitchen preparing our meal, an easy baked pasta with chicken and veggies. Duncan was upstairs in our bedroom. He'd just had a shower and was dressing before he came downstairs for dinner. I heard him crash to the floor, but at first I ignored the sound, not thinking; just kept chopping the parsley and thyme that I'd picked in the garden outside the back door.

I was thinking about a FIND REBECCA BUNDY Facebook message I'd received just a couple of hours earlier, some freak saying Rebecca was living in Houston, Texas. Such bullshit. Still, I'd asked for photographic proof, which I doubted would ever come, and never has. At the sound of Duncan falling, I did glance up with a vague question about what had caused the thud. How stupid of me. It wasn't until about five minutes later, when I had the pasta in the oven, that I went looking for him, wondering why he was taking so long to join me downstairs.

Duncan had had COVID in June, but he'd recovered. We were enjoying, as best we could, the rhythms of our daily routine in lockdown, each day blurring into the next. Like everybody else, we were both working from home. At the time, I had no sense that he was unwell. He'd not complained of anything. The only thing we were discussing was that he probably needed hearing aids. The two of us stared at each other, dismayed, that I had to continually repeat myself to be heard.

COVID restrictions meant only twenty people could attend his funeral, everyone distancing, wearing masks, which felt hopeless. We had to be restrained, couldn't hug or touch freely. In the end, we held the service at home, and even there in such intimate surroundings, we were cautious, standing apart. It was the saddest day of my life.

Duncan, my love, is buried just up the road in the cemetery at St Michaels. The epitaph on his headstone reads *Forever in Our Hearts*.

My grief has been immeasurable.

TWENTY-FOUR

2022

Dead leaves were scattered on the back lawn. Pretty rosehips among the bushes, some pink buds that never bloomed. Cold air infused with wood smoke. I felt the breath of another Scottish winter coming. I didn't mind, actually, the idea of staying inside. In some ways the lockdown months had suited the introvert in me.

I made a cup of tea and took it upstairs. At my desk I opened a manuscript I was editing; a series of short stories that didn't engage me, but it was something to do. I tapped away correcting typos, sorting out spacing. Page after page.

I was no better than Kate when it came to smartphones. Like a tic, my hand reached across my desk. I opened the news apps, read the latest headlines about the financial markets. Xi Jinping had a third term as China's president. Ukraine's infrastructure was damaged with cold months approaching. Next a scroll through Instagram. Followed by Facebook, which I only used for the FIND REBECCA BUNDY page. It'd been active for thirteen years and nothing concrete had ever come of it, mostly well-intentioned grief voyeurs. Sometimes other families with a long-term missing family member reached out, which was fair enough, but I didn't want to engage with anyone else's heartache. It was the psychics, fraudsters and religious nutjobs who had made managing the Facebook page so difficult. That alleged sighting in Texas came to nothing. Duncan had always been good at sorting out the liars and hoaxers.

There had been a couple of plausible sightings, the most significant back in 2013. A slim redhead, single mother, who lived in Yamba in north New South Wales went to the police to report a domestic violence incident. Her name was Bec Bundy, born in 1967, the same year as Rebecca, but a different day and month. That in itself should've been enough for us to let it pass. But you never knew. It might've been her. And that was the point. We didn't know. So Duncan and I detoured there on our way to visit Dad and Mum to investigate for ourselves. Kate didn't come. Since that awful trip back in 2010 she'd refused to return to Maryhill. Plus, in those teenage years, she was in love with her horse, Brandy, and didn't want to leave him. On our trips back to Australia she usually stayed with Karen, Duncan's sister. Anyway, when we got to Yamba it didn't take long to learn that Bec Bundy wasn't our Rebecca. Even allowing for the passage of time, they looked nothing alike. I suppose by then I was so used to disappointment, I wasn't really expecting her to be Rebecca. I think Duncan was more let down than me.

I looked at the time. Turned back to a short story about first-generation migration, but I couldn't concentrate. There was washing in the machine that needed to go into the dryer. I considered driving into Musselburgh to do some laps in the heated pool, then some grocery shopping. As I stood to go downstairs, a notification pinged on my phone.

A Facebook private message. I hesitated. A reluctant thumb press. It would be a desperate family reaching out to share something about their missing loved one. As I've mentioned before, you'd be surprised to know how common it is for someone to just disappear.

Ash Tennant.
My heart jumped.
Bull.

*Eliza, it's Ash Tennant here. You knew me as Bull, back
when we lived in Maryhill. Just wanting to say hello. I see
you live overseas in Scotland. Any updates on Rebecca?
Cheers, Ash.*

I sat back down, closed my eyes, brought Bull into my mind.
He was still nineteen years old. The cool way he stood, the easy
way he walked, more like a long-legged stroll. He had swagger back
then, and Rebecca loved him as best as any teenage girl could love a
teenage boy – which was with all her heart and body, with dreams
and hopes that they'd live happily ever after. Although that romantic
thinking was tainted with innuendo, the suggestion she'd been with
other men. None of that mattered anymore.

I realised that I'd missed Bull, an absence in my life. Those
innocent days when Rebecca lived at home with us. For a moment
I considered if I should've made more effort to stay in touch. But
that was just me being sentimental, rewriting the past.

I reread his message. Short, to the point. He knew I lived in
Scotland. He'd only made contact because he wanted to know about
Rebecca – and he'd know there was nothing to tell if he did a simple
Google search. All that came up was the old news about her last
day of high school in 1984. Her photo, a smiling seventeen-year-old
face with eyes that appeared sadder as the years went by. The *Gone*
podcast was online. And in 2019 a coroner's report said after almost
four decades it was assumed Rebecca was dead because there had
been no proven sightings of her. The eighty-four dollars and fifty-six
cents she had in her bank account had not been touched. And she

hadn't made any contact with her family. I'll give credit where it's due, it was the *Gone* podcast that activated the inquest. Dad and I attended and even though the outcome gave us no comfort, I emailed Virginia and thanked her. This time she gracefully replied.

Almost forty years had passed since that pointless fight between my mother and Rebecca at the showgrounds. I agreed with the coroner that my sister was dead, of course she was. Still, not knowing what happened to her was like an incurable illness that didn't have a name. No matter what I did, Rebecca thrived in the shadows of my mind.

I did the sums. Bull was fifty-seven. I searched his profile on Facebook to see if there were any photos. Only one, nothing of his face, just a hand holding the tail of a large silver fish. He'd only been on Facebook a few weeks, which I found curious and wondered why he'd only surfaced now. Plus, he called himself Ash.

> *Hi Bull, so good to hear from you. Of course I remember you and over the years have thought of you often. I've been living in a town outside of Edinburgh called Inveresk since 1998. My husband, Duncan, died twenty months ago. I have a twenty-two-year-old daughter, Kate, who's currently travelling in southeast Asia. She's joining me for Christmas in Maryhill. How are you? There's no news on Rebecca's disappearance.*

I wrote a hundred more words telling him what I knew. It felt good to tap out the sentences. That for more than twenty years my father travelled to Queensland searching. The orchard was sub-divided and my parents still lived in the same house, but only on thirty-seven acres. That after one rejection for a coroner's inquest in 2004, there was finally an inquest in 2019 that found Rebecca was most likely deceased. I finished off telling Bull it was still difficult not knowing what happened to her, an absurd understatement. I hit send then realised I had more questions.

Just wondering, Bull, why have you made contact now after all these years? And where do you live?

As I hit send for the second time, I was convinced I wouldn't hear from him again. The thought annoyed me, so I shut down Messenger and opened my Word file and started work again on one of the short stories; a good one, dark and imaginative. I kept reading, but my mind was constantly returning to Bull. I checked once more to see if he was online. Nothing.

I guessed Bull still lived in Australia, so depending on where, there was roughly ten to twelve hours' time difference between us.

And there in front of me, another message from Bull. How simple it suddenly was to be communicating with him.

I live in Darwin. Been up here in the Territory since I left Maryhill. Just decided to contact you, wondering about Rebecca.

Perhaps it was because sleet slapped the windows and I'd just put on a third layer. Another Scottish winter versus an Australian summer. I didn't know, everything was mixed up and I was alone. I missed Duncan more than I missed Rebecca, yet at least I knew what happened to him. I was there, thumping his chest, counting like an expert, outside of my body looking down as my husband died with me crouching over him.

I told Bull that I was due to visit my parents in Maryhill for Christmas, that I'd like to detour via Darwin.

*Are you okay if I come to see you? I'd love to catch up. Does
the third week of December work for you?*

I checked constantly, waiting for his reply. It took two days:
Yeah, no worries.

I told him I'd let him know my arrival date into Darwin.

Next, I opened WhatsApp and sent Kate a message in Vietnam.

*Hi honey, I'm flying into Darwin, then on to Melbourne. Have
you booked your flights yet? I plan to arrive in Melbourne on
23 December. It'd be good if we landed around the same time.
I'll send you my flight details. See you soon. Mum xxx*

TWENTY-FIVE

2022

Thick hot air, a sweet spicy smell like a chai latte. The Darwin hotel's air-conditioning wouldn't budge, sat on a permanent 23 degrees. The ceiling fan whipped the air. Out on the balcony I looked across the marina to palms, shade trees, rows of white frangipani, a grey muscular sky. In the distance was a wharf, a few boats. The towering apartments on the left and right looked deserted, there wasn't a person in sight. Already I didn't like the place. Or at least, I was struck by the extreme difference. When I left home it was 3 degrees, air so chilled my body could only be warmed by thermals, three layers, and when outside a down puffer jacket, gloves, scarf. In Darwin, my entire body was covered in sweat, and my clothes weren't suited to the humid, wet season climate.

The rain took me by surprise. All at once the sky became a water avalanche. A long flicker of lightning, a crack of thunder that made me gasp. It was dramatic, a theatrical performance on a grey and silver stage that I briefly videoed on my phone, but it was better to watch. The wind joined the show, blowing the rain sideways across the balcony. Ten minutes. Twenty minutes. Then as quickly as it started, it stopped.

In the bathroom, I peeled off my clothes and stepped into the shower. I braced at the cold water, forced myself to stand there letting it splash over me. Then dressed in the best I had, white cotton pants and a mauve t-shirt. I wanted to do better than that for Bull, but everything else I had with me was too heavy, firm-fitting, and there was no time for shopping. I studied my face in the mirror to see what Bull would be looking at in half an hour. It was too hot for make-up. I tied my hair up, strapped my sandals on.

And so, typically, I was ready early. I had studied where to go. Downstairs, I left the hotel, turned right, followed the shade. The air was heavy, frangipani infused. I was wary there'd be another storm so I walked fast, stepped around puddles. Peak Thai wasn't far, and it was thoughtful of Bull to choose a place convenient for me.

It was a large open-air restaurant-bar with fans spinning from the ceiling and mid-way up the pylons. From a hidden speaker, Elton John sang 'Candle in the Wind'. Red lanterns and fairy lights decorated the space. I looked around, taking everything in. The barman was wearing a Santa hat. Two young women, in sleeveless cotton dresses, sat close to the bar, each with a full-to-the-brim glass of white wine in front of them. At the far end there was a man seated on his own. Grey hair, light-coloured short-sleeved shirt, a beer on the table between his forearms. I turned away, unsure or anxious, as he glanced across at me.

He stood up, came towards me, a slight limp. When we were metres apart, he said, 'Eliza?'

I studied his face. It was Bull. The shape of his nose, forehead, mouth. But this man was puffy in the face, bloated gut, thick across the shoulders, stiff in his posture. And yes, his eyes were brown, but smaller, as if he'd spent years squinting against the sun.

I reached out to shake his hand, so formal, and realised he was as uncomfortable as me when neither of us stepped forward to embrace. We were strangers, and when I smiled he looked back at me impassively and I realised I didn't know who he was.

'It's good to see you,' I said.

'Wanna drink?'

I asked for a gin and soda.

I studied him standing at the bar, his back to me. The line of his body, grey hair cropped short. His beige knee-length pants and pale blue short-sleeved shirt gave the impression of newness. The horizontal folding lines, the crisp look of the fabrics, and I wondered if Bull had gone to special trouble for this meeting.

We sat opposite at the table with a furiously spinning ceiling fan directly above. It was good, the stifling air became a pleasant warm breeze.

I sipped my drink. Bull told me the gin was from a local distillery.

'Thanks for coming,' I said.

'No worries.'

'A coincidence, but it's exactly thirty-eight years today since Rebecca disappeared,' I said.

'Yeah.'

'So how are you? And what have you been doing all this time?'

He tilted his head, thinking.

'Working, mostly. Quit a couple of years back.'

I tried to merge the old man with badly stained teeth to the nineteen-year-old Bull. And the way he glanced at me, he must've been doing the same thing.

'We're both older. It feels strange,' I said.

He necked his beer, didn't have a comment.

'So where have you been working?'

'Up here with cattle. A few stations.'

'I've been living in Scotland since I was twenty-nine.'

'How'd you get yourself over there?'

Perhaps he asked the question out of politeness because he didn't properly look at me as I answered. He seemed preoccupied. I thought he was rude. Even so, we couldn't just sit there in silence. So I told him about those first years in London, how good it was to be away from my family. That I was able to put Rebecca in a secret place, like a box on a shelf, in my mind. It didn't mean I'd forgotten her, never, but I had to live, somehow.

I was talking too much, blathering on, because he was the first person since I'd left Maryhill who might fully comprehend what I was saying. My parents were stuck in the past, still waiting for the phone to ring. At least Dad had stopped his annual pilgrimage to Queensland.

I felt stupid, exposed, as I chatted away like he was an old friend, pretending he was interested.

'Duncan was a client. Fourteen years older than me, divorced with two daughters who lived with their mother. I moved into his family home in Inveresk, it's about twelve kilometres east of Edinburgh. I was pregnant when we married.'

I was on a roll. Started telling him everything about my life since I married, but when he looked over my shoulder, as if something other than me interested him, I shut up.

I took a long sip of the gin and soda. I was disappointed, sad, heavy in my chest. Bull wasn't who I wanted him to be. He was just a broken-down cattleman and we had nothing in common. I couldn't quite reconcile how the paths of our lives had spun so wildly apart.

'When I leave here I'm going to Maryhill to visit Dad and Mum,' I said.

'Yeah.'

'They're in their eighties now. Mum was diagnosed with dementia about four years ago. Dad is her carer, but he's wearing out.'

Bull nodded. And I guess it was fair enough he didn't have anything to say about them. We glanced around in awkward silence.

'We're strangers after all these years,' I said. 'Yet Rebecca is the link between us. How are you feeling about that time, you know, in 1984 and what happened afterwards?'

He shrugged. 'I don't think about it. Moved on.'

'You went to prison.'

'Sure did,' he said, his fingers pressing down his face like checking if he needed a shave.

'Was it worth it? Finding those men?'

'It was necessary.'

'Why?'

'I don't want to go there. History now.'

'So you've moved on?'

'Yeah.'

'That easy? I wish I could. I mean, I can sort of. It's like my brain is split in two parts.' I touched my head, explaining. 'That my life is on autopilot, just getting on with things, but the other half is always alert, watching, thinking. I see a girl with red hair, and believe me there are lots of them in Scotland, and I have to tell myself it's not her. Sometimes I follow a girl until I can see her face.'

I laughed nervously, high-pitched and for too long. 'And my twenty-two-year-old daughter Kate, would you believe, is the spitting image of Rebecca. I mean, that's the definition of cruelty.'

I was still talking too much, couldn't seem to stop. 'Do you have any kids?' I asked.

'Two boys.'

'Here in Darwin?'

'Perth.'

'How old are they?'

He looked to the side as if trying to work it out. 'In their thirties. They moved away with their mother when they were little.' Then he sat back, glanced around, uneasy.

'I'm sorry if my wanting to see you has made you uncomfortable.'

'It's all right.' He shrugged again.

'So why did you quit work? Did you retire?'

'Broke my back. Got kicked by a bull, spinal cord damage. Can't work.'

'I'm sorry.'

'At least I can walk.'

'So, you live here in Darwin?'

'A bit out of town.'

He moved in his seat, and I thought he was going to leave.

'I just wanted to see you to say hello after all this time. You knew Rebecca, you loved her. And I just live with a constant feeling of loss that, as much as I try, I can't shake off. Over the years, there's been a few sightings. People can be heartless, you know. Invented stories that gave us hope. For a few years we were pretty sure she'd hitchhiked because the police were told of a couple of sightings of Rebecca on the Hume Freeway just on the other side of Albury. Then the lunatics try and bait us with made-up sightings. You wouldn't believe it.'

'I told you at the time, Rebecca didn't go north,' Bull said. 'She was never serious about that.'

I looked at him and was reminded of who he was, a nice guy. And I saw he was ruined, still heartsick, that like me he'd dragged the loss of Rebecca around with him, a dead weight that never got lighter.

'The worst is the not knowing,' I said.

'Yeah.'

'I mean, Dad and Mum need to sell the house and move into Gyle. They're hardly managing, but Dad refuses in case Rebecca comes home. How insane is that? It's worn him out. And Mum's difficult at the best of times. I've got people coming and going to the house looking after them. These days I manage their finances, but it's crunch time. Something has to change. And I feel guilty because I'm living my life and not there to help them, but to be honest, I hate it, can't bear the place.'

'I'm sorry for your dad,' he said.

'I get that you have no time for my mother. I'm sorry she was so dreadful to you. She had psychotic episodes after Rebecca was born, a hormonal thing that wasn't properly diagnosed and my Auntie Helen said she never fully recovered from. I've been aware for most of my life she's had mental health issues, been on different medications.'

Bull pursed his lips, a small nod, and I knew what he was thinking. That Mum was the cause of Rebecca's disappearance. If it wasn't for her all our lives would've been different.

'I went to visit Mum before leaving for London. You'd left the mountain. It would've been back in 1991. On impulse, I drove to your old place. There were two men there, long beards. One was tall. The other one was big, muscled.'

Bull's eyes widened. 'Yeah, a couple blokes I met in prison. Gave them the place.'

'Scary guys,' I said.

I was about to ask him more questions when he leaned in. His brown eyes were smaller, tiny beads, or his face was somehow bigger.

'You know what kills me?' He pointed his finger at me. 'That I one hundred per cent know for sure Rebecca didn't take off to Queensland. We had plans to meet on that Saturday morning. I told everyone and no one believed me. No one. But I was the one inter-rogated as if I was hiding something. That's bullshit, and whatever happened to her, whoever took her, I've got no idea, but someone knows. That's why I gave those dicks a hiding, to find out for myself what they knew. And one more thing, seeing I'm stringing some words together here. I was never charged with anything in relation to Rebecca's disappearance, yet I was a marked man from day one. Lost my job. Cheryl couldn't go anywhere without people staring at her like she was harbouring a criminal. You've got no idea what it's like to be treated like a dog. So, you go off to Melbourne then overseas and build yourself a nice life. Good for you. What's more, it's not you that some smartarse copper comes to interview every few years. And the woman who did the podcast who kept at me to be interviewed. For fuck's sake. I just want it to be over.'

'At least the podcast led to a coronial inquiry,' I said.

'Big deal. They assume she's dead. How does that help?'

He picked up his beer and sipped, moved in his seat as if uncomfortable, didn't look at me, but he was waiting for me to say something.

'The thing is, Bull. In 1984 I was only fourteen. A powerless little kid living with a complicated mother and broken father. My whole life changed too and not for one day, one moment, do I ever forget Rebecca. A couple of weeks ago a redhead started work in one of the publishing houses I freelance for. I couldn't see her face but I followed her down to the staff kitchen to check her out. It's hopeless that after all this time I'm still looking for her even when I know it's not rational. And of course there's Kate.'

I took my phone from my bag, slid through photos, showed him a few of my daughter. And I remembered then, the photo Bull had of Rebecca in his wallet. The same smile, head tilt, bright eyes.

Bull glanced at it, turned away, didn't share his opinion.

I didn't understand his silences, his bursts of speaking, or why he was even there.

'It's too late now to be discussing theories on what happened to Rebecca, don't you think,' I said.

'All I'm saying is that someone knows what happened to her. She did not leave the mountain that night. I know that for a fact.'

'How do you know? You said you hadn't seen her since the previous Tuesday.'

He cleared throat. 'I've said everything I know.'

I waited, rattled the ice in my glass, took the last sip. He finished his beer.

I was suddenly deflated and impatient. I'd had some strange idea that Bull and I could be friendly towards each other, to reconnect somehow. But we were different. He wasn't what I expected or hoped for, and I was sorry about that. Yet, at the same time, I understood more than most how he'd suffered, how his life had so radically changed when Rebecca disappeared. I felt exhausted from dealing with all the repercussions, everyone's pain. Still, he'd been an important person in my life.

'Bull, can we stay in touch?'

He moved in his seat, and I was put off that he wasn't more affable, almost surly.

'Anyway, it was good to see you again,' I said. 'And if I ever find out anything I'll let you know. And I hope you have a good Christmas. Kate and I will be in Maryhill.'

I wondered if Bull was in a relationship. I assumed he lived on his own, that his whole life had been in some kind of suspension, that no other woman could be enough for him.

'Do you have a partner?' I asked.

'Debbie.'

I nodded, pleased about that. Then stood, gathered up my bag and turned to leave. I'd hoped to take a selfie of the two of us, but I didn't dare suggest it.

I was two steps away when he called me back.

'Eliza,' he said.

I turned.

Bull's head was bowed. 'I've got something to tell you.'

My heart went strange. I sat down, sat forward.

Bull swallowed, cleared his throat, then took his time slowly turning his empty beer bottle around in his cupped hands, thinking, deciding.

I watched him nervously.

'I've got a couple of things to tell you, actually,' he said. 'First of all, I've got lung cancer and my heart is buggered. The smokes finally got me, so serves me right. I've done a bit of chemo, but that didn't do much. I'm okay with that. Doctor reckons I've got six months.'

'I'm sorry.'

'You don't need to be sorry.'

A waiter came; I asked for another round.

When Bull started talking about Rebecca, I was startled, took a breath, and pinched my fingernails into my forearms.

'That day when she took off at the showgrounds and went behind the toilet blocks. Stinking hot day, it was, remember that? Well, she phoned me from the public phone at the Gyle post office and asked me to pick her up. I'd just knocked off, so I did. She was worked up about the way your mother acted crazy in front of everyone, bossing her around, trying to pull her into the car, and all of that. Accusing her of stealing money. You know what I'm talking about, right?' He glanced at me, and I nodded. 'Like I said, I was knocking off work anyway, so I did what she asked and picked her up. I was there in a few minutes. We passed you and your mum on the way up the mountain. I dropped her off at the bottom of your driveway, then went home and later had fish and chips for dinner with Cheryl. I've never owned up to that before. Didn't tell the cops I dropped her off. But they proved with Robyn in the shop about the fish and chip order that night, that the order was too big for a skinny old woman like Cheryl to eat on her own. What I'm trying to say is, I dropped Rebecca off and went straight home. I'm not bullshitting you. That's the absolute honest truth.'

'So, Rebecca was in the car with you when you passed us coming up from Gyle? And you dropped her off at the bottom of our driveway?'

'That's what I just said.'

'Why didn't you tell the police that?'

'Because your mother had it in for me, telling everyone I'd done something, or knew something. The cops had me in their sights and would've crucified me for certain. Earlier that year, I'd had a run-in with the cops over my gun licence. My point is, how could I prove anything when I was the last person to see her? It's why I shut up about it. Yeah, it was Cheryl's idea. She was onto me about staying quiet about dropping her off, so I did. But I know for an absolute fact Rebecca went home, and we had plans for the next morning and she didn't show up.'

I sat back, stared blind into the table, thinking. It didn't make sense.

A waiter put our drinks in front of us.

Bull was watching me, waiting.

'I can't believe what you just told me, actually,' I said. 'Because if you'd spoken up you would've saved my father years of slogging it out driving to Queensland, always hoping.'

'How would it have made any difference?' Bull splayed his fingers on the table to somehow make his point. 'I've thought about this millions of times. Take me out of the picture. The plain fact is Rebecca got out of my ute. I drove off. She walked up the driveway. That's the end of anything I know. So, what happened?

I've imagined it. She goes inside the house and your mother comes home. You reckon they started fighting again? Where were you? At the shop working, right? And where was your Dad? You told me he was off delivering an order somewhere. And where was that dickhead Bryce Jones?

'But that's my point,' I said. 'If you had spoken up and told the police exactly what you did then a whole lot of other questions would've been asked. Like what happened when Rebecca got home?'

'This is where we one hundred per cent disagree. I don't know what happened to Rebecca. No bloody idea. But maybe she and your mother kept arguing and carrying on and Rebecca did take off, took that travel bag, or whatever the story is about that. But if she did leave the orchard, where did she go and how did she get there? No buses going anywhere at that time. She didn't phone me to meet her. Everywhere else is too far to walk.'

'I don't know what you're actually saying.'

Bull sat back, wiped his mouth with the back of his hand.

'You know what?' He sighed. 'I'll go to my grave never knowing. But I just wanted to fess up to you about that bit of information that I never admitted to anyone before. It's a shit situation and I'm sorry for your father. He was good bloke by what Rebecca used to say.'

I was suddenly hot and exhausted from jetlag, menopause lingering. But something was niggling. I was missing something. There was a gap in all his confessing. I squinted as if it might help me concentrate. I started talking, heard my words as they left my mouth.

'I suppose I can understand, Bull, why you didn't say anything about dropping Rebecca off. But can't you see that if you had, the police would've been able to focus their attention rather than jump when every crazy person phoned with a theory? You've got no idea how insane it was. Hardly a week went by without some nutter phoning saying they'd seen her. Mystics had visions of her, knew where she was buried. Other times sadists would laugh, saying they'd raped and killed her and would tell us where she was buried if we paid them thousands of dollars. But we kept answering the phone in case it was her. And there were other sightings of her hitch-hiking on the Gold Coast. That was where we focused our attention, believing that she'd got herself to Queensland and something bad happened to her once she was there.'

'That's the point,' Bull said, 'and we're all buggered because of it. Who knows what happened? Anyway, I'll be dead soon. So, if you want to tell the coppers what I just told you, be my guest because I won't be around for much longer. End of story.'

'If the police are told you dropped Rebecca off, they'll doubt everything else you've told them, probably conclude you were more involved than that.'

'That's what I've been telling you and why I didn't say anything,' he said, enunciating each word slowly to make it clear he thought I was stupid, a bit slow. 'And right now I don't give a shit if anyone believes me or not.'

'Robyn from the shop knows something. She found one of Sinead's journals where she'd written letters to herself, hating Rebecca being in the house with Jacob when she wasn't there. And I've seen a photo of Rebecca with Jacob, her grinning into his face.'

Bull bit his bottom lip, thinking. 'It's bullshit,' he said.

'Why do you say that?'

'Because it's just another bleeding rumour. And lucky for Healy that he was already dead, because I would've given him a hiding too.'

'How'd you find out where Errol Soydan, Bryce Jones, and that other one, Jeremy McCourty, where they lived?'

A tiny smile. 'Wouldn't you like to know?'

'I would actually.'

'Ask your dad, then.'

'Did he give them to you?'

He raised his hand, no comment.

I had questions to ask, words were rising up bursting with emotion and confusion, but when I went to speak nothing came.

'I reckon I've told you everything I wanted to say,' Bull said.

As we stood, our drinks unfinished, it struck me how time moved slowly but determinedly, never stopping, and the path of our lives had landed us there. We faced each other, both much older than my parents were when Rebecca vanished. And I was bothered that we hadn't been able to slip into some kind of easy rapport formed out of our shared past and grief. I reached out my hand and Bull shook it quickly.

'It's been good seeing you. And good luck with everything,' I said.

'Thanks.'

I watched him leave. His limp came from his right hip, and there was stiffness in his back like vertebrae had been fused. His shorts sat under his gut forcing the crotch to hang too low. And I thought, Bull was beautiful once. Never had I seen a man wear a pair of Levi's like he had. And if Rebecca hadn't disappeared they might've married and had their own kids and all our lives would've turned out so differently.

I sat down, picked up the gin and soda. I would never see Bull again. I closed my eyes and tried to remember. That when Bull passed Mum and me on that mountain road, on the last day of school nearly forty years ago, I'd thought that maybe Rebecca was in the car with him. Bull had confirmed she'd been there in the cabin of his ute, hunched down so Mum wouldn't see her. I relived that moment again, like I'd done countless times before.

So, what happened after that? I went to work at the shop and Mum went home and would've found Rebecca was already there. Dad had driven to Coldstream to deliver an order of peaches for the agent to take to the Footscray market. I thought of Bryce Jones, saw his dark curly hair, weird eyes. He'd been having an affair with Mum and I didn't know when that had started or finished. Bryce would've been working somewhere on the orchard that day Rebecca went missing. Mum had always vouched for him, his perfect alibi.

I turned my right wrist over, looked at the soft white skin and the faint angles of a tiny star tattoo that I'd never finished. I put my left hand over it, as if to help that girl I once was, to hide it and pretend all that sadness never happened. But that fading star has never let me forget that day.

The overhead fans churned the heavy air. A family sat at an adjacent table. Mixed race, a happy father talking to their son, the mother looked on. I wished them well. I wished everyone well. I wished the whole fucking planet well.

I finished my drink. I was lighter, energy flowed through me because I'd just thought of something that had been with me all the time.

What time did Bryce Jones leave work on the day Rebecca went missing? And then I remembered something, a small detail. A footprint.

TWENTY-SIX

I've never minded an airport, wandering around. Kate's flight from Bangkok arrived almost three hours after mine. And there she was, coming through the doors. I'd not seen her in four weeks. She looked happy, her stride was long, her smile wide. As I pulled away from our embrace I saw a small bluebird tattoo on the side of her neck. I thought of Cheryl, that she had a similar one in the same place.

'What's this?' I asked. 'Is it safe getting a tattoo in Bangkok? You know, hygienic?'

'Mum, you shouldn't think that Thailand is inferior to the UK, because there's a lot going on there. You'd be surprised.'

I raised my hands in surrender.

'But why get it on your neck? It's so obvious.'

'Wait till you see the one on my back,' she said, laughing. 'And on both my butt cheeks.'

'You're kidding, right?'

She looped her arm through mine, smiling. 'I'm going to keep you guessing.'

It wasn't until we were on the Metropolitan Ring Road that I was comfortable driving the hire car, a white Hyundai. The indicator was on the opposite side to my Audi at home and clicked loudly, cicada-like. A transport truck passed, made the car shudder. I gripped the wheel and slowed down. Then out on to the Hume Freeway and that long boring section of road. Up a crest and over only to see another long stretch out in front. Again and again, it went like that for more than a hundred and twenty kilometres. But it was a good length of time for Kate and me to talk. She'd met an Australian from Sydney in Vietnam, Lachie, who she'd like to meet up with again. I told her I was thinking of selling Ramsey House; it was too big for me now that she was thinking of moving into a shared household with her best friend, Holly Stephens. I explained about her father's will, that settling with Duncan's first two daughters, Mary and Eve, had left me with less cash, and it made sense to downsize.

'It's not the same with your dad gone,' I said.

She reached across, squeezed my arm.

'So, who was the bloke you met in Darwin?'

I told her everything I knew about Bull, from when we were kids, to him passing Mum and me as we drove up the mountain, how I'd wondered if Rebecca was with him in the car. That he'd been to prison for assaulting three men who the police had eliminated as suspects.

'Mum never liked him,' I said. 'God, it was a mess, the way she never let up on him being involved somehow in Rebecca running off.'

'What did Grandpa think of him?'

'I don't remember him ever saying one way or the other. Somehow he was able to take Mum's side of things, yet at the same time keep the peace. If Mum was happy, Dad was happy, and it's still the same.'

'Coercive control,' Kate said.

'Who's controlling who?'

'Nan controls Grandpa.'

I thought she was right.

When we pulled into the Wallan service centre for a toilet and coffee break, I remembered it was three years earlier that I had been there with Duncan, before the borders were shut, fourteen months before he died. How strange it was to reflect on that. And there was Kate standing back, waiting for her name to be called with our coffees.

As we approached Gyle I phoned Dad to let him know when we would be arriving. His voice was softer than ever, a permanent whisper.

'I'll pick up supplies at the IGA on the way through,' I said.

'I went shopping yesterday,' he replied.

'Okay,' I said, knowing I was still going food shopping. Even though Dad could afford to buy whatever he wanted, he would've bought frozen meals, home brand everything.

'See you in an hour or so,' I said, indicating to turn off to Gyle.

I drove past my old school, which had a large new stadium where the basketball courts used to be. A right turn, we drove along the Deveron River.

'Where are we going?' Kate asked.

'You'll see.'

Through the granite pillars, I pulled up at the one-hundred-year-old Moreton Bay fig trees. Turned the ignition off, opened the window, let the breeze in.

'This is where we were all hanging out in the shade. Then Mum turned up in her Volvo. I was fourteen.'

Kate sat up, looked steadily through the windscreen as if she might see it happen again. 'Which bench was Rebecca sitting on?'

I pointed left. 'That one down there. Thirty-eight years ago.'

For me, returning to the showgrounds was like visiting a crime scene. A flicker of memory about the times I'd been there alone with

Andy. Being there had nothing to do with him, or that sad person I once was. I was there to remember my sister and what happened that day back in 1984 – a memory that was once intensely vivid, but after so many years, I could only rely on a fading replay. Still, I could see Rebecca sitting on a bench, a book held at chest level. She was calm, restful, happy enough in the moment. We glanced at each other, I recalled that. Just a whole bunch of kids keeping out of the heat. It was an ordinary day.

Kate got out of the car and went to where Rebecca had sat. I opened the car door, stepped around to the bonnet and leaned against it, watched her. Her red hair, their likeness, yet somehow it made me happy to see Kate sitting in that sacred spot. When she returned to the car, I pointed out the pavilion where Mum's wedding cakes used to be the star attraction. I told her about the blue-shirted man who stood watching us. His black dog. My heart was heavy with all the remembering.

'Did the police talk to him?'

'Yes,' I said, recalling Bull had given him a beating because of me. 'He was an electrician from Echuca with solid alibis.'

We drove back through the pillars and into town, up the main street. It was busy, no vacant car spots. Once I would've known all the faces, but everyone was a stranger. I stopped to let a young mother push a pram across the road. A hunched old man walked slowly along the pathway gripping his wheelie walker. The news-agency had the same awning from when I went to school. Up ahead another woman hurried across the road. I tapped the brakes. She was about my age, long dark hair, walked slightly bent from the waist, or was it the angle of her neck? Whatever, it was distinc-tive. Jasmine. My mind flew to what I should do next. Pull over and speak to her? She stepped up onto the kerb and headed towards the post office.

266

I can't explain my decision, but I indicated at the roundabout then angle-parked in front of the doctor's surgery.

'I know that woman,' I said to Kate, 'wait here.' She was staring into her phone before I'd even closed the car door.

I hurried to the post office and entered. Jasmine was standing in a queue. I was anxious, small, so I stepped outside, hesitated, then waited with no idea what I was going to say. I looked around, recalling being there as a girl in school uniform. The public phone box that Rebecca would've used to call Bull had been upgraded and was free to use.

When Jasmine came down the steps, I moved forward and called her name.

She turned, stared at me.

'I'm Eliza Bundy. Rebecca's sister.'

She looked around to see if it was me speaking to her. I took in her large deep-set eyes, too-black hair, the row of piercings along her ears, skinny jeans, black t-shirt. It was like she had just got older, but somehow stayed the same.

'I'm on my way up to Maryhill to see Dad and Mum, saw you so I pulled over to say hello.'

'Right.'

I didn't know what to say, and she didn't care that I was standing in front of her.

'It's thirty-eight years ago this week since Rebecca went missing.'

'I'm done with talking about all that,' she said. 'That podcaster woman bothering me when I've got nothing more to say.'

'I know how you feel. So how are you anyway?'

'Doing all right.'

'So you still live local?'

'Looks that way, don't it.'

'I live in Edinburgh, Scotland.'

'I know where Edinburgh is.'

Silence.

'I saw Bull earlier this week,' I said.

She brightened, a small eager smile. 'Oh yeah, what's he up to?'

'Lives in Darwin. But he's sick, cancer. It's not going well.'

'He got a raw deal with those coppers. I've never blamed him for what he did to those other men. Your parents could've done more. Spoken up for him.'

'That was never going to happen. My parents never liked him. That was half the problem.'

'What was the other half?'

I saw the hard set of her jaw, black staring eyes judging me.

'Anyway,' I said, 'I'd better get going.'

'I see your dad down here sometimes pushing your mum in a wheelchair. Funny how things turn out.'

'What's funny about an old man doing his best to care for his wife?'

'Nothing, I guess. It's just that your family used to be so high and mighty.'

'You don't know what you're talking about,' I said, scurrying away like a stupid fool. My heart was racing. I knew exactly what she was talking about. My mother always acted like she was better than everyone else, and I couldn't shake the feeling that maybe I wasn't much different. Or at least I'd changed since I left home and no longer fitted in to this place.

The truth was, I hated being back there.

Kate was still in the car, staring into her phone, thumbs like pistons. It'd be that bloke she met in Vietnam, Lachie. I told her I was going to the supermarket. She nodded, equal to ignoring me. I moved fast along the supermarket aisles, keeping my face averted towards the shelves in case I bumped into anyone else I knew.

Jasmine's words looped in my mind as I filled a basket with groceries that Dad wouldn't have bought, or even know what they were.

By the time I was at the fruit and veggie section I realised what had upset me the most about the encounter with Jasmine. She was right. I had been condescending. Me, telling her that Edinburgh was in Scotland. As if it was even necessary to mention where I lived, but I was bragging, thought of myself as better than her. So there it was again, the idea that I might be stuck up, not much different to my mother. That notion upset me.

The checkout girl's nametag said she was Elle. She was young, about the age I was when I used to work in the shop up in Maryhill. I recognised her enthusiastic efficiency, that she was proud, and liked serving customers. I wanted to tell her to be careful, that she should never take anything for granted. In my heart I wished her a lifetime of happiness. As Elle swiped my items and packed them in recyclable plastic bags she asked me, in a friendly voice, 'How's your day been?'

'Great,' I said, glancing around to see if anyone was watching me, whispering to someone else that the sister of the missing Bundy girl was in town.

TWENTY-SEVEN

Driving up the mountain, on that straight stretch, just past Hedge End Lane, I overtook a white ute, pulling a trailer carrying two Baldy calves.

'This is where Bull overtook Mum and me at high speed in his black ute with P-plates. Rebecca was hiding in the front seat beside him.'

Kate glanced at me, a slight frown, and I couldn't tell if she was properly engaged. All the talking about Rebecca, she might've thought I was obsessed. I probably was.

'He's the guy you caught up with in Darwin, right?'

'Yes,' I said. 'Two days ago. Up until then we weren't sure how Rebecca got home. Or even if she did come home. But he told me he dropped her off at the bottom of our driveway.'

'Why is that such a big deal?'

'Because it means he lied. He told everyone, including the police, he'd not seen her in about four days.'

'Why'd he lie about that?'

I explained to Kate how Bull and his grandmother were looked down on, especially by my mother. That she had it in for Bull even before Rebecca went missing, and for him to admit he dropped her off would've put the spotlight on him.

'Maybe that's right,' Kate said. 'If he lied about that he might actually know what happened to Rebecca.'

'That was his argument. No one would believe him if he was the last person to see her.'

'So, what do you think?'

'That he's telling the truth. And I understand why he lied.'

'So now that you know she got a lift home,' Kate said, 'how does that help anything? Maybe she did go home and pack and then took off to Queensland or somewhere else. You said there were sightings of a girl who said she was Rebecca.'

'It never ends,' I said. 'We actually don't know what happened.'

I told Kate how Bull tracked down other suspects, beat them up to get a confession, and was sent to prison for two years for aggravated assault, how at the time everyone was impressed.

'Did he find out anything?'

'No.'

'So why is that impressive?'

'You need to have known Bull. He was handsome back then, with a tough vibe about him. It'd seemed sort of brave and somehow gallant, a man trying to find out what happened to his girlfriend.'

'I'll take your word for it,' Kate said.

I was thinking back to that time, the way the *Gyle Gazette* likened Bull to Ned Kelly. How weird and frenzied everything was then, the rumours and anxiety.

On the right was a new planation of some type of bushy tree that I didn't recognise. Later Dad would tell me they were juniper berries. Some adventurous locals were starting up a distillery. Things on the mountain were evolving, new people had moved up there.

*

I slowed down when we entered Maryhill's main street. There was a woman, with a small child, in the front garden of Cora Engelman's old house. Cora died sometime back in the early 2000s. The Community Hall hadn't changed. There was a banner tied to the front fence promoting an Arts Festival. I remembered the Healys' funerals. The footy club Best and Fairest awards nights. The gala balls Dad and Mum used to take me and Rebecca to.

Across the road, on the right, was the old shop, renamed to Harts Café & Gallery owned by Frances, a cheerful woman, and her partner, Wayne. They prepared and dropped off three or four evening meals a week for Dad and Mum. I thought of Robyn, the Facebook posts she sometimes did. That her son, Fletcher, was now a parent himself. How strange, a sort of melancholy, to remember the past and bring it forward into the present.

Aside from the non-fruiting grapevine that was still there, wild and green, the place was very different. There were sculptures out the front, tables and benches under the shade trees, fire pits, an outdoor pizza oven. Inside there were tables and chairs, artwork on the walls, cabinets filled with fine pottery and handmade jewellery. On our last visit, Duncan and I took Dad and Mum there for pizza, the first time they'd ever eaten anything as exotic as Italian food. We thought it would be a treat. Mum couldn't manage the front steps, Dad almost carried her inside. And she didn't like the salami or mozzarella, just picked at it, looking around trying to understand where she was and why she'd been given such awful food. Dad thought it was too expensive. As for me, I ordered another glass of wine and struck up a conversation with Frances.

'This used to be the shop I worked in,' I told Kate.

We pulled up out the front, and I thought, *I'm here again, but without Duncan.* The phone box had been upgraded and moved further down the street.

I opened the café gallery door and entered. Kate followed. Frances was in the kitchen, which had once been Robyn and Gary's bedroom. She'd had the lefthand side wall taken down and fitted out with industrial ovens and stoves. There were two large fridges where the door into the hallway used to be. The storage cupboard was gone, replaced with an industrial dishwasher. Stainless steel glimmered. The walls were cream, the counter that I used to stand behind had been ripped out, a natural timber bench had replaced it.

When Frances heard the buzzer she turned. She was always friendly, although when she came towards me I heard her sigh, like she was tired, on duty without the energy to be cheerful.

'I just wanted to pop in and introduce you to my daughter, Kate, and to thank you for the meals you drop off for Dad and Mum.'

She smiled at Kate, then back to me, and said, 'It's not good up there. How long are you staying?'

'I know they're struggling a bit. But I'm here for a few days so will see what I can do. It's the same old story, I'm afraid.'

'You need to stay longer than that,' Frances said, frowning.

I swallowed her judgement and didn't remind her that my husband died only twenty months earlier. That the borders had been closed for two years. That Kate and I had our own lives. That, in the same way my parents had made their own choices, Kate and I were entitled to do that too. Well, even though I believed that, setting boundaries, expecting us all to be responsible for our own choices, there was an annoying quiet voice challenging me, saying I was obligated to care for my parents in their old age. I hated being trapped that way, and wondered if I was a selfish person.

'Did you get my email about Diane wandering off?' Frances said. 'She was found walking on the road two mornings ago in her nightie, with muddy slippers on. It was only about 12 degrees so she was cold and exhausted. To be honest I've got no idea how she made it as far as the bridge.'

I was confused. 'I've been travelling. Haven't seen it.'

I noticed the tiniest shake of Frances's head and realised she had a real problem with me. 'Your father is barely coping,' she said.

'I know that,' I replied, 'and I suppose the whole mountain is talking about it.'

'What people are saying is the least of your worries, Eliza. Something's got to change.'

I took her in, saw her small judging eyes, pale skin, the way her apron stretched tightly across her heavy waist and hips.

Jasmine's words returned, that the 'Bundys aren't so high and mighty these days'.

The buzzer went. An attractive fit-looking woman came in, swept back blonde hair, perhaps my age, early fifties.

Frances's face brightened, the two women smiled at each other, different to how I was greeted. I felt a small pang because I'd thought Frances and I were good friends. All through the pandemic we had kept in contact about my parents. We still chatted, via email, at least fortnightly about the meals she or Wayne prepared and delivered, but also other personal things about our lives.

'This is Angela McBain,' Frances said, 'and this is Eliza Bundy. You know, the old folk from the orchard. She's their daughter, and Kate here is their granddaughter.'

Angela looked at me unsmiling, saw whatever she wanted.

'It was Angela who found your mother on the side of the road, just over the bridge. She was the one who took her home,' Frances explained.

'Thank you,' I said, wanting to be friendly, wanting to not be there.

'I brought her to the shop because I didn't know who she was,' Angela said. 'Wayne told me. I was about to call the police.'

Those women didn't know me, who I was. They personified why I hated the mountain, standing in their presence when they thought they had all the answers.

'If you had called the police, it might've been a good thing,' I was speaking too fast, 'because then they'd be forced to intervene and I'd hope Mum would then go into care. The point is, they won't leave the house in case my sister returns.'

'That was almost forty years ago,' Frances said. 'She's not coming back. I listened to the podcast.'

'You're talking about my sister,' I reminded her.

Both women stared back as if I'd said something stupid.

Kate moved closer to me, her hand gentle on my arm.

'We don't know where Rebecca is,' I went on. 'Never have, so there's no closure for us.'

Still, they looked at me, as they shuffled backwards giving me the message that they were done with this conversation.

'All the same, something has to change,' Frances said. 'It's a disgrace the way they're living up there. Making the meals we send up there last for two or three days. They're both too thin.'

'I'm sorry to hear all this. And thanks for your help, it's appreciated.'

'It's good you're here so you can see for yourself what's going on,' Angela added. 'When I took your mother into the house last Tuesday morning about eight, your father was sound asleep on the couch with the radio on. The place was very untidy, dishes in the sink, and it smelled like old people, if you get my drift. It made me very upset, if you want to know the truth.'

'Let's go, Mum,' Kate said.

I straightened my shoulders. 'Thank you for your concern.'

Their stares burned into my back as we walked to the car.

And I guessed that within twenty-four hours everyone on the mountain would know Kate and I were there. That the gossip-mongering on the mountain was more effective than me personally posting on Maryhill's community e-mail tree that I had arrived.

TWENTY-EIGHT

I indicated and turned into our old driveway, which was twice as wide and sealed with crushed red rock. All that remained of the tall cypress hedge was the first couple of trees, rangy and unpruned. Even though it was twelve years ago when the trees had been bull-dozed, it still surprised me to see they were all gone. Wire fences with treated pine posts defined the four 20-acre properties. On the right a dozen or so alpacas grazed. A house with no verandahs was in the distance with an air-conditioning unit on the roof that looked like a nasty growth. All the properties and houses were similar. One had horses and jumps. Another had curved rows of commercial lavender. The last one on the left had several rusted-out cars, other junk, an eyesore.

Over the rise and to the right was Dad and Mum's place. Their thirty-seven acres were fenced off with the same wire and posts as the other properties. A steel wire gate blocked our entry into their driveway. In the past it had always been wide open, as if welcoming us. I stopped so Kate could open it, then drove through and waited for her to get back into the car. On previous visits Dad had always mown the lawns, everything tidied up and in good order before my arrival. Not this time. The grass was ankle high, dying roses that hadn't been deadheaded, broken tree branches hung. A red plastic bucket lay in the garden bed outside Rebecca's bedroom window.

I pulled in around the back, parked beside Dad's ute, and took a breath. I was never up for the closed-in feeling inside the house, the whole property – and mountain, for that matter. Out of the car I turned to Dunny Hill, obscured by wisps of lacy cloud, a bride's veil in a breeze, the large granite scar on the summit peeped through. I nodded to it in some kind of acknowledgement.

The metal swing set Dad had welded and painted white for Rebecca and me creaked quietly in the breeze. Little girls' laughter. Dad pushing us higher and higher. A single blue towel and two pairs of old lady undies hung on the clothesline. The tractor and packing sheds were on the flat ground past the sloped lawn. The last time I'd been here, before the pandemic, Mum thought the orchard was intact behind the sheds. I guessed that was what she still believed.

The gate squealed when Kate pushed it open. I followed her into the concreted patio that was covered in dust and fallen leaves. The potted geraniums were long dead. I looked inside the laundry, saw a basket of unwashed bedsheets on top of the machine. Dad's boots weren't beside the back steps, so he wasn't inside. Apart from the lack of upkeep, everything was always the same.

We didn't knock, but walked straight in. The door into the kitchen was unusually closed. I opened it.

Rays of light came through the kitchen window, and there she was in the corner. Mum in her recliner chair, legs elevated, and covered in a multi-coloured crocheted blanket. Head tilted to the side, eyes closed, mouth open, her chest rose and fell. Her hair was grey and thin and hung to her shoulders as if she was still too vain to have it cut short.

I went to her, bent down and touched her hand. Her eyelids fluttered open.

'Mum,' I said, 'I'm here.'

She blinked, looked confused, afraid. She was thin, skin like paper, teeth the colour of coffee. I breathed in the ammonia smell that would've become familiar to her.

'I'm Eliza, Mum. And Kate's here too.'

Kate smiled and leaned forward as if to embrace her. But when Mum saw her, she recoiled and shrieked in terror, her body shook.

'What's wrong, Mum?' I asked.

'She's dead,' she said, terror on her face.

'Who's dead?'

She gasped and looked away, pressed her head back.

I held her hand.

'It's okay, Mum. We don't know if Rebecca is dead.'

Her lips moved, 'Make her go. She's dead.'

'This is Kate, Mum. She's my daughter, not Rebecca. We don't know where Rebecca is.'

'She's dead. She's dead,' Mum said, lifting her hand weakly, pointing at Kate.

'Why are you saying that, Mum? How do you know that?'

Mum lifted her chin, her breath was sour. 'Because I did it. It was me.'

Kate gasped, put her hand to her mouth.

'What do you mean?' I whispered.

There was thick saliva around her mouth. Terrible sadness in her pleading eyes. She pawed the air in front as if trying to grasp onto me, as if she was falling and wanted me to catch her.

'Tell me again, Mum. What did you say about Rebecca?'

As if letting go, falling into a void, she closed her eyes and rested back in the chair. For a moment I thought she'd just died. Then her chest slowly rose.

'Mum, what did you do to Rebecca?' My heart was racing, a pulse ticking in my neck.

She was perfectly still, a tiny hiccup.

Then Kate leaned in. 'What did you do to me?'

'Kate, no,' I said, 'don't.'

She ignored me and gently shook Mum's arm as if to wake her. 'It's me. Rebecca. Tell Eliza what you did to me.'

Mum blinked awake and stared into Kate's face, crying and mumbling, 'No. No. Go away.'

She was afraid, quivering, but Kate kept going. 'Tell Eliza what you did to me.'

Kate moved in closer.

'It's time to speak up, Mum,' Kate said. 'Tell Eliza what you did to me.'

When Mum stared back at Kate, I saw her eyes were wet with tears. Her lips moved as if trying to find the words. I wondered where Dad was. This was cruel. But I was dumb, transfixed.

'It's okay, Mum,' Kate said, 'I've forgiven you. I want you to tell Eliza what you did to me.'

Again, Mum closed her eyes, but Kate put her hand on her shoulder, gave a little shake. 'Wake up, Mum. You need to tell Eliza what happened. It's okay. I forgive you.'

'Maurie. I want Maurie,' Mum pleaded.

'Kate, that's enough. Leave her,' I said.

We stood back and stared at each other, incredulous.

'Did you hear that?' Kate loudly whispered. 'She admitted killing Rebecca.'

'She didn't. She's got dementia and is confused,' I said, my heart thumping, terrified that I may have just heard the unbelievable truth.

'No way. She said it more than once. She did it.' Kate pushed her shoulders back, emboldened.

'Please don't say that, Kate. She just got confused when she saw you because you look a lot like Rebecca.'

'That's the point. She couldn't understand why I was there because she knows Rebecca is dead.'

'That's enough,' I snapped. 'Help me bring our stuff in from the car.'

But as we were wheeling our suitcases in, backpacks slung over our shoulders, I wondered. I replayed the words Mum had spoken, *She's dead, she's dead. I did it, it was me.* She had dementia, couldn't be trusted to know what she was saying. Still, I kept thinking, trying to make sense, adding it to what Bull had told me. That he'd left Rebecca at the bottom of the driveway, so she was likely to be home before Mum arrived. She'd already dropped me off at the shop. Dad was doing an apple delivery to the agent in Coldstream. They would've been alone in the house.

When Kate went to the bathroom to shower, I went outside looking for Dad. He wasn't in the garden. Down at the tractor sheds, I called out, 'Dad, Dad!' Then further down the hill I entered the packing sheds. I imagined the smell of apples, the busy days when harvest was on, packers standing at the grader, the forklift moving bins into position. And there he was. Dad was standing in front of the wooden boxes filled with irrigation drippers, thousands of them, tiny black nozzles that used to supply fat droplets of water onto the apple trees.

'Dad,' I said.

He turned, smiled at me. 'You're here already.'

I didn't remind him that I'd phoned him as we entered Gyle, told him we'd arrive about then. I leaned in for one of his awkward hugs, his lovely familiar smell. 'What are you doing down here?' I asked.

He laughed. 'Came to get the lawn mower, but got busy sorting out these things.'

'We should sell them, or take them to the tip.'

He shook his head no. 'I'll work it out, gives me something to do.'

'But, Dad, you've got plenty to do already. Looking after Mum.'

'Diane's all right.'

'You're both looking a bit skinny. Are you eating properly?'

'Don't fuss. We're fine. There's people coming and going from here all the time. Can't stand all the bother.'

'I heard that Mum wandered off the other day. And was brought back to the house by a woman new to the mountain.'

'How'd you hear about that?'

'You know how people talk up here.'

He studied me, unsure if to believe me.

'Come up to the house and see Kate,' I said.

Dad's stride had become shorter so I slowed down to match him. On the uphill path towards the house, I told him what Mum said about Rebecca being dead. That she did it.

We were almost at the woodshed when he stopped, and said, 'Pardon?'

'She said she did it. She killed Rebecca.'

He stared at me, a twitch of his lips. I saw something.

'Mum thought Kate was Rebecca, got confused and frightened because they look so alike. Remember the last time Kate was here when she was ten? Same thing as then.'

Still, Dad just stood there looking at me.

'What, Dad?'

'Your mother has dementia. She's confused and not responsible for what she says,' Dad said, firmly, matter-of-factly.

'That's what I think. Still, there's something I need to tell you.'

We sat on the bench beside the water tanks, the wisteria was lush and wild, fronds in all directions. I told Dad about seeing Bull in Darwin. How he'd contacted me on Facebook. That I'd decided to travel there on my way to Maryhill.

'Bull's got lung cancer and not much time to live. He contacted me to tell me something.'

'I think he was a smoker. I remember that,' Dad said.

'He told me that when Mum and Rebecca had that fight at the showgrounds, Rebecca went to the Gyle post office and phoned him to pick her up and take her home. So he did. Rebecca was home before Mum on the day she went missing. I was at the shop working. You were two hours away making a delivery to Coldstream. Bull didn't tell the police because he said he'd be incriminated in her disappearance. But he swears it's the truth.'

Dad stared straight ahead into the purple rhododendron. His Adam's apple moved like a stone was caught in his throat.

'If he's only come up with that now, what else does he know that he's not told anyone?' Dad said finally.

A husky screech came from inside the house.

We were on our feet. I was faster than Dad, up the back steps, flung the door open, across the verandah.

Mum was in her chair, eyes wide, lips trembling, her hands shaking.

'What's wrong?' I said.

But I didn't wait for an answer. Down the hall I went looking for Kate. The bathroom door was open, steam on the mirror. Into my bedroom, and Kate was sitting on the bed, hands clasped in a knot.

'What happened?' I asked, sitting beside her.

'I can't stay here,' she said. 'After my shower I went into the living room and Nan started up again about me being dead. It's bullshit.'

'What did she say exactly?'

'Something about killing me and I needed to go away.'

It couldn't be true.

I saw my mother that night after I'd returned from working at the shop, when Rebecca still wasn't home. She was lying in bed, Dad beside her, holding her hand, shushing her to sleep. She'd changed out of the white-and-yellow polka-dot dress and was wearing a blue denim dress with a zipper up the front. That day Mum had been crazier than ever. Followed by all the drinking. The sex with Bryce Jones. The medication she went on to settle her down into someone more tragic than eccentric.

There was a tap on my bedroom door. Dad came in.

'Hello, Kate,' he said.

She made no attempt to greet him further than a nod. We were all serious, there was unusual energy in the room like we were about to hear bad news.

'We need to talk.' Dad was looking at both of us.

Kate glanced at me.

'We should go to the kitchen then,' I said.

'Let me put Diane to bed first.'

'But she's not had dinner yet,' I said.

'Don't worry about that. I'll take her a tray later on.'

'Let me come and help you,' I offered.

'I can manage.'

I was about to stand up and insist I lend him a hand when he stepped out and closed the door.

'This is getting seriously weird,' Kate said.

I swallowed.

We waited. Kate was back on her phone.

I heard laboured movements as Dad ushered Mum down the hallway. The toilet flushed. Seconds passed. Their bedroom door closed. I knew if I put my ear to our joint wall I'd be able to hear them.

So I did. Kate watched me, eyebrows raised.

Mum was whimpering. Dad was talking so quietly I couldn't make out a word.

I heard Mum say 'Rebecca', other words I couldn't pick up.

Their bedroom door opened again. A short burst from the bathroom tap. That would be Dad getting the water for Mum to swallow whatever medication she was on. This wasn't right. I wanted Duncan's calm gaze on me, to hear his rational voice.

Dad was back in their bedroom.

I waited. Kate still staring into her phone.

Perhaps it was ten or fifteen minutes later that I heard Dad open their bedroom door again. Then came into my room. He told us he'd see us in the living room. It was like I was still a child, being summoned from my bedroom where I'd spent so many hours waiting to be allowed to come out.

We filed down the hallway into the kitchen.

'Should I make us tea?' I asked.

'If you want,' he answered, dismissing me, pulling out a chair, sitting down.

'Got anything stronger?' Kate joked.

She sat opposite Dad while I put the kettle on. Noticing it was a new kettle cheered me. So things did get sorted out around here; it wasn't all about the past.

Mugs, teabags, milk, teaspoon. My back was to them, but I didn't hear Dad make any attempt to talk to Kate, ask her anything about her life.

I sat beside him. And so, with mugs of steaming tea in front of us, the moment had come.

Dad didn't pick up his mug. I sipped. Kate watched us, cat-like.

'Quite a few years ago now,' Dad said, 'Diane had a car accident in Benalla. 2011, I think it was, the year after we demolished the orchard.'

'I remember.'

'After Rebecca disappeared, Diane acquired a drinking problem. She was convicted of dangerous driving, and we were able to avoid anything worse than a fine and her licence being suspended, because no one was injured and the judge understood the strain on her from losing her daughter. My main concern was keeping it quiet.'

I moved in my chair, decided not to interrupt. Kate continued studying us.

Dad looked into the woodgrain of the table, thinking.

Silence.

His body shuddered.

'I've not told anyone else this and never thought I would. But you being here for the next few days is going to be very difficult.' Dad looked across at Kate. 'Your likeness to Rebecca is obvious and upsetting to Diane.'

'It's not Kate's fault, Dad.'

Dad raised his hand to silence me. 'Rebecca lost her footing after your mother hit her. She must've had a haemorrhage, or something like that. What I'm saying is, Rebecca died accidentally. I know the law calls it manslaughter. But I call it an accident. She told me about it after the car crash I just told you about. She broke down and said Rebecca was already here at the house when she got home from the showgrounds. Remember? It's like Bull said. That's the bit I wasn't sure of. Well, they continued on arguing, pushing and shoving and so forth. Rebecca went into her bedroom and starting packing the travel bag. Diane believed she was going to Bull's place and tried to stop her. Anyway, in all the struggling, Rebecca cracked her head on the footboard at the end of her bed.' He glanced sideways to the hallway, up where Rebecca's bedroom was.

'Dad,' I breathed, my hand on my throat, gaping at him.

I had no words, no breath. My heart thrashed in my chest.

'Are you *kidding* me?' Kate was glaring at him.

Then I remembered that time Dad had his long-handled hoe, digging around in the rutted dirt when the orchard was bulldozed.

'So that time when the orchard was demolished and you were looking for Rebecca's body in the churned-up dirt, did you know then?' I said.

'No. Your mother told me after that, the following year. At the time I was just speculating because I'd not found Rebecca anywhere else. I didn't know where she was.'

I supposed because he'd had so long to digest what had happened to Rebecca he seemed oddly calm, like he wasn't fully aware of the seriousness of what he'd just said.

'Dad, this is insane what you're telling us. Why didn't Mum just admit what happened at the time? It was an accident, for God's sake. Look what we've all been through.'

'She's suffered the most,' Dad said. 'Hated herself for what happened to Rebecca.'

'Dad, all those trips to Queensland. All the years of not knowing. I've experienced anxiety, spent thousands on therapy trying to come to terms with Rebecca's absence. And here you are still caring for Mum, protecting her. I can't believe this. It's too much.'

'What did you expect me to do? Contact the police?'

'Yes!' Kate snapped.

I couldn't think, blood was rushing through me, smashing in my ears. I covered my face with my hands.

'Diane promised me she'd stop drinking and driving if I kept the accident with Rebecca to ourselves. In a way, I was relieved to know. It meant I could stop those long trips north with the idea that we'd get back to some kind of normal existence.'

'How could anything ever be normal again after that?' Kate said.

Dad glanced at Kate, then down at his hands. A slight trembling in his fingers.

'But what about *me*, Dad? That was eleven years ago and I've been living every day since wondering about my sister. And Duncan and I visited here four or five times since then and you kept it a secret from us. How could you do that?'

He turned to look at me straight on. 'I'm sorry you feel that way. But you were living your life with Duncan and Kate in Scotland. I am glad you were there away from all this. All those hiking trips you took. Busy working. Kate with her horse. Why would I put what happened onto you and ruin all that? You didn't need to know.'

I was speechless.

'Grandpa,' Kate said, 'you don't understand how Mum is always anxious about Rebecca. She's a happy person, but never stops trying to work out what happened to her sister.'

Dad picked up his tea, drank.

'So what are you proposing we do now?' I asked, cautiously, watching him.

He shrugged.

'What do you expect Kate and me to do with this information?' I asked again.

'Why would you do anything? Your mother is eighty-two years old. Neither of us have much time left. And the other thing I'd like to say is this. Our family has been through enough without the accident with Rebecca being blown up in the newspapers and on the television. We don't need any more harm done. We've had more than our fair share of problems. So no one needs to know.'

'Dad, I don't know how you've been able to live with Mum under these circumstances. She's put us all through hell and you just carry on, protecting her. She lied. She lied over and over for years.'

Dad closed his eyes, I thought he wasn't going to answer. Then he breathed deeply. 'I accept it's difficult for you to understand. Your mother and I have had our troubles. Most married people do. It wasn't her fault that her nerves went on her after Rebecca was born. Of course, I wish everything had turned out differently, but in spite of what happened, your mother and I care for each other. And I don't believe I need to explain our relationship to you more than that. I'll make one final point in the hope it helps you come to terms with things. Your mother didn't intend for Rebecca to hit her head. It was an accident. A terrible accident. Keeping that in the front of my mind has helped me.'

'It's not called the accident, Grandpa. It's called Rebecca's *death*.'

Dad stared back at Kate, impassively. It was like he wasn't fully with it. Perhaps there were two demented people living under the one roof? But that wasn't true. He was sitting there rationally stating facts that made sense.

I needed to think, so stopped talking. There was a confusing feeling between us all. Nothing was resolved. I went down the hallway to Rebecca's room, to the end of her bed, put my hand on the timber footboard, saw the panic, heard the screaming, slapping, pushing, grunting. Kate came up beside me. All those times since 1984 that I'd visited Rebecca's room, stood at the door wondering.

'I never thought it was Mum,' I said.

'Why would you? This is too weird. And why wasn't her body ever found?' Kate asked.

'Because no one ever looked for it.'

Kate put her arm around me. 'Are you okay, Mum?'

Sick with shame that my family was so messed up, I felt an urgent need to explain to her how it was back then.

We sat on Rebecca's bed and I told Kate about the Healys' bloody deaths. 'Sinead was six months pregnant. It was like a massive bomb exploded in Maryhill and everything else faded into the background. And Rebecca was a bit wild back then. At first the police were dismissive, saying she'd come home when she was ready. And when she didn't the rumours started and never stopped. The point is, I guess, that because the police were so distracted it was easy for Mum to keep her lie. No one was properly investigated. They never spoke to me.'

'This mountain is so fucked,' Kate said. 'What are we going to do?'

'I don't know. But they can't keep living like this.'

Dad was still sitting at the kitchen table, waiting. When I sat down he turned to me, pleading in his eyes. He was afraid.

'I told you about your sister because Diane can't seem to separate Kate from Rebecca,' he said. 'For her, they're the one person. That for the time you're here it's going to be hard for her.'

'I know that, Dad. Let's talk more in the morning. I need to think.' As I turned, I thought of an obvious question. 'What happened to her body?'

Dad looked forlorn, helpless. 'Let's leave that for another time.'

'Why?'

'Because it's upsetting,' he said, 'and I'd prefer not to talk about it.'

I was astonished that Dad seemed so matter-of-fact about everything. But then, he'd had a long time to absorb what had happened. As for me, my mind was spinning. Years flashed by, how I'd lived in the house for a time after Rebecca disappeared, the hours and hours dealing with Facebook searching for her, the false leads, the endless worry. My whole life had been upended. All the while my mother kept her vile secret. Her lies, hysterics, all the nonsense we'd put up with, for what?

*

In the morning I let Kate sleep in and stepped into the hallway. Dad was moving around in the kitchen. The radio was on. I opened the door to Dad and Mum's bedroom. There she was, curled on her side, asleep. The room smelt – urine, stale air, a trace of Chanel No. 5 – but it looked entirely different to when I lived at home. Sometime, maybe fifteen years ago, Mum redecorated. Everything in the room was in shades of blue and white, like they lived near the sea. New furniture too, and presumably a new mattress. The TV was mounted on the east wall facing the bed. All the secrets that room held were buried deep in the walls, painted over in a shade of blue that was too dark.

'Mum,' I said, as I sat on the side of the bed.

As she stirred I tried to fathom how a woman who looked so old and vulnerable could be so cruel to those she professed to love. How did I feel about her? I didn't know, still disbelieving, yet it all made sense. 'It's me, Eliza.'

She smiled, weakly.

'How are you feeling this morning?'

'Maurie is bringing me tea and toast.'

'He looks after you very well, doesn't he?'

'Mostly.'

'When doesn't he look after you?' I waited, thought she'd forgotten the question, so I repeated it. 'When doesn't Maurie look after you?'

'I don't know.'

'Mum, I've got a question to ask you.'

She looked up at me, so ancient.

'Remember Bryce Jones? That workman with bright blue eyes who used to work for us?'

'Yes.'

'Did he help you bury Rebecca?'

'Oh yes, I couldn't do it.'

'Was he your special friend?'

'Who was my friend?'

'Bryce Jones, the workman.'

She sparked up, looked around the room as if she might see him. 'Where?' she asked.

'He's not here. But you liked him, didn't you?'

'I think I did,' she said, putting her white chicken-claw hand to her forehead as if it might help her remember.

'It doesn't matter, Mum. I just wanted to know how Rebecca was buried. The ground would have been too hard for you to dig.'

She nodded, but I wasn't convinced she understood.

'So, did Bryce bury Rebecca for you?'

'What did he do?'

'Bryce buried Rebecca for you because the ground was too hard.'

She turned to the side, trying to catch the memory. 'Rebecca,' she whispered.

'What about Rebecca?'

'She's dead.'

'Did Bryce Jones help you bury her?'

She did it again, looked around the room as if Bryce might have been standing somewhere. 'Where's Maurie?' she asked, wringing her hands as if nervous. She stared at me; her eyes looked blind.

'Mum, are you okay?'

'Yes,' she said, a strange smile as if something was funny.

Then, a feeling washed over me. I stood and turned.

Dad was standing at the open door holding Mum's breakfast tray. I'd not heard him enter the room.

'Dad,' I said.

His lips moved, no words came, as he stepped in front of me and placed the tray over Mum's lap. Then with his arm around her, he carefully lifted her so she was sitting up. He positioned the pillows. Then he turned away from me and left the room. I followed him down in the hallway. 'Dad, what?'

He was standing at the kitchen table, head bowed, scratching his chin.

'Dad, did you know about Mum and Bryce Jones?'

He was pale, hollowed out, mouth open, shrunken eyes behind his glasses. 'How do you know about that?' he asked.

'On that first trip you made to Queensland, one day I stayed home from school. Mum didn't know I was in my bedroom. I heard them.'

He took a breath, shook his head. It was like he was ashamed, couldn't look at me.

'It's not your fault, Dad. You've carried the load for this family. Rebecca vanishing. Caring for Mum even though you knew about her and Bryce. I actually don't understand how you've been able to keep going.'

'I don't want to discuss this,' he said.

'But Bryce was an accessory to Rebecca's death.'

'I believe that.' He nodded.

'So when Mum sent him away from the orchard, why didn't he dob her in? He had that hanging over her.'

'Because they were in a romantic relationship at the time he helped bury Rebecca. I don't know exactly what happened on that night. Was Bryce around the house? Did Rebecca see something that caused a row? I'll never know. But the point is, if he went to the police about what happened, then he would've been arrested. Anyway, he's dead. Died in 1998 in a car accident.'

'How do you know that?'

'Because I went looking for him.'

'When?'

Dad pulled at his bottom lip, thinking. 'I can't rightly remember. Soon after your mother told me.'

'What were you going to do when you found him?'

Dad stared into my eyes. 'Find out where he buried my daughter.'

I gaped at him, disbelieving that we were talking so factually, clinically. After all that time, it felt like we'd come to the end of it. Part of me wanted to curl up on the floor and rock with grief and hurt that I'd been so taken for granted with no consideration of my experience.

I gathered my thoughts, 'So do you know where she's buried?'

'I told you he died in 1998.'

'And Mum doesn't know?' I asked.

'That he's dead? Or where Rebecca is buried?'

'Buried,' I said.

'She wasn't involved in that part of it.'

'Dad, this is so unbelievably crazy. How have you been able to care for Mum knowing she had an affair?'

He took a breath.

I waited.

'Because I made a vow. Sickness and health. Also, I love her and have memories of happy times. And I'm probably not an easy man to be married to. Besides, I don't know what else I could've done. Your mother didn't mean for Rebecca to die. It was an accident. Just a very bad accident.' And then as an afterthought, his voice almost a whisper, 'When I found out about what happened it was a very hard time. Your mother and I talked it all through and decided to work it out and try and find some kind of life,' he said, exhaustion on his face.

I thought he might cry.

'I'm sorry Dad, it's been so awful for you.'

'Not just me. All of us,' he said, pulling a chair from the kitchen table and sitting down. I sat too.

'So Bull didn't do a proper job beating up Bryce to find out what he knew,' I said.

'Seems that way.'

'Do you know how Bull got hold of those men's addresses?'

'I gave them to him. Got them off Jeff, sort of indirectly.'

'What?'

'Bull came to see me and asked me. Told me his plan. We shook on it that he wouldn't say where he got them from. I told him he'd be sent to jail for it, but he said it'd be worth it. I sort of envied him.'

'But it backfired, because he didn't get anything out of them.'

'I visited him in prison a couple of times.'

'Why? You never liked him.'

'I know this won't make much sense. But when he went after that Soydan fella, I was glad of it. I thought he had it coming. And in spite of Bull not getting anything out of Bryce, I'm happy he got what he deserved. He's one man I would've liked to front up to.'

My gentle father, talking about violence. I couldn't imagine it. We sat in silence. The faint whoosh from the overhead fan, a creak in the walls.

'What about Rebecca and Jacob Healy? Were they just rumours?'

Dad shrugged, bowed his head. 'I don't know. Probably nothing.'

He wasn't convincing, more like he was telling himself a story. His beautiful girl couldn't have been having sex with a married man. As for me, I was past caring about that.

'It's time, you know,' I said.

'What for?'

'For Mum to go into care. You can't keep this up.'

'But you've not thought this through,' he said. 'What if she's in that place in Gyle and tells someone else about what she did to Rebecca?'

'Is that why you've been so resistant?'

'Maybe.'

'Dad, Mum's off with the fairies a lot of the time, no one will believe her. And if they do, which I doubt, just ignore them, say it's the dementia.'

I saw his vulnerability and tiredness.

'Dad. Let me make you a cuppa.'

'Thank you,' he said.

*

The track up to the workman's cottage was different, somehow narrower, probably through lack of use. Sometime during the subdivision, the pines were cut down leaving a long row of broad stumps. There was more sky. Bare paddocks on either side had gone to weed. Sturdy thistle bushes and capeweed dominated. The dam was still there, but smaller as if the banks had shrunk, the water shallowed. The waterlilies, those graceful ballerinas, had disappeared.

Kate was beside me. We'd walked along this track before, and together we were pointing out all the changes. I was still on the lookout for snakes. Around the dogleg corner we headed towards the workman's cottage, which was part of Dad and Mum's acreage and so avoided the bulldozer. I can't explain how the boundary worked, but the cottage had morphed into the state forest, as if it belonged there. The liquidambar at the front steps had survived, towering over the cottage, protecting it.

The front windows were broken, some effort to tape them up wasn't working. Cobwebs, leaves, dust on the front verandah. A few dead moths. Some boards were rotted through.

We didn't go inside, but sat on the step.

I remembered the other times I'd been in the same spot.

We talked about Rebecca and the things we'd learned since we arrived.

'I can't believe Nan had an affair with the workman and covered up her death. It's like we're in an episode of *Shetland*.'

Of course, she was right. But I couldn't reconcile that for most of my life my mother had let me suffer, wilfully letting me live with the constant not knowing. And the same for Dad, too. I hated her. But then I reminded myself that she had a mental illness. Was that an excuse?

'We should go to the police,' Kate said.

'You think that would make anything better or different?'

'But we're aware of a crime. Nan committed manslaughter. That Bryce person, the workman, was an accessory. Even Grandpa has been covering it up for a decade.'

A scarlet robin darted into the liquidambar. Involuntarily, I made a wish and remembered that I'd done the exact same thing on the steps before. It might've been that day when I wagged school and heard Mum and Bryce in bed. It was only weeks after that I left the mountain. This time it was a different wish. *Rebecca, what should I do now?*

'I've looked it up,' Kate said. 'It's a serious offence to kill someone accidentally, an indictable offence. It'll go to court.'

'Kate, Nan has dementia. We don't even know if any of what she said actually happened. In literature, she's what we call an unreliable narrator.'

'That's bullshit, Mum, and you know it.'

I twisted around to look at her square on. 'Kate, for thirty-eight years this family has been living with trauma. I'm not going to have my parents live out the few years they've got left having to front up to police questioning. And even if I did report them, really? Mum can't speak for herself. Bryce Jones is dead, good riddance. That leaves Dad to tell his version. He's been through enough.'

'What would Dad do?' Kate asked.

I thought of Duncan and was immediately certain what he'd say. 'He'd agree with me,' I said, trying for his accent, 'Let them be. That poor old bastard, Maurie, give him a fecking break.'

'I don't know what to do,' Kate said. 'I can't be in the same room as Nan because she goes nuts.'

'Why don't you fly to Sydney, see Lachie?'

'Are you serious?'

I shrugged. 'Why not? But don't go thinking you're in love or anything like that.'

She pulled her phone out of her pocket.

'I can drive you to the airport tomorrow.'

'Really?'

'Okay, stay here with me then.'

She leaned across, kissed my cheek. 'What are you going to do?'

'I'm hoping Dad will now agree for Mum to go into care. So I'll stick around to sort that out.'

'Will he stay here on his own then?'

'One step at a time,' I said.

TWENTY-NINE

2023

It is autumn, wood smoke and pine in the cool air. The maples along Josephs Road in Maryhill are tall and golden, a beautiful contrast to the grey overcast sky. As I drive, Dad and Mum are sitting together in the back seat, holding hands. As far as I can remember, I've never driven them anywhere before. And here we are now. In the tray of Dad's ute is Mum's wheelchair and two suitcases filled with a selection of her clothes, all labelled with her name in cursive font. A new lilac dressing gown, three new nighties, also labelled. A pair of new slippers. I put Rebecca beside me in the front passenger seat and speak to her in my mind, like I've been doing on and off for almost forty years.

Down the mountain, the wide valley in front. A big grey sky rises above. The green hills remind me of parts of Scotland and I feel the call to return there. Kate's home and waiting for me. She's just started a new job working for Scottish Legal Aid. Lachie, the Sydney boy she met in Vietnam, is coming to stay with us over Easter. That's my deadline to get everything sorted out here so I can join them. We're going to the Isle of Arran for a week's hiking.

On the left is a new grand house that distracts from the view across the flatland north of Gyle. It's high on a ridge, looks like two oversized shipping containers joined together with a smaller one. It reminds me how everything keeps changing and moving forward. The years pass quickly.

Dad and Mum are quiet in the back seat, like a couple of well-behaved kids. In the rear vision mirror I see Dad is very solemn. He's dressed up for the occasion, his brown trousers with a shirt and beige V-neck jumper. His hair is parted and neatly combed. His glasses sit on that indent on the bridge of his nose, the frames must be twenty or more years old.

As for Mum, she looks tiny, narrow shouldered. I feel strangely detached from who she was when I was child. Perhaps because she's now so frail and vulnerable, I can't help but feel concerned for her, also pity, which she'd hate if she knew. Dad has dressed her up. Navy trousers, a white silky shirt with a frilly collar, and a pink cardigan. In spite of me taking her to the hairdresser for her hair to be neatened up, she refused to let it be cut. It hangs thin and limp on her shoulders. With her free hand, she grips the handle of a large black leather handbag, like it's a lifebuoy.

When we arrive I'm efficient. There's no turning back and this has to be done. Out of the car, I have the wheelchair in place, ready. Dad knows the best way of holding her, his arm across her back as he gently pulls her from the car and into the seat. I release the brake ready to wheel Mum through the double doors, but Dad steps in front and pushes her himself. We don't speak, just walk ahead. The glass doors open and close behind us.

We're welcomed by Linda, an Irish woman I'd met previously when I organised Mum's admission. She smiles and greets us like it's her own home. The hard part is coming. We follow Linda around a corner, down a corridor. She presses a code into a pad beside the door. A buzzer goes and the door opens. It's the dementia ward, called the Memory Support Unit. In we go. Dad wheels Mum through a communal area, past four sleeping residents sitting in armchairs in front of a large-screen television. Whatever is showing, it's got subtitles. One elderly woman holds a baby-sized plastic doll wrapped in a cotton blanket. A skinny balding man walks fast up and down the room. Another younger man wearing a captain's sailing hat is sitting on a chair staring at the door as if waiting for his chance to escape.

Mum's room is at the end on the right. It's barren, hospital-like. It seems impossible that we'll have the courage to leave her here. I look at Dad. Tears are running down his face, but because his hands are on the wheelchair handles he doesn't wipe them away. I leave him to his misery. This has to be done.

It's when Linda leans forward to help Mum out of the wheelchair into the bed that she becomes alert, fear in her eyes. She's still gripping onto her black handbag and I wonder what's in it.

'Maurie?' she whimpers.

'It's all right,' Dad says, now wiping his face with a white handkerchief.

Mum starts to tremble, her lips quiver. 'Maurie?' she asks again.

'I'll sit here with you for a bit,' he says, trying to tug the handbag off her. Still she won't let it go, so he leaves it in the bed with her.

I can't stand it here, can't breathe.

Linda says we can stay as long as we like to settle Mum in. There's only one chair in the room, not much sunlight. When I'm unpacking Mum's suitcase, the woman cradling the doll comes to the door, stands there and stares at me for a few seconds until Linda gently walks her away.

I watch Dad lean down and hesitate before he brushes his lips on Mum's.

'Get some rest,' he tells her. She looks like she's already asleep.

Then he stands and looks across at me. 'Let's go,' he says.

'You don't want to stay a bit longer?'

'No. Let's go now before I change my mind.'

'What's in the handbag?' I ask.

'I put her make-up purse in it. And a few other things she likes.'

Before we left the house, Mum knew something was up. The fuss Dad made dressing her up, combing her hair. He held a mirror for her to apply lipstick and dab skin-tone powder in her face.

I heard him explain that she was going to hospital, that the nurses there were kind.

'Why hospital?' she asked.

'Because sometimes you get confused.'

Mum nodded in agreement, seemed satisfied with his explanation.

My once-powerful mother. She was so contradictory, beautiful and ugly, strong and weak, loving and cruel, hardworking and lazy. Would I ever make sense of who she was and what she'd done to our family? Would I ever forgive her? Perhaps this won't make any sense, but I've looked into explanations for my mother's ability to keep her evil actions to herself for so long. How was it possible for her to allow Dad to make all those long drives to Queensland, for me to leave home when I was only fifteen? And all the rest of it. There's a psychological condition known as the illusory truth effect. It's a state of mind where a person after repeated exposure to a lie starts to believe it's the truth. I'm certain Mum convinced herself that Bull really did know what happened to Rebecca. She'd never let up on it. I don't know, but it's the only thing that makes any sense to me.

THIRTY

Now that Mum is finally in care and everything is more settled, I have something to confess. It's taken me all this time to build up the courage to say it. Or perhaps I'm a coward, now speaking up when it doesn't matter any longer.

It's late afternoon. Cockatoos fly across a delicate mauve sky to their nests in Dunny Hill and the state forest. The light is quite beautiful, muted, yet vivid. My footfall out in front, along the dirt track where once the line of pines threw long shadows. On the right, Granny Smith and Golden Delicious apple trees used to grow. I recreate the landscape to how it was when I wandered along here with Rebecca.

The dam is up ahead. Memories of ballerinas and girls' laughter. Around the corner and up ahead is the workman's cottage. I'm still a hundred metres away and from that distance see the liquidambar towering above the cottage. There's a few Hereford cattle grazing close by; Dad is agisting a neighbour's cattle to keep the grass down. I turn at the windbreak, open the gate, walk up the steps.

I put my shoulder to the front door and enter. Nothing different, just shabbier, a heavy layer of dust, the stink of rodents, living or dead I wouldn't know. Because the liquidambar blocks out what little light there's left in the day, I pull my phone out and follow the torch's conical glow.

Into the kitchen. The rusted nail still pokes up from the floorboards, the nail I'd jammed my foot into, those days when I was so ridden with guilt. I know exactly where to squat. With no further mucking around, no pretending or holding back, I put my hand inside the hole in the skirting board and plaster. My fingers tickle around, a moment of shock when I can't find it. But there. I roll the jar forward, ply it out of the darkness. It's been hidden there since that first time I came here looking for Rebecca.

I wipe cobwebs off the jar cap with my hand. It's stiff, I have to put all my strength into twisting it open. I tap out the roll of notes. One hundred and seventy-five dollars. Three fifties. One twenty. One fiver. Lauren Reinhart's wedding cake money. Yes, it was me who stole it out of Mum's purse. Think about it.

Obviously, there's no satisfactory defence for stealing the money on that last day of school, back in December 1984. It's just that Rebecca got all the attention. She was the beautiful daughter. I was the plain one. She ignored me, treated me like a kid. All those fights she had with Mum, in their own negative way, was her getting attention from our parents.

I actually had no plan for what I was going to do with the money, except to probably put it back. Not for one second did I ever think my raid on Mum's purse would have any consequences for Rebecca's life. All our lives.

I'm sorry, Rebecca, I say.

If she has something to say back to me, I don't hear it.

I have checked on the jar, with the cash inside, a few times over the years. In the days immediately after Rebecca went missing, I had tried to tell Dad the truth, but the words never came. Once, I nearly told Duncan about it. And a counsellor with huge red glasses almost got my confession. I suppose that makes me a pathetic human being. See what I caused? I've ruined so many lives. Aside from my family, I'm thinking of Bull and Cheryl.

But I'm done with it all now. I put the cash back into the jar, recap it and push it back into the hole. Someone might find it one day and wonder who put it there. A housewife's get-away money.

I stand up. Dust my hands off on my jeans.

Out through the back door and onto the path. The sky is lava red, startling. Around the side of the house I walk to the corrugated iron shed. The door is completely off its hinges. Rabbit traps still hang from the rafters. The kid's bike. Paint cans, shovels and spades, a pickaxe.

There's rye grass and capeweed under my feet. But that first time I came here there were fresh footprints in the dry dirt. I bet Bryce Jones once stood in this exact spot.

I turn to Dunny Hill, see the dark wingbeats of the late arrivals to their nests.

She's up there somewhere. I look around. Anywhere here. I'm glad Dad kept this parcel of land in the subdivision. It's like Rebecca's memorial.

I bow my head and say goodbye to her.

I tell my sister I'm sorry one more time. Even though I want it to be, I can't vouch it'll be the last time I say those words.

As I head back to the house, I'm suddenly in a hurry. I walk fast, faster. That's how it is for me, always getting away from that crushing ache in my body. It's been a long time since I've deliberately hurt myself, but I'm suddenly reminded how good it'd feel to have the guilt excised. Don't go there. Move on. Right now, I could swim thirty laps, and be guaranteed to feel better afterwards.

Back at the house, Dad is waiting for me so we can eat together. He's heated the lentil and vegetable soup I made earlier. The toast is buttered. We sit at the dining table in our places. Two seats are empty. For a man who's just left his wife in a dementia ward, he seems all right.

'How are you feeling, Dad?'

'They called me to say she ate dinner. That she was watching the TV.'

'Have you thought more about what you're going to do? It'll be very quiet here without Mum.'

'Haven't you noticed? I like the quiet,' he says, a tiny smile.

It feels irreverent to be experiencing a kind of lightness, a simple happiness. But I think Dad has earned it. Good on him.

As for me, I deserve nothing, but I feel it too.

ACKNOWLEDGEMENTS

Loren O'Keeffe, founder of The Missed Foundation, does incredible work providing support to families with a long-term missing loved one. Her podcast *What's Missing* provided me with real life heartbreaking insights into ambiguous loss – the emotional and psychological impact on individuals and families who cannot get resolution when a loved one disappears. I'm grateful to her for the work she does and the resources she makes available. For more information and to make a tax-deductible donation, please refer to **missed.org.au**.

For many years I've been fortunate to be part of a Melbourne-based writing community, led by Antoni Jach. My connection to this group has been significant and I'd say my writing achievements partly relate to the incredible support I've received from the collective and individuals. Special mention to Jane Leonard, Janine Mikosza, Ellie Neilson, Vikki Petraitis, Tiffney Plummer, Jane Sullivan, Honeytree Thomas and Lyn Yeowart. Of course, my sincere gratitude to Antoni for his generosity and ongoing commitment to my work and that of many other writers.

My appreciation and thanks to my first readers Jane Sullivan, Amanda Tokar and Georgie Videan. Jane's considered opinion on the book's structure and her overall positive approach helped me improve the book. Amanda has been a regular listener on the novel's progress and I've valued her advice and guidance. And Georgie's enthusiastic response, after reading the final draft, emboldened me to hope this story would eventually get published.

Julia Banks, Jill Bartlett, Carolyn Bell, Jill Cook, Ann Eldred, Jo Fisher, Dawn and Peter Hartley, Helen Kennett, Rhonda McKenzie, Chris Power, Christine Talbot, Meg Webster, and Karen Williams – each in different ways – have provided support and encouragement during the drafting of this novel. Thank you. To my awesome aqua friends, who I meet regularly at the local pool, I value your friendship and interest in my writing. A special acknowledgement to Leah Allison, my very talented cake decorating niece, who gave me advice on wedding cake decorating, all of which was given to Diane.

Thank you to Shelley Burr, Vikki Petraitis, and Lyn Yeowart for endorsing the book. I'm humbled and grateful for the time they took to read the manuscript and the fabulous testimonials they gave.

To my literary agent, Sarah McKenzie, I owe special thanks for her valuable critical feedback on the manuscript that most certainly improved it. I'm very happy to have her in my corner.

And to the Penguin Random House team, it's been wonderful to work with you all again. Special recognition to Bev Cousins, my amazing, insightful and hard-working publisher, for her belief in the book and expert guidance through to publication. Also to my fabulous editor Kalhari Jayaweera for her thorough interrogation and editing of the novel and Jocelyn Hungerford for her detailed proofread. Huge thanks and appreciation to Elena Kaloudis and Chi Chi Zhu for their publicity and marketing support. Also to Veronica Eze for her expert production of the audiobook.

Finally, to my children. Narelle, Denise and Daniel, thanks for your encouragement and being part of my publishing journey. And also my grandchildren, Sasha, Ethan, Olivia, Joshua and James.

To Alistair, my husband, best friend and writing collaborator, thank you for all that you do.

BOOK CLUB QUESTIONS

1. What did you enjoy most about the novel?
2. The term 'ambiguous loss' is a psychological term to describe a grief that cannot have closure. How do you think the author depicts the trauma of 'ambiguous loss' within the Bundy family?
3. Could the family have done anything differently to support Diane's mental health?
4. Eliza started self-harming soon after Rebecca disappeared. Why do you think this made her feel better?
5. The stories circulating about Rebecca suggest that she might have been involved with other men aside from her boyfriend, Bull. Do you think any of those rumours were valid, or just gossip?
6. Was there anything the Bundys could have done to salvage Rebecca's reputation?
7. What are your thoughts on Maurie Bundy? Do you see him as a strong or weak person? Give examples.
8. Could a more focused investigation have discovered what happened to Rebecca back in 1984, if the police had not been distracted by the Healys' murders?

9. Auntie Helen became a vital mentor for Eliza. How important are non-parental mentors in the lives of (particularly troubled) young people?

10. Maurie's trips to Queensland started as following up on leads and sightings of Rebecca, but did these trips have a greater purpose for him as the years went by?

11. What are your thoughts about Eliza living in Scotland, away from her elderly parents? Should she have done more to help them?

12. Discuss the differences between rural and city living. If the Bundys lived in a city, what might have been different after Rebecca went missing?

13. Do you think Maurie, and eventually Eliza, made the right decision to withhold their knowledge about what happened to Rebecca from the police?

14. The 'illusory truth effect' is the tendency to believe false information to be true after repeated exposure to it. Do you think it could have applied to Diane's insistence that Bull knew what happened to Rebecca?

15. At the end of the book, Eliza confesses to something. What are the ramifications of her not revealing her secret immediately after Rebecca went missing?

ABOUT THE AUTHOR

After a successful career in overseas aid, and as a senior executive with a global food company, Glenna and her husband spent several years living and working on their cattle property in rural Victoria. During that time they also owned and operated a commercial blueberry orchard. Glenna's time in the country enables her to write authentically about life in the city as well as in remote locations. She now lives in inner Melbourne with her husband. She is also the author of *Blueberry* and *Stella and Margie*.

Discover a
new favourite